NEXUS CONFESSIONS: VOLUME FIVE

Other titles available in the Nexus Confessions series:

NEXUS CONFESSIONS: VOLUME ONE
NEXUS CONFESSIONS: VOLUME TWO
NEXUS CONFESSIONS: VOLUME THREE
NEXUS CONFESSIONS: VOLUME FOUR

NEXUS CONFESSIONS: VOLUME FIVE

Edited and compiled by
Lindsay Gordon
and Lance Porter

Always make sure you practise safe, sane and consensual sex.

Published by Nexus 2008

First published in Great Britain in 2008 by
Nexus
Virgin Books
Random House, 20 Vauxhall Bridge Road,
London SW1V 2SA

www.virginbooks.com
www.rbooks.co.uk

Addresses for companies within The Random House Group Limited can be found at: www.randomhouse.co.uk/offices.htm

The Random House Group Limited Reg. No. 954009

Distributed in the USA by Macmillan, 175 Fifth Avenue, New York, NY 10010, USA

A CIP catalogue record for this book is available from the British Library

ISBN 9780352341440

The Random House Group Limited supports The Forest Stewardship Council [FSC], the leading international forest certification organisation. All our titles that are printed on Greenpeace approved FSC certified paper carry the FSC logo. Our paper procurement policy can be found at www.rbooks.co.uk/environment

Typeset by TW Typesetting, Plymouth, Devon
Printed and bound in Great Britain by CPI Bookmarque Ltd, Croydon CR0 4TD

2 4 6 8 10 9 7 5 3 1

CONTENTS

Introduction vii

Hello, Boys – *Yummy Mummy knows best* 1

Life of a Salesman – *A breast man has his hands full at a sales convention* 14

Teasing – *Some girls just love to flaunt it* 23

Poor Little Rich Girls – *A firm hand mends spoiled ways* 29

The Summer of Sixty-Nine – *Getting to know the girls next door* 39

The Newsagent's Wife – *A top-shelf magazine fuels a cuckold fantasy* 55

The Nurses' Home – *Caught spying and smothered into submission* 63

Girl on a Motorbike – *A MILF is tempted by her future daughter-in-law* 75

Lucy Takes Liberties – *A rich bride-to-be has a weak spot for workmen* 82

Win-Win – *Girls will be girls* 98

A Financial Arrangement – *When a wife makes her husband pay* 108

A Night at the Opera – *A cultivated lady submits to a dominant lover* 115
Couple Cruising – *A woman's first swinging experience* 122
The Tent – *Bi-curious?* 137
Female Bonding – *Two young students become more than best friends* 142
Male Chambermaid – *An intimate encounter with a Hollywood actress* 150
Dirty Girl – *A back-garden exhibitionist gets more than she bargained for* 157
TV Bitch – *Punished for wearing his wife's lingerie* 168
Designing Women – *High heels, hosiery and a passion for legs* 175
Tango – *He leads and she responds* 185
Mercy – *A soft-hearted girl who likes to please* 191
The Way Things Are – *A dominant wife lays down the ground rules* 197
Sparks – *A young apprentice finds his Mrs Robinson* 203
Body Search – *Stripped bare for her mistress's pleasure* 209

Introduction

Who can forget the first time they read a reader's letter in an adult magazine? It could make your legs shake. You could almost feel your imagination stretching to comprehend exactly what some woman had done with a neighbour, the baby-sitter, her best friend, her son's friend, a couple of complete strangers, whatever . . . Do real women actually do these things? Did this guy really get that lucky? We asked ourselves these questions, and the not knowing, and the wanting to believe, or wanting to disbelieve because we felt we were missing out, were all part of the reading experience, the fun, the involvement in the confessions of others, as if we were reading some shameful diary. And when Nancy Friday's collections of sexual fantasies became available, didn't we all shake our heads and say, no way, some depraved writer made all of this up. No woman could possibly want to do that. Or this guy must be crazy. But I bet there are readers' letters and confessed fantasies that we read years, even decades ago, that we can still remember clearly. Stories that haunt us: did it, might it, could it have really happened? And stories that still thrill us when the lights go out because they have informed our own dreams. But as we get older and become more experienced, maybe we have learnt that we would be foolish to underestimate anyone sexually, especially ourselves.

The scope of human fantasy and sexual experience seems infinite now. And our sexual urges and imaginations never cease to eroticise any new situation or trend or cultural flux about us. To browse online and to see how many erotic sub-cultures have arisen and made themselves known is to be in awe. Same deal with magazines and adult films – the variety, the diversity, the complexity and level of obsessive detail involved. But I still believe there are few pictures or visuals that can offer the insights into motivation and desire, or reveal the inner world of a fetish, or detail the pure visceral thrill of sexual arousal, or the anticipation and suspense of a sexual experience, in the same way that a story can. When it comes to the erotic you can't beat a narrative, and when it comes to an erotic narrative you can't beat a confession. An actual experience or longing confided to you, the reader, in a private dialogue that declares: *yes, if I am honest, I even shock myself at what I have done and what I want to do.* There is something comforting about it. And unlike a novel, with an anthology there is the additional perk of dipping in and out and of not having to follow continuity; the chance to find something fresh and intensely arousing every few pages written by a different hand. Start at the back if you want. Anthologies are perfect for erotica, and they thrive when the short story in other genres has tragically gone the way of poetry.

So sit back and enjoy the Nexus Confessions series. It offers the old-school thrills of reading about the sexual shenanigans of others, but Nexus-style. And the fantasies and confessions that came flooding in – when the call went out on our website – are probably only suitable for Nexus. Because like the rest of our canon, they detail fetishes, curious tastes and perverse longings: the thrills of shame and humiliation, the swapping of genders, and the ecstasy of submission or domination. There are no visiting milkmen, or busty neighbours hanging out the washing and winking over the hedge here. Oh, no. Our readers and fantasists are far more likely to have been spanked, or caned, feminised into women, have given themselves to strangers, to have dominated other men or women, gone dogging, done the unthinkable, behaved inappropriately and broken the rules.

Lindsay Gordon, Winter 2006

Symbols key

Corporal Punishment

Female Domination

Institution

Medical

Period Setting

Restraint/Bondage

Rubber/Leather

Spanking

Transvestism

Underwear

Uniforms

Hello, Boys

My three boys always used to tell me I was pretty when they were little, sitting on the stairs watching me put on my lipstick to go out. But when they hit puberty and turned into greasy, spotty Kevin from the telly, boy, was I an embarrassment. Just being a mother, an adult, was enough to put a sneer on their faces. Frank and I were ‘the olds’. Being a man, Frank didn’t notice, didn’t care, basically stayed the same. But the taller and hairier my boys got, the fatter and uglier I felt. One or two of their gang might grunt the odd hello or thank you if I chucked a piece of toast at them, like that Kevin’s ugly mate who tugs his forelock all the time, but frankly by then I barely noticed.

Heard of empty nest syndrome? Not this nest. When our youngest, Robbie, finally left home and went to work in New York, we were very proud of them all, obviously, but now it was our time. My time, really. Frank had never stopped having his time. In fact, he got promoted then, and I hardly saw him. I went back to work at the art gallery, and lost some weight with all that running round London. Waited for an invitation to the Big Apple, which hasn’t arrived yet.

So I’m in the garden one scorching summer day, crawling about in the herbaceous border, photographing the privates of an overblown rose. The gallery wants to exhibit some of my flower pictures: the Baileyesque vaginal ones, all dark reds fading to white-pink, labial petals radiating from that tightly-wrapped bud, that dark little hole refusing quite to open. They sell well in monochrome, too, as suggestive greetings cards. Well, I'm happiest seeing the world through my viewfinder. And they look glorious blown up.

There's jazz playing in the house, and bees buzzing in my ears, but otherwise I'm alone. Frank's playing golf at Gleneagles. Did I say I don't miss my boys? Well, the work and the photographs and my new life keep me busy, but I'm still a soppy mare. That's why I'm wearing Robbie's old jeans, the baggy ones he used to wear with the crotch round his knees. I wear them loose round my hips, tied with Johnny's old school tie. A striped business shirt of Frank's is knotted under my tits like I'm Doris Day or someone. I lie back, hair tangled in the dry grass, bare feet in the hidden damp soil. The sun hums on my face. Christ, far too hot for clothes. No one here, neighbours can't see, why not just peel everything off?

I start to undo the jeans, wriggle them down my legs. Hot sun on my skin. I run my fingers up and down my thighs, tickling the tender parts so that little spasms shiver down me. OK, sunbathing in Chiswick isn't all that great. And as for masturbating in the open air . . . fuck, it's so humid. Don't give a damn. So sweaty.

Robbie says that after work he goes to swim in a rooftop pool and you can see over Manhattan. Imagine that!

I stretch out, let my knees flop apart. Dreaming about my boys now. Must talk to Frank about a trip somewhere when autumn comes.

The ground vibrates under my ear. Must be my heartbeat. But then several more thumps, footsteps, shake the earth. Someone grabs my shoulder, a big shape blocking out the sun. I yelp and sit bolt upright.

'Hey, Mum! Surprise!'

I shield my eyes with my hand.

'Robbie, you little monster! Scared me half to death!'

I yank my jeans, his jeans, over my pink knickers, scrabbling on all fours. He crouches down to hug me. He's gotten so big. 'What are you doing here? It's lovely to see you darling, but – why didn't you call?'

He shrugs. 'Thought you'd be pleased.' Wearing a suit, poor boy, in this heat. Dazzled as I am by the glare, he could be in his school uniform again. Tie askew, unshaven, ash-blond hair on end. So like his big brothers and his father now. 'Sent us back for some meetings. Thought I'd stash the expenses and stay here for the weekend.'

'Of course I'm pleased, sweetie.' I stumble to my feet, dizzy from the heat and the surprise. My hair is stuck to my forehead as if I've got a fever. I lean on him, buttoning my flies. 'But Dad and I could have been away gallivanting in St Tropez for all you knew.'

There's someone else here. Just a silhouette with dots dancing all over it until I can focus. Standing on the terrace, hands in pockets, kicking the tip of a very shiny shoe at my potted lilies.

'Yeah, right. St Tropez indeed.' Robbie slouches back towards the house. 'Could we have shepherd's pie, do you think?'

'In the middle of July? Your poor mum. She looks overheated as it is.' It's a very deep voice, coming from the terrace.

'Oh yeah, Mum, you remember Jake, don't you? Would you believe he's working in the same block as me downtown? And was on the same flight back? Wake up, Mum! He was always round here eating toast.'

I follow Robbie across the strip of parched grass towards the shade and the tall stranger standing there. I must look like shit. I furiously rake my fingers through my matted hair, breathe my stomach in, wipe sweat from my upper lip.

'Jake? The spindly polite one?' I remember something else. 'The guitarist?'

They both laugh and wave their air guitars. I try to look nonchalant, but I can't take my eyes off him. He's absolutely gorgeous. Like a young Marlon Brando, not that he'd know –

'Still doing it, Mrs Epsom. Robbie and I play in a jazz band in Greenwich Village on Friday nights –'

'Jake?' I repeat, tongue-tied like a schoolgirl. 'But you're all grown up!'

'We're not kids any more, Mum! Hell, Jake's already a tycoon.' Robbie steps back into the house. 'And I'll be earning more than Dad soon!'

I smile at that. 'Bring it on, I say! And you can lose the American accent now you're home!'

I catch Jake's eye. I don't remember seeing his eyes before. Youngsters never look at you straight, and he was always hidden behind a messy curtain of thick black hair.

I hear the fridge opening, the cool clink of bottles. In the old days his mate would have shuffled off after him. I half wish he would. My armpits are practically liquid. But he stays right where he is, staring at me. At my open, wet mouth. My throat, streaked with pollen and sweat. My breasts, pushing out of Frank's striped shirt. I'm breathing too fast, making them heave and wobble. At least I updated all my underwear when I lost that weight. I don't even go in the garden these days without something jewel-coloured and lacy. And yes, today's fuchsia pink bra is showing too.

'I'll come and help you, darling!' I start to push past Jake, but he puts a warm hand on my arm, just next to my left breast, and I have to stop, right up close to him. I can't believe how he's changed. He's so tall. He even stands differently. Something very still about him. He's looking down at me, rather than sideways. And forcing me to look back at him. And he smells gorgeous. Hot, and spicy. Christ, what's the matter with me?

'Is it OK if I stay? I know it's taking the piss. Robbie should have checked –' He has to bend down to speak to me, grip loosening but not leaving my arm. 'I can always go back to the hotel.'

He's like a Mexican bandit next to my blue-eyed Aryan boy. Glossy hair, expensively cut but flopping boyishly over his black eyes. He's neater than Robbie, but I can see the dark stubble pushing through his tanned skin. It's evening, after all.

'Of course you must stay. I love having my boys around me,' I squeak as I try to tug my shirt closed with my free hand. I'm so hot and seriously bothered.

Suddenly he runs his finger down between my breasts, down the slippery damp crease, and lifts off a squashed greenfly. I ought to slap him. Instead I'm pinned there. My nipples spring up, poking against the cotton. I can see his tongue. My tongue runs across my mouth. He runs his finger up my cleavage again, and down, watching me. My breasts feel swollen. I want to press up against him, pull open the shirt, show him, give him my big hot mumma's breasts to fondle and squeeze and lick and suck. But I also want to cover myself up, run away and hide, because he's so young.

Inside the house Robbie's roaming about, slamming doors, making himself at home. Outside, on the terrace, my heart is hammering in my ears. I can't tear my eyes away from Jake. A part of me is waiting for him to make fun of me. Silently he lifts the finger that has been stroking my cleavage and puts it in his mouth and sucks my sweat off it.

'Where did you learn to be so dirty?' I whisper, shaking my head slowly and stepping back. 'You, Jake, were the only boy who ever said thank you.'

He pulls at me roughly so that I bang against him and feel the long hard outline of his cock against my stomach. He puts his mouth in my hair to say something.

'And you, Mrs Epsom, were the only mother any of us wanted to fuck.'

They make so much noise, boys. After months of

virtual silence it disturbs and excites me. Up in my bedroom, I'm cool at last. I'm in front of my mirror, wet from the shower and naked. Downstairs they're clattering about, turning up the music, dropping spoons, running taps. Up here I'm looking at my body. Downstairs they're making the supper. Amazing. It was Jake who suggested it.

Jake. He said that word, *fuck.* It keeps ringing in my ears. He, they, whoever, wanted to fuck me while I was mashing spuds? What did I look like back then? What do I look like now? Christ, it's only five years since they left school and look at the transformation. They've become men. Do we oldsters change much? On my dressing table there's a picture of me at Robbie's eighteenth. Two stone heavier. Frank with that awful moustache.

They're laughing downstairs, that mocking male laugh. Chairs are scraping. A wine bottle pops.

I look better now, actually. I run my hands over myself. I'm slimmer. My hair is longer, and better highlighted to an ash-blonde. You can see my cheekbones again. I'm honey-coloured all over, just from the last solitary week or so in the garden. My tits have always been good. I run my finger up and down where Jake ran his, between my tits, and gasp. I watch myself in the mirror, voices murmuring now downstairs. I push my breasts together as Jake might have done if I'd opened my shirt for him. Big, full breasts. Not like those pert Pussy Cat Dolls my boys run around with. I pinch my nipples, feel my breasts swell with pleasure. How would it be to shock him as he shocked me, tangle my fingers through his silky black hair, press his face into me, feel that young stubbly mouth nibbling and sucking?

My hands move down between my legs. They're OK, too. My breasts are thrust towards the mirror, nipples brushing the cold glass, and I gasp again. They're so sensitive. To hot, cold, wet, dry, touching, licking, the slightest stimulation – I push my finger into my cunt, feel it hot in there and wet, the lips closing greedily. Spasms of desire zigzag down my belly. I hear myself moan, and that fires me up. Think of those handsome boys downstairs, all unaware. I rub my breasts against the mirror, my breath misting the glass, my hand working harder between my legs, driving faster into urgent friction against my cunt, speeding up so I'll come, quick, before I'm interrupted –

'Mum! It's ready! Jake's worked wonders!'

I spread my legs wide and there, I'm coming, standing in the room above them, frisking myself and whimpering and making myself sweaty all over again.

I know Robbie's bigging up his mate's achievements to make up for inviting him to stay. But he doesn't need to apologise. His mate told me he'd like to fuck me. He can stay as long as he likes.

But get real. I twist away from the mirror, splash my neck and wrists with cold water so as not to smudge my lipstick. Sure, Jake says he wanted to fuck me. But that was then. I bend to put on knickers. Think of Jake sitting next to me on the terrace, those long legs in their smart trousers, that young cock hidden in there. How hard would it get if he knew I wasn't wearing any knickers? I kick them away.

I drop a pale-blue silk dress over my head. It whispers over my skin like a kiss. I'm still breathless, and hot again, but I run down the stairs and out onto the terrace.

Johnnie's materialised, too. My other big handsome son come to surprise me. They are all watching me. I feel as if I'm on fire.

'Hello, boys!'

The shepherd's pie dish is scraped clean. I've picked at mine, listening to the bravado round the table. Jake has Johnnie enthralled with the fascinating deals he's been doing, some clients of Frank's he's met, how he and Robbie bumped into each other one morning running in Central Park. He doesn't look at me particularly. Why would he? *You were the only mother* . . . That was then. A teenage fantasy. A wet dream.

And now?

'We're off to the pub, Mum. Wanna come?'

I press my hands on Robbie's cheeks. He's looking a bit pale now. Johnnie and Jake are halfway out the front door already.

'First time you've ever asked me, but no thanks, honey. Need to edit some photographs.'

I take a big glass of wine down the garden. The air is warm like soup. My studio, tucked into the corner of the garden and buried under ivy and clematis, is like an oven. I leave the door open and switch on my laptop. My camera feeds in the images of the roses I took today, and they start to slide across the screen. I take a swig of wine and bend to study them. The big roses, lilies, tulips, all blossom out of the ether, some blood-red, some sepia, petals falling open to show the bud within, its hole tightly wrapped. Sweat trickles down my back and my flimsy dress sticks between my thighs. I can feel the silk snagging on the little strip of hair left over my pussy. I can *smell* my own aroma, hot like perfume, from creaming myself earlier.

'You always looked as if your mind was somewhere else, even when you were grilling pizza.'

I jump round. Jake is right up behind me, blocking the fading light, blocking any air.

'I thought you were at the pub?' My voice is hoarse and dry.

'Jet-lagged. They're in for the duration. Johnnie's playing pool and Robbie's bumped into an old flame.'

He looks over my shoulder. I reach to switch off the computer. They look so genital, those roses, so spread open, so blatantly on display. Like big wide fannies. I start to blush. 'No. Let me look at them.' He stops my hand, but instead of resting it on my wrist this time he winds his fingers in mine and pulls my hand back over my stomach. His weight is heavy behind me. 'Christ, nature at its sexiest,' he says, his mouth in my hair again. My neck prickles in response. So does my cunt. 'They're like floral centrefolds. You can't look away. They're such a turn-on. Just asking to be touched. Opened up. Fucked. Know what I mean?'

I'm breathless again, still bent forwards. I grip the desk for support. The roses slide relentlessly across the screen, close-up, soft-focus. Cunts asking to be fucked. And yes, there's Jake's cock, pressed right into the crack between my buttocks. Now my pussy is really getting wet.

'You should get to bed, Jake. You said you were tired.'

He chuckles, but instead of moving away he starts to slide my dress up my legs, exposing my bottom to the sticky air. I try to press my legs closed.

'Always the mother, eh? I don't want to go to bed. Not on my own, anyway.'

He starts to stroke my bottom, his fingers fanning out over the cheeks, tugging them apart, creeping underneath to probe at my pussy. I gasp, I can't help it, feel my legs giving, arching my back with pleasure.

'I can't go to bed with you, Jake.'

But I can't stop him. Worse, I'm straining my pussy upwards really obviously, tilting myself towards his fingers.

'Then we'll have to do it here.'

I half laugh, half sigh. Oh, he has all the permission he needs. He spreads my cheeks open, pushes more fingers between my sex lips and I can feel them throbbing but also tightening to grab him, suck him in. We both hear the wet slick sound as he parts them. He presses down over me, fingers probing and pushing, flicking near but not touching my clit, juices already moistening my cunt as he pushes my legs open with his knee. The fabric of his trousers is rough on my skin. I moan loudly and reach behind to grab at him, fondle his balls inside the trousers, and he unzips them for me.

'How did you get so dirty, Jake?'

'The art mistress at school taught me. Then my boss. I've always fancied – women your age.'

His big cock thumps into my hand, warm and pulsating like an animal. I can't see it, but its size makes me gasp. It's rigid and thick and long and it's already nudging through my cheeks. He takes my hips and tilts me, easing it into me, into my sex. My cunt feels like a little mouth, nibbling, eager to suck him in.

I fall forwards onto my desk, arms outstretched on either side of my laptop. The vaginal roses still glide past. I let him manhandle me, push his cock in, helpless as I am. As he opens me up I am reduced to one sizzling little hole. My hot body vibrates with desire as I thrust myself backwards onto his waiting cock. We both hear the soft wet pop as it penetrates. It slips in so easily. I close my eyes, bite my lip as Jake's cock goes on and on slipping easily inside.

'I'm a big boy now, Mrs Epsom.'

His silly words, straight out of *The Graduate* (but he wouldn't remember that film, either), just turn me on even more. I moan as my cunt grips him inside me, his cock filling me, already thrusting me across the desk, the hard surface pressing against my stomach, my buttocks banging against his strong thighs. Now he's fucking me, hard, and I want it like that, furious and hard and his cock is so huge and my cunt is so tight round it and it's amazing and rough. I'm nearly there but he comes first with a couple more violent thrusts and a deep groan and that excites me so much that I come straight afterwards in a wild, exhilarating burst.

We lie there, panting, for a few minutes. It's quiet, but any moment now my sons could come home. I can't breathe. He pulls me upright. Then walks out into the garden without a word. What now? Has he won a bet?

I can barely walk, but I have to get out of the studio.

He's flicking shut his mobile. His eyes glitter in the darkness.

'They're going to a party.'

Then we're kissing and I'm already turned on again, his stubble rough on my face, his tongue flicking and licking, me greedy to suck on it, and then he's pulling the straps of my dress down and my breasts are falling into his hands and I'm straining against him as he starts to squeeze.

'Christ,' he groans, and stops.

I freeze, juddering with every heartbeat, holding my breath so as not to betray my excitement. I try to pull away, almost sobbing with frustration and embarrassment.

'I'm too old,' I pant, trying to pull my dress up. 'A mistake –'

'Christ no, let me, these are just gorgeous, I used to dream about this, used to watch you – you're even more gorgeous, what's happened to you?'

The suave young man is still there, just, but he's disintegrating into a hungry beast as he pushes his face between my breasts, breathes on them, runs his tongue up them, over the swollen skin, the jutting nipples, and his teeth close round one sore tip.

'No, darling. It's what's happened to *you!*'

And then he's sucking my tits, hungrily at first and then more slowly, luxuriously. Of course he's done this before, with those other lucky women, but he makes me feel like I'm the first, the best, and then we're falling down onto the grass. Hidden from the house, but even so, any minute –

'Jake, this is crazy –'

'So tell me to stop, Mrs Epsom. I do as I'm told.'

But the night dew is delicious under my knees and now I'm on top of him, pulling open his white shirt, opening my legs to straddle his young body. I cup one breast and offer it to him. I rub its taut dark nipple across his mouth.

His tongue flicks across the nipple again, and I nearly scream out loud. His hands squeeze the breasts together until they sing with delicious pain. Then his soft lips nibble up the little nub of the nipple, the tongue laps round it. He draws the burning bud into his mouth, pulling hard on it, and begins to suck. It makes my whole body ripple with desire.

Electrical currents are streaking from my nipples through my body to my empty, waiting cunt.

He turns from one bulging breast to the other and I can't help wondering how it was with the others, but it's so gorgeous hearing him breathe heavily, groaning, biting and kneading harder and harder as if he owns me.

His mouth is getting rougher, more ferocious, and I'm pushing more roughly against him, daring him, searching for more pain to communicate more pleasure. I'm on top of him, my tits dangling down over him, their size and weight accentuated by hanging there, the soft globes pale in his brown fingers. I tilt my pussy desperately towards his groin and rub it briefly against his gorgeous cock, then take it in my hand and start to slide it up and down my wet cunt.

He raises his hips obligingly, and I moan desperately. God, it's a work of art. Its surface is smooth like velvet, the mauve plum emerging from the soft foreskin which wrinkles back to show itself all gleaming. I weigh it in my hand and as I do it he bites my nipple so hard that I do scream out with delight. I lean over him, settling myself just above my new toy.

I want him to think he's died and gone to heaven. Any minute now I'm going to heaven, too. I'm just preparing the way.

Greedily I press him down, tilting myself over him. We've moved some way from the studio now.

'See how beautiful it is,' I croon at him, showing him the length of his shaft encircled by my fingers. 'See how well it's going to fit.'

I smile as I raise myself on my knees and aim the tip of his cock towards the bud wrapped tightly round the hidden hole. I let it rest there, at the opening, just nudging it past my wet sex lips. I wait. I smile again, lowering myself a little more, gasping as each inch goes in. I reach under him to cup his balls in one hand and he bites his lip with another loud groan of surprise.

This tension is ecstasy, but I can't hold on to it for much longer, and slowly, luxuriously, I let the boy's knob slide up inside, all the way to the hilt. It's so tempting to ram it, let our hips start jerking, but once it's right in I force myself to pull away again. He frowns, impatient for action, but I just ease myself down again, moaning and tossing my head back, and the next time I do that he's with me, pulling his own hips back, waiting when I wait.

'So I'm telling you to be a good boy, and fuck me, Jake.'

I keep my eyes open the whole time. He's so beautiful. I try to see the spindly boy he used to be but all I see is this stud, who wants me and is fucking me and I'm riding him, pushing him back into the grass, his lips on my tits and his cock ramming me and we're coming again, we could go on forever, there on the grass. We'll go on doing it until the boys come home.

'Christ,' he says, when eventually the lights in the house come on. 'I guess that makes me a mother fucker, in the nicest possible way.'

My sons come out on the terrace, watch us walking across the grass. They don't notice me shaking, the grass stains on Jake's shirt.

'Hello, boys,' I say.

And my invitation to the Big Apple? He wants me out there soon as I can, boys. Just as soon as I can.

– Sophie, Chiswick, UK

Life of a Salesman

It had been a long hard day at the convention booth. Jennifer and I had gotten a few nibbles that may or may not translate into sales somewhere down the road, but the strain of smiling and making nice all day had left me with a mild headache and a sore face. I packed up our pamphlets and said, 'Well, Jen, that's it. I'll load everything in the van now, so we don't have to waste time in the morning. Why don't you grab a table in the restaurant and we can have some dinner . . . and drinks?'

She looked even more tired than I felt. 'I don't know . . . To be honest, I'm exhausted. I think I'll just take a shower, order some room service, and then go to bed.' She smiled. 'I'll see you in the –'

'Come on, Jen. It's our last night in town. Then it's back to the grind at the office. I'll tell you what, take your shower and order some room service and we'll eat it together. It's a lot more fun than eating alone.' I grinned. 'Maybe we can break into the mini-bar, too, and get some more mileage out of the old expense allowance. What d'you say?'

'I don't know. I –'

'I'll see you in half an hour,' I said, and scooped up a box and hightailed it out the door and into the parking lot.

This was it, I thought. Showtime! I had worked with Jennifer for almost a year now, and had lusted after her hot body every hour of every day of every month of that year. She was a tall babe in her late forties, which put her about twenty years up on me, but age had been very, very good to her. She wore her long blonde hair in a ponytail or piled up on her head in a professional manner, and had warm green eyes that could blaze with fire when she got passionate about something. Her skin was tanned a light brown, and her waist was slim and trim – obviously the result of plenty of early-morning, or late-night, exercise. Her legs were long and smooth, and held the promise of bliss at their axis.

But what really made Jennifer sweet, sweet Jennifer, was her beautiful bountiful tits. She was easily a 38D, and when she walked towards me and those magnificent tits started bouncing, it was all I could do to keep my tongue in my mouth and my hands in my pockets. And when she took off her suit jacket, the business ends of those tits were clearly and rigidly outlined against the thin material of her blouse; no doubt, in my mind, yearning to be free of their cloth and lycra confines and frolicking openly in my loving hands.

I gave my head a shake, noticed a group of Japanese tourists laughing and pointing at me. I sheepishly turned my back on them and tried to think away my spontaneous hard-on with thoughts un-Jennifer.

'That was a great meal,' Jennifer said. 'I'm stuffed.'

Not yet, I thought, not yet.

She got up from the small table and walked over to the mini-bar. I watched her every move. She was dressed down in a pair of tight faded-blue jeans, and a thin white T-shirt that did nothing to hide her enormous chest.

'Would you like another drink?' she asked, bending over and opening up the mini-bar.

Her firm rounded ass was a sight to behold. 'Huh? Uh . . . sure,' I responded. 'I'll have whatever you're having.'

She pulled out a couple of tiny overpriced bottles and brought them back over to the table. She poured the contents into a couple of glasses, and we both quickly downed them. She left a rim of lipstick round the edge of her glass, and I pictured such a rim being left round my cock. I stifled my erection for the time being, however, and we shared a few laughs about the people we had met at the convention.

When she brought over our fourth set of bottles, a slight stumble in her step, she put them on the table but didn't sit down herself. She stood in front of me, not six dick-lengths away, her big chest heaving like she had just run round the hotel a couple of times. I could have been chivalrous and stopped staring at her tits, but being knighted wasn't on my list of long-term goals, so I gazed at her breasts like they were some sort of optical illusion.

'Like what you see?' she whispered.

The air in the room suddenly grew very, very hot, to go along with my face. I gulped, my tongue swollen in my dry mouth, and had trouble getting wind into my lungs. Her womanly scent and the heat from her body smothered me in a lust embrace. 'I'd . . . I'd like to see more,' I said, choking. I'd seen a fair bit of feminine action in my day, but nothing approaching a woman of Jennifer's size and experience.

'So would I,' she replied. She pulled a couple of clasps out of her hair and her silky blonde tresses cascaded down her back and shoulders. Then she pulled her T-shirt up over her head and tossed it aside.

I swallowed hard and my throat creaked. Her tits were huge, the nipples large and dark inside her satiny pink bra. 'Wow,' I said softly.

I think Jennifer smiled then; I'm not really sure. I was watching her hands as they rubbed the sides of her slim, naked upper body, and then slowly rose up and caressed her breasts. She moaned slightly – I know that because I could hear it – as she squeezed the sides of her tits. Then she cupped her monstrous melons and hefted them slightly for my inspection.

'Yeah,' I stated eloquently.

She massaged her tits through the silky material of her bra, then slowly undid the fastener on the front. I held my breath. When she squeezed her breasts together in the action of unlocking her treasure chest, I swore that I could've lived contentedly for the rest of my natural life in that deep, deep cleavage. She slipped off her bra in slow motion and her tits spilled out into the open. Free at last!

They were even bigger and more beautiful than I had fantasised, and I had long imagined the shape and texture and suckability of those titanic tits during many, many an office bathroom jerk-off session. They were a sun-burnished brown like the rest of her body, and huge and smooth – sagging not a bit. And her two glorious sun-kissed mounds were peaked with thick brown inch-long nipples that stood erectly to attention in the air-conditioned cool of the hotel room. She lifted her tits with her hands, squeezed them together, shook them, rolled the long rigid nipples between her fingers, moaning an accompaniment to her sensual tit-play. Her massive breasts were obviously sensitive to the touch and, hopefully, taste.

'You're beautiful, Jennifer,' I said, stating the obvious.

'Suck my tits,' she hissed, more to the point. 'Suck my tits, you big tit-hungry stud!'

My eyebrows shot up along with my cock. So, she liked to talk dirty. Dirty it would most definitely be. I jumped up, brushed her hands aside, and grabbed onto her tits for the first time. They were as full and heavy and hot as I'd imagined. They were more than a handful. I squeezed them, kneaded them, rubbed them with shaking fingers and sweaty hands. I lightly pinched and rolled her impossibly large nipples. I fondled those incredible tits like a blind man shopping for watermelon.

Her body trembled at my touch, and her eyes glazed over with lust. Her lips opened and closed like she was already on the verge of a cataclysmic orgasm. But she managed to give voice to her filthy feelings, and my filthy thoughts. 'Explore my tits with your hands and your mouth and your tongue!' she said, in a quavery voice thick with passion. 'Then stick your big cock between my tits and spray them with hot sticky come!'

'Sweet Jesus,' I mumbled. I shoved her tits together and was about to apply some suction and saliva when her legs buckled and she collapsed backwards onto the bed. I was on top of her in an instant, and I was holding nothing back. I frantically sucked on her right breast while I squeezed her left.

'Yes, suck my fucking tits!' she screamed, twisting her head back and forth, her body writhing around on the bed.

The lady's tits were of the super-sensitive variety, just as they were super-sized, so I poured on the oral stimulation. I tongued her mocha nipples, teasing them till they swelled even further in my mouth, and became drenched in my saliva. I sucked and sucked on them, bouncing my head from one to the other, licking and biting them, all the time squeezing and rubbing the mammoth mammaries on which they stood to damp, rigid attention. Then I inhaled as much of Jennifer's right tit as I could cram into my mouth, which wasn't much, and flattened my tongue against her nipple and sucked long and hard.

'Fuck, yes!' she wailed, her hands in her hair, my hair. 'I'm coming!'

I almost choked on her tit. This was one goddamn passionate MILF! I pulled back for a second, keeping my hands on her tits, always on her tits, and stared down at her bronzed upper body, her tits spit-soaked and polished, her lower body still spray-painted jeans. It was a picture worth a thousand come-shots. I couldn't admire it for long, however, as Jennifer desperately grabbed my head and pulled me back down to her chest.

'Suck my tits, lover!' she cried.

It was hard to imagine at that moment that this wild brazen woman was the same cool professional business-person who walked the impersonal hallways of the office back home. I didn't give it much thought, though – I had my hands full. I shoved her fleshy mounds together and sucked relentlessly on one nipple and then the other, flapped my tongue across the both of them at the same time.

'Yes, baby! Yes!' she yelled, then grew ominously rigid. Her fingernails dug into my scalp and her eyes flew open and she stared desperately at her approaching ecstasy, her muscles tensing with the onslaught of all-out orgasm.

I lapped joyously at her nipples, buffing her tits with my tongue. She let loose a muffled scream and her body began quivering like a sexual divining rod at an orgy. I didn't stop for a second. I sucked and bit on her nipples, fondled them with my fingers, kneaded her beautiful tits with my hands. She gasped for air, then shut her eyes and gritted her teeth, as her body was ferociously jolted by orgasm after orgasm after orgasm. White-hot sexual ecstasy tore through her body and her tits and burst into my greedy mouth. I desperately fought to maintain contact with her jouncing tits as her body bucked and bounced all over the bed.

After what seemed an eternity in come-time, but was only a minute in real-time, she finally came to rest with a groan. Her face and tits were soaked. I lapped at the sweat on and between her tits, and it tasted clean and salty and good.

'Thank you,' she murmured, and smiled up at me.

'I know how you can,' I said.

'Help yourself. Anything.'

I grinned like I was her personal bra-fitter, then stood up and tore off my shirt and my pants and my shorts. My cock sprang out into the come-humid air and pointed arrow-straight at her lush chest.

'Tit-fuck me, baby,' she said softly, reading the thoughts in both our heads.

She slid further onto the bed and I jumped on top of her and straddled her chest. I stared at the slick path between her gigantic tits and readied myself for action. She beat me to it. She grabbed my cock and began stroking it, slowly, sensuously at first, then faster and faster, until her hand and my brain were a blur. I felt come boiling at the base of my cock, and I closed my eyes and tossed back my head – the only things of importance in the world becoming her hand and my cock, my cock and her hand.

She pulled me back from the precipice of ecstasy by tugging me down into the cleft between her tits. 'Fuck my tits, baby!' she urged. 'Then spray your come all over them!'

I opened my eyes, gave my head a shake, and reached down and shoved her tits together – against and over the top of my cock. The sensation was like nothing I had felt before. I let my cock bask momentarily in the damp super-heated pressure of her giant tits, then started sliding it back and forth within her fleshy canyon.

'That's the way,' she said, replacing my hands with hers.

She pushed her tits together even harder and the pressure on my cock became unbearable. It felt like I was plundering a virgin's tight pussy for the very first time. I moved my hips and shoved my cock back and forth between her pillows as best I could, until she temporarily loosened her hold on her tits and spat on my cock and into her love tunnel, lubricating both for better action. She pressed her tits back together again and I thrust my slickened cock back and forth between them. I groaned when the fiery head of my cock poked through her tits and she licked it.

'Suck it, Jen!' I encouraged her, stopping my rocking motion so that my cockhead peeked out from between her tits, pointed at her mouth.

She bent her head forward as far as she could and tongued and sucked on my swollen cockhead. Her lips and tongue were warm and wet and soft. My body shuddered like I'd been plugged into an electrical socket dick-first when she bit lightly on my purple head, and her tongue slapped across my slit.

'Yeah,' I moaned. Pre-come seeped out of my dick and she greedily lapped it up and swallowed it.

'I want more,' she hissed. 'I want you to come on my tits and my face . . . and in my mouth!' She nipped angrily at my cock and I knew that she meant it.

I picked up the rocking rhythm again, tit-fucking that gorgeous woman for all I was worth. She smiled wickedly up at me in anticipation, then pulled back her right tit and sucked on the engorged nipple. I could stand it no longer.

I slammed my cock in and out of the tunnel between her tits, the tension towering to the exploding point in my balls. I grabbed onto the headboard and frantically pounded away at her huge tits, my cock on fire as it rubbed her breasts and chest. The bed rattled with my frenetic tit-fucking, until I smashed through the point of no return and the hot slick friction on my cock forced the come to shoot up from my balls and out the tip of my blazing cock.

'I'm coming!' I screamed.

'Come all over my tits!' she screamed back.

I grabbed my bursting cock and pumped it frantically over the top of her tits. White-hot jism rocketed out of my dick and splashed down onto Jennifer's tits and face. My body jerked and my legs quivered as I doused those glorious tits and that beautiful face with what felt like gallons and gallons of super-heated come.

She groaned as my come rained down on her and coated her nipples and tits and face in long hot thick ropes. She opened her mouth and stuck out her tongue and hungrily captured and swallowed as much of my come as she could.

'Fuck!' I shouted, my cock spurting my lust onto her face and body. I tugged at my meat desperately, milking it of its gigantic load, painting Jennifer's tits white with my jism.

Then my body spasmed one final time, and the last of my sizzling semen shot out of my cock and found a home in her wanton mouth. I dropped my cock and used both of my hands to hold myself up on the headboard. Sweat poured off of my face and onto Jennifer's face and tits, mixing with the steaming puddles of semen that she hadn't yet licked clean.

She looked up at me as I gasped for air, my chest heaving. 'Help me clean up this mess?' she asked with a naughty smile.

'Sure,' I groaned, fighting to stay conscious, totally and absolutely drained. I bent down to kiss her on the lips and her tongue snaked out and I tasted come.

She cupped her breasts and pointed them at me. I flopped down on top of her and began licking her massive tits, tonguing sweat and come off her breasts and then depositing it in her mouth. She greedily took it in, swallowed it down, sucking my tongue to get all of the come out of my mouth and into hers. I shoved her giant tits forward and we lapped at them together, sucked on her nipples, passionately frenched till all of the come was gone.

When her huge tits were finally mopped clean, she smiled at me and asked, 'Do you do bottoms, too?'

– William, Chicago, USA

Teasing

I've always had a thing about being looked at. It's not that I'm an exhibitionist in the sense of always going around in short shorts or tiny miniskirts, and I don't like the sort of guy who talks to my tits any more than the next girl. It's different to that, and it's not something I generally tell my friends because most women find it creepy. So do I, in a sense, but it's the sort of thing where you have to separate fantasy from reality.

I like to be spied on. OK, so maybe it is a bit creepy, but it's a thrill, and the thrill comes from the thought that somebody's watching me, and wanting me, but knows they can't have me. So it's not like I have rape fantasies or anything heavy like that. I just like the idea of a man yearning for me so much that he's prepared to risk public humiliation, maybe even arrest, to see me in even a mildly erotic situation.

They say that that sort of thing gets into your head quite early, and maybe that's true for me, or maybe it's the other way around and I never knew how much it excited me until the first time something happened. I suppose I was a bit of a Queen Bee at school. Not the bitchy sort, or I like to think not, but I was always one of the popular girls and my parents were really generous and made sure I had lots of stuff. My boyfriend was Dan Calloway, which meant everyone envied me, although I really only went out with him because I could and looking back I realise he was a complete jerk.

He was really possessive, but I liked that, especially when he got tough with other boys because they'd been looking at me, or he thought they had. OK, I was young, all right, but it turned me on. He used to like to show me off too, making me wear tight crop-tops and stuff and always snogging me and groping me where we'd be seen. I still don't know if he got off on other people's jealousy or from making me do sexual things and show off in public.

I knew what I got off on though, knowing that people were watching, but I didn't dare push it too far in case Dan thought I was flirting. He was like that. It was OK for him to show me off, even to make me go commando in a sports skirt so there was every chance of people seeing my bare bum, or worse, but if I'd done the same when he hadn't told me to he'd have gone ape.

In the end I grew out of him, but not before I'd figured out what it was about showing off that turned me on. I wanted my watcher lost in helpless admiration for something he could never have, just as the other boys at school knew they didn't stand a chance while I was with Dan. At first I thought it would be enough to wear sexy clothes and dance a lot, making sure the men around me could get a good eyeful. That didn't work though, because the sort of men I met were pretty confident they could get me or, if not, then another girl, so they just enjoyed the view without being all that bothered.

The beach was better, with more of a mixed crowd and lots of older men, alone or even with their wives and keen to ogle the girls. I'd deliberately buy bikinis a couple of sizes too small, so that my boobs and bum were bursting out at the seams, a bit embarrassing sometimes and I never went like that unless I was on my own, but a real turn-on when I knew all the men were trying to watch and hoping I'd fall out of my costume. Twice I got so turned on I let it happen, once by running along a beach in Somerset until my boobs popped out right in front of a middle-aged guy who was trying to put up a sunshade for his wife, and once by pretending I was doing exercises until the inevitable happened and my cups came up so high my nipples were showing to a whole group of OAPs who'd just got off their bus.

All that was fun, but it didn't really get me there. I wanted some individual attention, and to know that somebody was truly desperate for me. My first real chance came when a group of us went on holiday to Kos. The north coast is really lonely, and you can strip off completely without any real chance of being seen, which was what the other girls wanted. Not me.

Some of us were with partners, others weren't, me included. I'd been flirting with a guy called Dean, not because I wanted to get with him, but because I knew this other guy, Paul, really fancied me. Paul was really short and had red hair, not my type at all, but just the sort of guy I could imagine getting really steamed up over me. So I spoke to the other girls who were in couples and suggested we spend an afternoon skinny-dipping, but instead of just sneaking off without telling Paul or the other two spare guys I made a point of saying what was happening but that they weren't wanted, even managing to imply that it was somehow perverted for them to see us in the nude when it was perfectly OK for each other's boyfriends.

I knew they wouldn't be able to keep away, and I had the best afternoon. We'd found a place with lovely soft sand and dunes behind covered with bushes, so nobody was likely to see us unless they knew we were there. Paul and the others had followed and I knew they were watching, so I was able to go in among the bushes to strip off and make sure they saw everything. I could feel their eyes on my body as I undressed, and I made sure to do it slowly and to show off. I was so turned on by the idea that I even made a point of bending down to give them all a peep of pussy from behind, not something I'd usually do, and once I was stripped off there was no stopping me.

We went in the sea, stark naked, mucking about in the waves and even touching each other a bit to get our boyfriends going, but for me it wasn't Dean I wanted to turn on, it was Paul, in among the bushes with his eyes glued to my body. Sunbathing was even better, laid out on my towel without a stitch on, first on my back, then propped up on my elbows to read my book, knowing full well the position left my boobs dangling down and everything on show. Even naughtier, I turned around, as if the sun was too bright, and lay with my thighs just a little apart so that he could see every detail of my bare bum and between my legs. By the end I was so horny I wanted to touch myself, but obviously I couldn't, not with the other girls there, and I didn't want to go with Dean, who'd probably have expected all the attention on his cock anyway, because he was a selfish bastard.

Going all the way had to wait for another time, but I was getting to be quite the expert by then. Whatever the situation, so long as there was an excuse to go nude or show off without making it obvious I was doing it on purpose, I could usually work it so that somebody got a good eyeful. This time me and two friends had taken a house in Spain, more of a chalet really, and right back from the coast. The beaches were no good, too crowded for any real fun, but right from the start I'd realised there was something much better to be had. We had a patio, just right for sunbathing, and it was overlooked by another house, where two old guys would come out and sit.

They could see me, but if I hadn't been looking I'd never have noticed them, because their place was right up above us and their heads only just showed above some olive trees on the slope. It was perfect, and I'd go out to sunbathe at every opportunity, first in my bikini, then topless, and in the end nude, all the while knowing they'd be watching me and wanting me, but they couldn't do a thing about it.

By the time we'd been there about a week both my friends had picked up guys. They didn't want to leave me on my own, but I insisted I'd be all right and one afternoon I finally made my fantasy perfect. I knew the guys were there, they seemed to spend half their lives there, and I made a big show of laying out my towel and getting together my sunblock and some water and stuff. I wanted it to be slow, so I did it gradually, first undoing my bikini top, then taking it off to go on my back, all the while glancing around as if I was shy and wanted to be sure I wasn't being watched by some pervert, but never looking up to them.

By the time I took my bikini pants off I was so horny they were wet. I made a really big deal of rubbing my sunblock in, standing up and doing myself all over. I already wanted to touch myself, and the idea was to make it look as if rubbing in the sunblock was turning me on, so I could pay more and more attention to my boobs and bum, then pretend to get carried away and do the business. I didn't have to fake it.

Just standing there rubbing sunblock into my boobs and knowing full well they were watching me would have been too much, but doing my bum and bending over to let them see pussy pushed me over the edge. I lay down, on my front, still creaming myself, incredibly horny at the thought of their eyes on me as I let my thighs come apart to show it all. I was to do it, go all the way, and you know how it is when you start to get close and you just want to be dirtier and dirtier. It was like that for me. Soon I was holding my bum-cheeks open to let them see between and rubbing the sunblock in my crease and over my pussy, just as if I was in the most private place possible. My fingers went everywhere, and I do mean everywhere, right inside and everything, and when I got there it was like I was going to pass out. I was sticking my bum right up too, so I was completely open to them and, do you know, at that moment if they'd just had the guts to come down the hill they could have had me, one at each end, the way footballers do the girls at their dirty parties.

Anyway, that was the first time, but you can bet it won't be the last.

– Lucy, Newport, UK

Poor Little Rich Girls

My friend Meena and I are members of a country and sports club. Well, we're not paying members, obviously – our fathers are. We're still in our gap years before university. We like the Club because it has a pool and tennis courts and a nine-hole golf course (Mummy likes me to partner her), as well as a spa with all the girly stuff we prefer best like facials and massage.

And it has Jeff.

Jeff is the caretaker in the sports hall where the gym equipment and the climbing wall are. He's a big, rough-looking man who always has blue stubble by the afternoon. He's not good-looking like the tennis pros, and he's got a bit of a belly starting, and he always smells of cigarettes even though there's a strict No Smoking ban all over the grounds. He scowls all the time, even when he's whistling to himself as he walks the corridors. I don't think he likes sassy girls like Meena and me much. In fact he doesn't like anyone who uses the equipment because they always leave it for him to tidy up afterwards. I've seen him complaining to the personal trainers and the other staff.

But Jeff has this thing. Well, this really big . . . thing. That's what the rumour is – I heard it off Rebecca and she said she heard it off one of the girls who does the seaweed wraps: Jeff has this absolutely *gigantic* cock. Well worth a look at.

Not that Meena and I are experts on cock, really. I mean, I've blown a couple of my boyfriends, but Meena's dad is really strict and wants her to have a big traditional wedding eventually so she only gives hand-jobs to hers. I guess things will change when we get to university and we've got our own space, but it's hard work getting private time when you've got families like ours. That doesn't stop us thinking about cock all the time. And talking about it. And keeping our eyes open. Ramon the Pilates instructor has this huge bulge in his Lycra pants, but everyone knows he's gay so we're not likely to see much more of that.

But there was Jeff in his baggy overalls. The mystery cock. You couldn't see anything, but the rumour was enough to get us giggly, and that was enough to make him glare at us as we passed him in the corridor.

So it started as a dare. Meena said, 'I bet you wouldn't dare ask him for a look at his prick.' And I said 'Nor would you!' Then it became, 'I bet you wouldn't dare hide in his office and watch him getting changed!'

Because he has an office, you see, all of his own, where he keeps tools and stuff. It has a door that locks automatically when he leaves, but hangs on the latch for a good minute before it snaps shut that final inch. We knew that because we'd spent a few hours sitting in the window seat on that corridor watching the men playing tennis on the court outside.

In the end, inflated by our giggles and speculation, we did what we both said we would do if the other were up for it: we waited one day after tennis until Jeff left his room, then jammed a golf-tee in his door. Once he'd turned the corner and was out of sight we could saunter back down the corridor at our leisure and slip into his room.

It was a bit of a mess really. There was no window, just a row of cupboards and a little table covered in paint stains and a couple of chairs. There were all sorts of sports-club bits and pieces standing about; a basketball hoop, some netting, climbing harnesses, a floor-polisher, the pieces of a rowing machine. It smelt of cigarettes too, and male sweat. We had a poke about, giggling nervously. We thought he'd be back quite soon because it was nearly the end of his shift and he hadn't got out of his overalls yet. See, we'd planned this. We weren't stupid.

I checked the cupboards, making sure there was one we could hide in. Then Meena found a magazine in the desk drawer and squealed under her breath. I hurried to look too. I was expecting one of those top-shelf magazines with the glossy pages and the beautiful models, but this wasn't like that. The paper was cheaper-looking and so were the girls. Some of them weren't lookers at all, and some had fat bottoms and cellulite. There were a lot of bottoms on display because this was a magazine about spanking. The models were posed over knees and desks or just bent at the waist and braced, their bums thrust out at the camera and their plump shaven pussies on display. Their bum-cheeks were usually bright red, but sometimes they had pale weals across the pink, or red stripes across pale cheeks, because they were all being spanked in some way – by men just off-camera – using canes or hands or leather paddles. Some of the pictures showed the models' faces screwed up in pain or dread, or wide-eyed in shock as the blow landed. We turned the pages, hardly believing what we saw. 'That's disgusting!' hissed Meena, but I was feeling funny and I couldn't stop looking. It was strange, because they weren't nice pictures at all, but my own pussy had become hot and I felt all squirmy and dirty.

'We should go,' Meena said. 'He's weird if he likes this stuff.'

Then we heard it; his whistle. He always whistled the same tune as he strolled around; something old-fashioned. 'Annie's Song' I think it's called.

'He's coming back!'

'Quick!' I shoved the magazine back in the drawer and we dived into the biggest cupboard, squashing up together on top of a load of hockey sticks. We were so close Meena's boobs were crushed against my arm. I pulled the door closed, but it had louvred panels so we could see out between the slats. Then we held our breath as Jeff came into sight, shutting the outer door behind him. He sat at one of the chairs, facing our cupboard, and lit up a cigarette.

'I'm scared, Flis,' Meena breathed in my ear. I pinched her to stop her talking and she quivered.

The caretaker opened the drawer of his desk, got out the magazine and laid it on one knee. I felt my heart, which was already racing, bang against my ribs. He was looking at pictures of girls' bare bottoms, and we were only a few feet away. And for a while that's all he did; smoke his cigarette and turn the pages slowly, tilting his head a little. Meena's breathing seemed really loud. Then he dropped his tab-end on the tiles and ground it out with his foot. His hand, free now, drifted to his crotch and groped thoughtfully.

Oh good grief, he was touching himself. Meena squirmed against me, and I didn't know if it was excitement or terror she was feeling. We watched, wide-eyed, as he rubbed the bulge in his coveralls until it was at a stage that obviously satisfied him, then undid his buttons one by one from the neck down. He didn't need to take them off further, nor the clothes peeking from underneath; he just slipped his cock out through his open fly, easing it into view. It was big all right, as we'd been promised – and veiny too. It wasn't like the neat slim things I was used to with the boys I'd known. This was all lumpy and discoloured, and as he pulled back his foreskin the helmet bulged dark red and winked its wet eye.

Then he began to jack off slowly and deliberately, looking at those pictures of punished bottoms – and to my disbelief he got *bigger*. He was *enormous*. I couldn't help it: I gave a little quiver and my foot slipped and one of the hockey sticks fell and rapped against the side of the cupboard.

He looked up straight at where we were hiding, his face knotting into the scowl we knew. Then he stood. He didn't hurry; he put his magazine aside and – with obvious effort – tucked his erection back inside his trousers. There was absolutely nothing we could do, except watch as he came over and flung the cupboard door open, revealing us clinging together and staring up at him with huge eyes.

'What the fuck do you think you're doing?' he asked. He didn't raise his voice. I don't think he ever raised his voice in all that was to happen after that. He just looked furious. Of course, we couldn't answer him, so he reached in and grabbed Meena by the arm, hoiking her bodily from the cupboard. That was my chance; I ducked and ran under his other arm as he was distracted, and nearly made it to the door.

'You going to run out on your friend then?'

I stopped and turned at that growl. Meena's face was blank with fear.

'And leave her with me?' he mocked. 'Coward.'

'Let her go!'

'Not until you come back here and face me.' His voice was deep, but he wasn't shouting. 'Come on. *Here.*'

So I came back, reluctantly, wriggling in my skin. I felt like I was ten years old again and facing the headmaster in disgrace. But at least he dropped Meena's arm.

'What's your names?'

'Meena,' she whispered.

'Felicity.'

'And what were you doing in my cupboard?'

'It was just a bit of a laugh.' I knew my face was crimson.

'Uhuh? Watching me get my cock out? Want me to tell your fathers what you were up to?'

Meena's eyes widened. 'No!' Her dad would be furious, I knew; he might even stop her going to university.

'We'll tell them what sort of things you've been reading!' I blustered.

'Oh? So first you read through my porn magazine, and then you hide in my cupboard to spy on me. That's going to look good, isn't it? You think they'll approve of their dirty little girls?'

'Don't,' Meena begged.

'Dirty, naughty little brats trying to get a look at my cock.' He smiled, in a twisted way. 'Did you like what you saw? Was it . . . nice?'

She shook her head. I thrust out my lip. 'You're filthy.'

'Not half as filthy as you. Well, it's your choice, girls. Either I tell your fathers or . . .'

'Or what?'

He wet his lips. 'Well, you've been reading my magazine. You know what I like. And you've already had a look at mine. Fair's fair: you let me have a look at those bottoms of yours and I'll let you off. This time.'

'You're not hitting me!' Meena protested as we both guessed his game.

'Only a couple of slaps, say. Haven't you ever been spanked before?'

Not for years, in my case. Meena pouted and admitted, 'Mummy would hit the backs of my calves with her slipper.'

'Well, it's not that bad, is it? Someone's going to have to punish you, after all. Your choice.'

I took a deep breath. 'OK.'

He lost his scowl. 'OK?'

'But you don't get to take our knickers down.'

He nearly laughed; I could see him trying to hide it. 'All right then, blondie. Get those two chairs. Put them side by side.'

'Flis!' hissed Meena anxiously, but I pulled a face at her.

He directed us to kneel up on the chairs, side by side, and lean over the backs to present our bums. We were still wearing our tennis clothes; short white skirts, bare legs and white trainers. I gripped the back struts of the chair, worried about overbalancing, feeling very exposed. He walked behind us. I could feel him looking at our skirts, our thighs. Then without a word he lifted my skirt up and laid it on my back, revealing my panties. They were plain cotton tennis knickers I was wearing that day. When he touched my bum I nearly fell off the chair.

'Hey –'

'Quiet,' he rumbled. And I realised he wasn't pulling my panties down; he was tugging them up – pulling the material into the cleft of my bottom to bare my cheeks. So I shut up, even when he ran his hand over those bum-cheeks. His fingers were calloused but his touch was warm and gentle. It felt nice. I felt braver.

Then he went and did the same thing to Meena. I turned my head to watch her expression as he did it, seeing the humiliation and trepidation and reluctant relief flutter across her flushed face. My friend is very pretty, with her glossy mane of hair and her big dark eyes, but I thought I'd never ever seen her look as pretty as she did then.

'Look at those two beautiful brat bottoms,' he murmured to himself. 'Just perfect. And never been spanked.' He patted us both, one hand to each of us. I clenched my buttocks automatically; maybe that goaded him, because he started with me. Facing my heels, holding my hip with one hand, he brought his hand down stingingly on my cheeks, first one then the other. Automatically I gasped, but the pain was gone in a heartbeat, leaving only the shock and the heat.

'Brat. Dirty, cock-hungry little girl.'

I was glad he took it slowly, giving me just enough time to recover from each swat. I was determined not to scream, but I did gasp. I could feel my flesh plumping, swelling, growing hotter. I knew my pale skin would be going as scarlet as the girls' in the magazine. In between blows he would pause and caress my burning skin, and that was more than a comfort – it felt wonderful in contrast to the stinging pain. When I was nicely warmed through by his reckoning he turned his attention to Meena, and I watched her take his punishment. She gasped and struggled more than I did, and tears ran down her cheeks: she'd always been a bit on the soft side. She would have slid off her chair if he hadn't held her. He called her a cock-sucking slut: I was jealous. Then out of the blue he struck my wobbling arse twice more, once on each cheek and harder than he'd done yet, and stepped away so that he could survey his handiwork.

Oh how my poor bum burned! I writhed on my knees, seeking relief. I thought it was all over. But he closed in again to touch us. Not with blows. One hand each, it turned out, straight on the panty-gusset, fingers probing. 'You dirty girls,' he groaned. 'Do you know how wet you both are? You're dripping with fuck-juice, both of you. You're begging for it. You wanted cock, didn't you? – shall I stick my big hard cock into these two snatches?'

'Nooo!' squealed Meena though clenched teeth, but she was pushing back onto his hand and I could see it. My pussy seemed to have caught fire from my thrashed cheeks, desperate for pleasure to balance the pain. Jeff poked at us through the wet cloth strips.

'No? I think I'm going to have to punish you harder for being such cock-teasers.' He stepped away briefly, but only to pick up a coil of rope, the kind used on the climbing wall. He took most of the coil in his left hand but a short tail in his right. 'Hold still,' he told me, pulling up my knicker gusset even tighter. 'Stick that arse out properly.'

I obeyed, burning with fear and shame. The crack of the rope-end across both my cheeks was quieter than his hand, but hurt far more. I hissed and writhed, sweat springing out on my skin as the pain grew bigger and redder and deeper.

'One more. Two stripes each for the slutty girls.' I took another, but at her first lash Meena squealed dangerously loudly and burst into tears.

'No – don't!'

'Shut up,' he growled. 'You spoilt brat.'

'I'll take it,' I gabbled. 'I'll take hers.'

'That's better.' So he planted a third stripe across my outthrust bottom, right at the crease between thighs and cheeks. Then he stroked my skin and I could tell by the catch of his fingertips there would be welts there. I sobbed and wriggled, trying to swallow my own tears. 'You're so wet, both of you,' he mused, pushing the gusset of my knickers up into my pussy, and presumably doing the same with his other hand to Meena. The indent of my cunt was an easy target, wanting to swallow his fingers. 'Wide fucking open too,' he observed, scratching his fingers over my clit. Meena let out a moan, helpless and humiliated and too excited to stop. 'Gagging for it,' he sneered, frigging us hard. 'You both got a good spanking and you're still begging for cock. Letting me touch you like this. What've I got to do to teach you a lesson? You look like good girls but you're just *sluts*.'

That's when I came. I don't know if Meena did but she was noisy enough.

After that Jeff lost patience. He walked round the front of our chairs, whipping out his cock again, pumping it like a shotgun. 'Lick it,' he commanded Meena, and she did – right from the root to the tip. Then he took its head in his hand and shoved his length into her mouth until her eyes bulged. He didn't keep it there long and switched to me instead. 'And you, blondie.' His gnarled prick was slippery with my friend's spit. I wrapped my lips around his swollen helmet and sucked hungrily. This is what we'd wanted, wasn't it? A good close-up of his spectacular cock? We were getting everything we'd asked for now.

'Both of you!' he gasped, dragging the chairs together so we could lick him simultaneously, but that was too much for him to watch; he shot his load almost at once, strings of sticky come jetting up into my face, splattering my eyelids and clinging to my lashes, then more gouts spurted on Meena's cheeks.

The last thing he did before he let us go was make us lick his jiz off each other's tear-stained faces.

We didn't tell on him, of course. We were too embarrassed. Meena now goes pink at the mention of a game of tennis. My own marks took a day or so to fade and I had to be very careful nobody else saw them. But I'm biding my time. I'm going to have to deal with this, the only way that makes sense. I'm going to go back and face up to Jeff again. And kneel on that chair in that dirty, stuffy little room and beg him to spank my bottom scarlet – and this time to stick that huge cock of his up my pussy and fuck me properly.

– Felicity, Harrow, UK

The Summer of Sixty-Nine

The first thing that would surprise you is how young we were at the time. I'm a little ashamed to tell you exactly, but suffice to say both my and Nicky's ages had an '8' in them.

It was summer, and we were being treated to a short but well-appreciated sunny fortnight of low-cut tops, short shorts and nipples standing out in the breeze. At least that's how Nicky and I were dressing most of the time.

I had just finished further education and, as I had decided against university, I was enjoying my last truly free summer before nine to five drafted me to active duty. Nicky, my closest friend throughout college, was in rather the same position and we hung out together all the live-long day, strutting around shops in hot pants, trainers and vest-tops, or working on our tans in the park or on the front lawn. My mother kind of frowned on us flaunting ourselves in full view of neighbours and passing strangers alike, in lime-green or pink bikinis, but she never did anything more than pass a disapproving comment.

It did not take long for our sun-worshipping to attract attention, from adolescents at first, who cycled past craning their necks every five minutes, apparently unaware that when you ride past the same spot ten times in an hour, your motives become a tad transparent. Nicky and I smirked at each other when we saw them – we both knew they would be storing images of our shiny tanned bodies away in their mind's eye, for masturbating over later.

Soon, though, we attracted a more focused form of attention from our next-door neighbour, Martin, who stopped to say hello one afternoon as he cleaned his car, and then the following afternoon as he mowed the lawn, and then again the afternoon after that as he dug his garden. We were both pretty suspicious that he had suddenly found all these chores to do, coincidentally while two teenagers were sunbathing near-naked in the front garden, and we speculated what job he would find to do as an excuse to get a look at us on that third day: we did smirk knowingly at each other as he emerged from his garage with a spade in his hand, as it was near enough what we had predicted.

After lunch that afternoon I renewed my lotion, smoothing it down my legs, then up inside my thighs, and over the part of my pelvis and hips exposed by the cut of my bikini bottoms. I needed another splurge to cover my abdomen and a few more squirts for my upper body. It was vain of me, but I was rather proud of the effect that glistening film of oil gave to my flesh.

'Do my back, would you?' I said to Nicky as I rolled over, turning my arse to the sky.

Nicky put her book face-down on her towel and sat herself astride my backside as if it were a pair of cushions. From there she undid my bikini top and applied the creamy lotion over my back. It felt very good indeed to feel the emollient seeping into my skin, and especially good as Nicky was intent on turning the whole exercise into some kind of therapeutic massage.

'Hmmm, what are you up to?' I asked her as she began to knead her thumbs in-between my shoulder blades.

She leaned forward to whisper a reply in my ear: 'Let's give him a show,' she joked.

I tutted and groaned at the frivolous idea but as it really did feel surprisingly good and relaxing I didn't protest. However, while she was very good at the massage I don't think she made a very convincing lesbian lover as all shc could really think of doing was moaning playfully and squirming a little. Anyway, it seemed to havc the desired effect of attracting Martin's attention: he looked up from his digging and laughed quietly to himself at our antics, one eyebrow raised.

Once Nicky had rolled back onto her own towel and our silly giggling had died down, we were surprised to see him deposit the blade of his spade into the ground with a thrust of his arm, and walk over to talk to us.

Martin was in his late thirties, and had always been one of those friendly avuncular types ever ready with a joke and a smile for the kid next door. He had made me giggle many a time as a child, for example, when he tried to join in or goof around with one of our games – you know the sort he was, I am sure. He knew the value of a silly voice and never complained about balls going over the fence into his garden. We didn't anticipate that Martin would be a neighbour for much longer though; his wife had caught him with another (younger) woman and left him a few months ago and we couldn't see how he could maintain himself in a large house with just the one income and a divorce settlement on the horizon. His face was regular and masculine, with laughter lines appearing around his mouth and eyes even at his relatively young age, giving him a cheeky, impish look.

'Looks like I'm having dinner with you tonight, ladies.' He smiled.

At first I thought he was making some stupid attempt at getting one of us to go on a date, but he soon explained when he saw the puzzled looks on our faces.

'Did you not know? Your parents have invited everyone over for a barbecue,' he said.

I looked at Nicky. No, I didn't know.

'Oh, right,' I said vacantly. 'See you then.'

He turned out to be right and I shouldn't really have been surprised: my parents had pounced upon the great weather and taken full advantage of it, taking the cover off our little pool and eating barbecue practically every night, so I suppose it was only a natural progression that they would start showing off and feeding the whole neighbourhood.

Martin came round early. My folks were borrowing his picnic table and when he came round to deliver it, mum could not resist offering him the hospitality of the back garden and the first beer out of the fridge. Nicky and I were sent out to chat with him while meats, sauces and salads were prepared inside. The conversation was pretty benign at first, that was until Martin had got through half of his beer and become a bit more relaxed.

'So, are you girls trying to kill me out there, flaunting your naked bodies every day?' he asked.

I looked askance at Nicky but her sardonic expression was no help.

'We're not naked,' I pointed out.

'Not yet,' he said, more to himself than anything.

'Don't get your hopes up, her mum wouldn't allow it for starters,' Nicky cut in.

'Ah, so if you were allowed to sunbathe naked, you would then?'

We both gave him a withering look.

'That's not what she meant,' I said.

'But would you?' he insisted, smiling broadly.

'No, because that really would kill you,' Nicky jibed, glancing at me for my approval. I think she was quite proud of her comeback.

I laughed and Martin seemed to accept he had been out-manoeuvred for the time being. He had to watch his tongue for a while anyway as my parents came out to have a drink and a quick break from the preparation.

'You want me to help, Mrs T?' Martin offered like a good guest.

'No, you sit and relax, you're a guest,' my mum replied like a good host as she headed back to the kitchen with my long-suffering dad in tow.

The three of us were alone again and Martin didn't waste time trimming the course of the conversation so it was once again parallel with his one-track mind.

'So you had many boyfriends, Debra?' he asked, swigging his bottle nonchalantly.

'Many,' I replied with a smug smile. Perhaps it was a little exaggeration.

'I bet you've been all the way with a few of them, yeah?'

I gave him an admonishing look and anxiously glanced over toward the patio door, wildly conscious that my parents might be able to hear. I could see them moving around in the kitchen, blissfully unaware that their daughter was the subject of a lewd interview from a man over twice her age.

'That's none of your business, Martin,' I replied. It was hard to know how to frame my reply. I didn't want to prudishly shut the door on the conversation and look like an embarrassed virgin, but at the same time I wasn't about to reveal my magic number. A lady would not do that, unless it had a '1' in it maybe, which mine did not.

'Probably not, but I still want to know. You know, Nicky, don't you? How many is it?'

'Leave me out of it,' replied Nicky, waving a hand at him.

'Let's just say it's more than you,' I finally replied, swigging my own beer triumphantly.

'Don't be too sure of that,' he said, winking.

I really wasn't sure how to take this side of Martin. I had always liked him and even found him attractive. What girl doesn't have a thing for the attractive mature mentor? But his sexuality was something I had never had occasion to factor into my evaluation of him. It did not fit right with his wholesome image (recently tarnished by the gossip about his affair, admittedly). I certainly hadn't considered the possibility that he would come on to me, but he appeared to be preparing for that. How would I – how should I – respond?

The doorbell went: the first of the other guests had arrived and I stood up to answer it, interrupting the conversation.

'How ever many there were, I wish I was one of them,' he murmured as I walked away. The most infuriating thing about his comment was the broad cheeky smile on his face as he said it – it made it impossible to hate him. Not even when I felt his eyes burning into my arse as I wiggled away from him back into the house.

The conversation retreated to more of a PG-rating during the barbecue. With over a dozen respectable folk enjoying a meal and a drink together – two of them my parents – Martin had to watch his words. He would have known that having essentially forced his wife from his home, many of them would have been reviewing him on a probationary basis right now, so he was treading a bit more carefully.

After everyone had eaten their fill of steak, sausage, chicken legs and burgers another box of wine was opened and things started to become a little more relaxed. Martin proved just how much he was trying to improve his image by insisting on doing the clear-up and quite adamantly persuading those who stood up to help to sit back down and enjoy their wine.

'Debra and Nicky can help me,' he said. 'Come on, girls.'

The crafty beggar. He knew we couldn't really refuse in front of everyone and so we got up and began to clear away the plates and bowls just as he had hinted, and ferry them into the kitchen.

After the first run he patted my bum as we passed at the back door, knowing that with plates in my hands I couldn't really fend him off. I felt his middle finger curl up and brush my crotch and my soft fleshy vulva through my panties. Surely that had been an accident? He wouldn't have, would he? Not deliberately? I tried to ignore the slight wetness it gave me inside.

Nicky and I collected the last of the crockery from the table and made another trip to the kitchen. I was expecting Martin to pass by again, copping another cheeky feel, but to my surprise he did not emerge. Instead he was waiting in the kitchen for us.

'I suppose we should wash up too, eh?' he suggested, ushering us in and closing the back door behind us.

He stood there for a moment, right near the door that had just been closed behind us, right in our personal space, and looked at us. He smiled the cheeky, impossibly infectious smile at me again, and I saw him look at my lips. My heart skipped a beat and I felt my fingers start to tingle with nervousness. Before I could think what I was doing, I glanced at his lips. It was only the most subtle of weaknesses that I had shown him, and the only encouragement I had given him the whole time, but it was all he needed. He wrapped his left arm around me and drew me in, pressing his lips to mine and flicking his tongue at my resistant – for the time being at least – lips.

I felt my legs wobble; I have never felt so nervous. The fear that we would be discovered, the thrill that it was so wrong, and the lust at being swept into such a passionate kiss, all combined to send me into some kind of momentary erotic trance. I held back though; I was far too conscious of Nicky standing there with us like a gooseberry and, of course, of my parents, pillars of the community as they were, out in the back garden, enjoying wine with, well, other pillars of the community. Needless to say not a one of them would look favourably on teenagers snogging thirty-somethings when they're supposed to be doing dishes. After those few seconds, in which so many darting thoughts passed through my mind, I think Martin sensed the conflict within me and pulled away. Neither of us said a thing.

Despite his silence, he was not finished. He turned to Nicky and, fixing her with a smouldering gaze, he gave her the same treatment. Nicky even moaned at the release of tension she felt as she received her kiss. I watched, my heart thumping like mad, and my pussy gradually moistening.

Martin pulled away again with Nicky's captivated gaze upon him. We were both frozen to the spot, dizzy with it all, motionless. I glanced nervously at the window, so frightened that someone would look in or pass by.

Martin was not so nervous. He grabbed our arms and pulled us both nearer to him, then, cradling both our necks, he pushed us towards each other. My heart nearly choked me, it pounded so hard in my throat. The nervous thrill I was feeling intensified beyond anything I could have imagined; my fingers, toes and tongue all tingled like crazy as I contemplated kissing my friend. I must have been mad with the excitement of it all, for I did not withdraw, and neither did she. Softly, our lips met, caressed, then parted and I felt her soft feminine tongue play with my own. I moaned as a contented sigh escaped me, and we pressed our mouths to each other with a passion and lust I had never felt before.

When eventually we withdrew, Nicky's face was a picture of quizzical delight, and it mirrored my own. I did not know what to say or do at that point, and Martin knew it. The wily old sleaze took full advantage of our racing young minds by grabbing both our hands and leading us out of the front door, across the front lawns to his own front door, and inside his house. I wondered if any of our guests had seen us leave. I doubted it very much.

Once inside, he kissed us again, this time grabbing a buttock and pulling it away from its partner. I felt the fabric of my shorts brush my pussy and anus as my buttocks were stretched apart, and this time I knew when the tip of his middle finger stroked my camel-toe, it was deliberate. After he had kissed Nicky and subjected her to the same titillation, I moved in on her, unprompted this time, pressing my small pert breasts against her fuller mounds, feeling them squash against me as our tongues danced.

We were both trembling now and, for comfort somehow, we held onto each other's hands for this great trip into the unknown. Martin pointed upstairs and Nicky was the first to react. I followed her close behind. For the first time in my life I watched her as a sex object, observing the way her arse swung as she took the stairs in her shorts. I reached out and held her on the hip as she climbed ahead of me.

Halfway up, I felt the tickling of Martin's fingers on my gusset and I gasped as I felt a finger wiggle its way to my flesh, burrow softly between my labia and, making use of the juices I was producing, press slowly inside me. Martin simply held his finger there, letting my tunnel grind upon it as I took the last few steps onto the landing.

I stopped at the top of the stairs to allow Martin to finger me more vigorously. Nicky joined in, putting her arm around me, wetting the tip of a finger of her own on her cute little tongue and using it to softly rub my clitoris. It felt good to say the least, and my legs were soon wobbling with my first little orgasm. Nicky kissed me to stifle my moans as I peaked. By the time I had recovered from my little climax I was thirstily sucking my own juices off their fingers.

'Come on,' said Martin, urging us into the bedroom.

It, like the rest of the house, was well kept and decorated. Clearly he and his estranged liked to live in plusher surroundings. The bed was massive, an ambassador I think they call the size, and covered in a thick silk-covered quilt and a pile of pillows. I began to wonder why Martin's wife had chosen to leave this luxury –

surely, if he had been the transgressor, she had the leverage to force him out of the marital home and remain to enjoy the nightly delights of wallowing in this welcoming pile of feather and foam.

We sat on the bed, Nicky and I, still holding hands as if we were sitting together on the school bus. Martin stood expectantly before us, unbuttoning the linen shirt that he had worn for the summer evening. I knew what he wanted, so I reached forward and fed his belt strap back through the loop, unbuckled it, looked up at him, popped the button and prised the zip open. Martin continued to take off his shirt as he watched me removing his trousers.

I still could not quite believe what was going on and I glanced at Nicky, almost to say: 'Should we be doing this?' but she just smiled in encouragement. Emboldened, I pulled Martin's jeans down to his thighs and regarded the head of his penis pressing out against his briefs. I noticed the tiniest spot of pre-come soaking through the fabric – not much, just a pin-prick really. Glancing once more at Nicky, I pulled down his briefs, allowing him to spring forth and harden fully before our widened eyes. I took it in my hands and wanked it softly. Nicky budged up nearer to me and jabbed me with her elbow.

'What?' I said.

She said nothing, merely flicking her head in the direction of Martin's cock. It was obvious what she meant. Egged on by her, I complied, leaning forward to kiss the head and collect that tiny dribble of come on the tip of my tongue. Martin seemed to enjoy that.

'Go on,' said Nicky, nudging me again.

'I know, I know, don't rush me.'

I cupped Martin's scrotum with one hand and guided the head into my mouth, sucking hard on the bulbous end with my lips and tongue. I glanced up at him coyly, which seems a little silly now that I describe it, as the last thing you are with a penis in your mouth is coy, but he seemed to find it sexy. I sucked harder and harder on his helmet and it really began to become intense for him: he moaned and shook, pressed down on my shoulders and bent over double, but I did not relent until he was begging me to stop.

'God! You're going to kill me!'

'I haven't even started yet.' I smiled at him as I came up for breath and dove back down on his cock again.

This time I slowly worked my way down and up the shaft, twisting the head as my lips passed over it. I gave him another look as he expressed his approval. I repeated the exercise over and over, quickening the pace until his whole penis was covered in a sheen of my saliva. Nicky nudged me again.

'Come on, let me have a go,' she said.

I passed the penis on to my friend, like it was the baton in a relay, and watched as she stretched her lips around it and started to bob her head up and down. She looked like she was enjoying it; her eyes were half closed and she was moaning quietly.

'Can you taste your girlfriend's spit on it?' Martin asked her lewdly as she sucked.

Nicky nodded as she sucked and moaned louder. She seemed to like Martin talking to her and Martin sensed it, and took advantage of it.

'Do you like the taste of cock as well, Nicky?' he asked.

'Mmm-hmm.'

Again she seemed to get a big thrill from answering him, becoming more and more eager to blow him. She was sucking him with attitude now. I continued watching, really getting into the show, reaching down to finger my clit.

Finally, Martin pulled back and pushed Nicky firmly back on the bed. She reluctantly let of his cock and lay back on her elbows, looking eagerly back up at him. We both looked up at him. He was very much in charge; we weren't exactly virgins, as you may have guessed from our skills at fellatio, but we were very young and at that moment I think we saw Martin as kind of our mentor in love-making. In effect, that made him the director of this pornographic movie (being acted out for no cameras or audience of course). We were very much waiting for his direction as we lay there on the bed staring up at him and his glistening erect cock.

'I think you want to taste each other now, don't you, ladies?' he asked, somewhat rhetorically.

It was something of a surprise to hear him say that. Not that it was an unreasonable thing to say, but because it threw into sharp relief a reality that Nicky and I had accepted subconsciously the moment we had kissed and let our tongues dance together in the kitchen, but were yet to acknowledge on a conscious level. Where else did we think this was going if not inevitably to the two of us tasting pussy for the first time?

We looked at each other, right in the eyes, and I felt a melting lust wash over the both of us. There was no doubt for me that the answer to Martin's question was 'Yes.'

I practically dove for Nicky's crotch, wheeling around so that my own sopping wet lips were aligned with her face. Martin removed her shorts for me and I began by licking and nibbling at the inside of her thighs. I reached under her buttocks as I did so and allowed my finger to gently massage her anus and perineum.

I could feel her pulling down at my shorts and yanking away my knickers as she gasped in response to the work of my busy little tongue. She pulled them both over and around my arse and as far down my thighs as she could work them. Excited, I diverted the attention of my tongue to her vulva and anus – I was trying to imagine or recreate the kind of oral stimulation that I like to feel from a man's tongue, that is, to feel it slowly and gently working the entire area before homing in on my clitoris, and, eventually, slipping inside my vagina.

Nicky seemed to agree on this policy – I felt the warmth of her little tongue tickling at the inside of my thighs, around my anus, pressing on my perineum, and tracing the sides of my vulva, teasing me wonderfully as I got more and more aroused and excited.

Martin distracted me for a moment. I could tell he was enjoying the show, but he interrupted my work, looking for a couple of sucks on his penis to keep him going. I was happy to oblige and, as I bobbed my head up and down on it, I groaned deeply as I finally felt my best friend's tongue pressing and playing on my clitoris. I kissed a temporary farewell to Martin's piece and dove straight down for Nicky's bud to return the compliment.

I had never felt so at one with someone: our bodies meshed so perfectly in that famous position as we imparted symbiotic pleasure to each other and knew within ourselves exactly how and what the other was feeling. I was overcome with an ecstatic contentment.

'Go on, girls, make each other come for me,' Martin said, as he kneeled on the bed next to us, appreciatively pulling on his penis.

We moved on to each other's pussies, tongue-fucking slowly and deliberately. Every now and then we went back to the clitoris, just to keep it interested (that's important, right, girls?) before returning to lapping at each other's pussies. Nicky's moans were making me more and more excited and now I really was building to something. I lapped and tongue-fucked harder and harder hoping that Nicky would take the hint and reciprocate. She did, and soon I was coming again, but just that little bit harder this time around.

The sight of me biting my lip and pressing my pussy down hard on Nicky's face excited Martin greatly and he could wait no longer. He moved around behind me and I felt him parting my lips and pressing his glans against the entrance to my vagina. I sighed and readied myself for what was now a much-needed cock as he toyed with me, rubbing it between my labia, perhaps to collect my juices upon it.

I was neglecting Nicky's pussy and clit, I know, and, to my knowledge at least, she had not come yet – some friend I was turning out to be! Well, I was trying to think of her, I promise, but this was my first threesome and the thick shaft of hot flesh knocking at my door was distracting me somewhat. It distracted me even more when I felt it push inside and thrust at my pussy like a piston. I managed eventually to gather myself and get back to work on Nicky's sacred place whilst still enjoying my fucking from Martin's cock.

I could hear her whimpering with pleasure as I dug in to the tasty flesh with my tireless tongue. Soon enough she responded with an orgasm of her own, bucking and writhing as best she could, trapped underneath me as she was.

I lapped more casually now at her juices and savoured the feel of Martin's rod ploughing into me.

'Yeah, lick my balls while I fuck her,' I heard him say to Nicky. She responded with another one of those moans of excitement, just like when he had talked dirty to her before. I looked down between my legs and saw, right enough, she had extended her tongue and was lapping at his dangling scrotum as it passed by with each thrust into me.

Martin rammed it hard up me three times – and I grunted in appreciation at each – before withdrawing from me.

'Give me that other pussy,' he said bluntly. He was quite aggressive now, in a sexual sense at least, but I didn't mind, it was actually very sexy in its way.

We inched down towards the foot of the bed so that Nicky's bum was right on the edge and Martin could enter her from a standing position. We were still in the same position, Nicky and I, and I was treated to a very close-up view of Martin's thick cock entering Nicky's pussy. I held her labia apart to ease the passage.

Nicky buried her face right in my entrance as she felt the quickening rush of a penis's first invading pushes. The vibrations of her cries of pleasure played on my clitoris like the tip of a dildo as she tried her best to muffle her noises in my soft, wet pussy.

Soon Martin had reached his rhythm and I watched the very erotic, very arousing show of his juice-smeared shaft moving in and out of her, inches from my face. I flicked my tongue at the shaft and at her clitoris as the fun played out before me. Behind me, Nicky did her best work on my clitoris as she savoured her seeing to.

Martin powered on, speaking to Nicky in the way he knew she liked, telling her how wet she was and how much her pussy was loving it. I had never heard such talk before, being so young and innocent, but must admit it was kind of thrilling to hear. Nicky's pussy responded by soaking the shaft of his penis with more of its sugary fluid.

Martin cried out very loudly and slowed right up with his fucking, trying, I think, to stop himself coming. He withdrew again, and told me to bring my pussy down to the foot of the bed. I was content to do as he asked and I turned around, so that now I was lying on top of Nicky, pressing my breasts to hers and kissing her fervently, allowing our pussy juice and saliva to intermingle upon our taste buds.

I felt Martin's penis push inside me once more, pounding me fast in a build-up to climax. I began to want his come inside me and to anticipate it bathing my vagina. But I could not have it all to myself it seemed, as he withdrew and, adjusting his position, slipped it inside Nicky's pussy just a couple of inches below mine. It must have made quite a sight for Martin, those two hungry honey-pots aching for his come.

I knew he was getting close now and I actually started to feel some jealousy that my friend was going to receive the full consignment of warm spunk and I wasn't going to get a drop, so it was with some relief and no little ecstasy that I felt him pull out of Nicky and re-enter me again, thrusting away in pursuit of his orgasm.

It did not take long after that for the moment to arrive and my pussy thrilled to the feel of his pulsating penis pumping a hot dollop inside me. He was crying out in pleasure as I felt him withdraw again, sprinkling a few drops on my pussy as he pulled back, and enter Nicky, where he pumped the rest of his load inside her. It was quite a manoeuvre on his part and shows, I suppose, one of the advantages of taking an experienced lover!

Nicky and I giggled as we kissed and writhed, rubbing the dribbles of semen between our pussies as we came down from our stratospheric high. Martin flopped onto his back on the bed next to us breathing heavily and looking very satisfied indeed. We could faintly hear the revelry going on in our back garden next door and for the first time I was afraid that our activities might have been noticed.

'Oh my god, do you think anyone heard us?' I asked.

'Nah. But we'd better not hang around here too long, or they'll miss us,' said Martin. 'We'll just say we went for a stroll before tackling the dishes.'

'You've obviously got experience at making up cover stories,' observed Nicky as I rolled off her and reached for my shorts and knickers.

He just winked at us and pulled up his trousers.

– Debra, Milngavie, Scotland, UK

The Newsagent's Wife

Late at night and both naked, my husband and I were indulging in what was our occasional amusement. It was our habit to read each other the stories in the sex magazines from downstairs in our newsagent's shop. He would usually read me one or two and then he would enjoy me reading to him while I was impaled on his erect prick. His favourite position was with me on top with my bum pointing towards his face. I reckon that he preferred this because he could feel me gripping his cock tight and stare at my spread buttocks. Probably he imagined the face and body of the heroine of the letter attached to that bum, which was OK with me as I could imagine he was someone else too. Brown-skinned, black-skinned, white-skinned – it was my choice.

I would read aloud, shifting up and down, feeling his cock deep inside me, right where I wanted it. Occasionally the feelings would be so exquisite I'd have difficulty holding on to the magazine and keeping my eyes focused on the words. As a consequence, I would often improvise, making up whole sentences until the feeling in my sex subsided slightly and I could once more see what I was supposed to be reading. But I soon realised that it was just as effective for us both if I made up almost the whole story. He loved to hear of cuckolded husbands whose wives took well-endowed lovers. So I invented tales of wimpish men forced to observe as their sexually voracious spouses writhed ecstatically on the end of hard cocks and moaned and screamed in ways that they never would for their husbands.

I stroked his balls beneath me and felt him twitch inside me when I told him that I had found a story which he would absolutely love. It was about a young couple who had a corner shop like us. He was often away sorting out business, at which times she was left alone to run the shop and manage the hired help. She had been a shy village girl from India but quickly grew in confidence and learnt enough English to master the daily banter needed to deal with customers. She had been surprised at first by how much attention male customers paid to her, having never considered herself to be attractive. When they complimented her she became quite flustered and sometimes had to fight to remain composed and carry on serving. One particular customer, a young white guy, had started hanging around that little bit longer than necessary, chatting about harmless things like the weather or the day's headlines. But then he started asking more personal questions and even made a joke about whether Asian woman wore panties under their saris.

As I reached this point in the story, I could feel my husband's cock twitching. He reached his hands forward and grabbed my hips, urging me to move on to where the action started. I pretended that this was the way it was set out in the magazine and turned a page as if checking what happened next. I squeezed myself around his dick, promising him more action soon.

The interested customer was tall and muscular and the wife felt tiny in his presence. Occasionally he offered to help her move boxes or bundles of newspapers. At first she declined but one day, when an elderly customer wanted something off a high shelf, she had been forced to accept his assistance. As she reached up helplessly, he had stepped forward, sweeping her arms aside with a stroke of his palm and lifting down what she wanted. After the pensioner had departed with his purchase, she could still feel the touch of the man's strong hand on her skin.

After that her admirer would linger in the shop almost every day and she began to enjoy his company and looked forward to his visits. Not only was he entertaining, he was also very complimentary about her looks, making clear his preference for dark-haired and petite women. Occasionally she caught him staring at her breasts or her bottom as she moved around the shop but he never appeared threatening. He was just open in his admiration for her. Her husband had never complimented her figure: it made her feel desirable and even sexually aroused to have so much attention paid to her.

Then it became her habit to make him tea if she was having a cup. Once he had play-wrestled with her, offering to make the tea for her. As he reached around her for the kettle, she was conscious of his muscular body pressed against her and of a hardness at his groin. She smiled to herself, wickedly proud that she was the cause of his excitement.

In response to my husband's demands that they 'get on with it' and the urgings of his stiff cock, I pretended to skip forward in the story, to the point where the wife invited the man to take his tea in the flat upstairs while the morning assistant covered the shop. I was rewarded with a few casual bounces on the mattress, and I had to pause to catch my breath as I rode the pleasure rippling through my body.

The wife made the promised tea and sat beside him on the settee. He asked about her husband and she blurted out that he would be away all day. Her admirer muttered that he would never leave such a beautiful and sexy woman alone if he were married to her.

I was reaching the point my husband liked – the prelude to adulterous sex – and I could feel him growing even harder between my legs.

'What happened next?' he gasped.

‘They kissed,’ I told him. ‘The man offered to dispel the neglected wife’s doubts that she was sexy by making love to her.’ My husband responded by arching his body so I was suspended on the spike of his prick, just off the bed. I squealed at the sudden jolt of pleasure this caused and almost dropped the magazine I was pretending to read. ‘The man told the wife to trust him. He kissed her hard on the mouth and then pulled her top over her head. She panicked and clasped her hands across her bra, hiding her chest.’

‘Go on, go on,’ my husband urged, stabbing me with his cock to emphasise his words.

‘He slowly coaxed her hands away from her breasts, all the while kissing her collar bone, the back of her neck, her arms.’ I was gasping with pleasure. I could picture every detail of the scene in my head and my sex was clutching greedily at my husband’s thrusting cock. ‘He called her breasts magnificent, stunning, beautiful, the most perfect pair he had ever seen. She had never felt so sexually desirable or turned on before and she surrendered to his touch as he stroked her bare back and belly.

‘Gently, he slipped his hands into the waistband of her trousers and started to tug them down. He knelt at her feet to remove her shoes and helped her step out of the trousers. She realised with a shudder that he could ask anything of her and she would consent. Still kneeling, he stroked her thighs and kissed her trembling knees. Gradually his kisses moved upwards, his lips tracing soft lines along the inside of each thigh.’

My husband was holding his breath under me, clearly imagining the ascent of the lover’s mouth, perhaps wishing it was his own mouth making that erotic journey.

‘The wife tenses and suppresses a moan. She is both excited and appalled when her lover plants a kiss on her pussy through the plain white material of her panties. No man has done this before, brought his lips so close to her yearning sex. And no man has done what he does next –

presses his tongue against the fabric and traces the line of her slit.

'Now he slides her panties down and kisses her sex without any barrier. He teases and tongues it and the wife almost collapses with pleasure. This is something she has never even imagined, not even with her husband. His tongue sneaks into her and unconsciously she opens her legs wider to allow him access. Soon his face is pressed against her dark bush, his nose resting on her swollen clitoris. He moves his mouth and flicks his tongue across her open sex, swirling it round the excited little stalk of flesh.'

I urge my husband to imagine what effect this would have on a woman, as I 'read' further. 'The wife is groaning, loudly,' I tell him. 'She grabs his head and holds him tight to her flesh, suddenly discovering a pure animal excitement which shocks her. She has never had sex with a white man. She has never enjoyed sex like this before.

'She desperately wants him inside her now and to enjoy the type of sex she is accustomed to having with her husband. She tugs at him. But he will not move. His mouth is clamped over her sex and he continues to tease her clit and slide his tongue in and out of her. She can hear him slobbering as he drinks the moisture that is dripping from her, sucking extravagantly on her juices.'

I can feel my own moisture oozing down over my husband's balls as I conjure the images and give voice to them. I can tell he is more excited now. He is almost shuddering as I relate the tale of this seduction. He urges me on to read more.

'The wife surrenders to her lover's expert mouth and almost collapses as she comes, jerking her hips against his face. He grabs her bum and holds her steady, forcing as much of his tongue as possible inside her. Her sex muscles grip it tightly and her eyes close, her mind blank but burning. When she is once again aware of what is happening, he is still kneeling at her feet, face buried in her crotch. She pulls him up – successfully this time – and he slips her bra from her and begins to kiss her breasts. He mumbles that she is gorgeous and that her breasts are divine. He teases her nipples with his lips.

'He is still fully clothed, while she is nude, and she tries to undress him. But he will not allow it. He brushes her hands away and begins to stroke and caress her whole body. She can feel herself glowing, as if he is stoking the embers of her orgasm, spreading the warm sensation over every inch of her skin. His fingers slide between her legs and one of them is soon reaching stiffly up inside her, much further than his tongue did.

'She starts to shudder. At first she thinks she is shivering but then she realises it is a purely sexual response and that she cannot stop this reaction to his probing fingers. He is touching her somewhere secret, somewhere special that is known only to the two of them. Her body jerks and twitches in response. Her thighs are damp now, soaked with her own juices, and she is begging him to enter her, to complete his control of her body.'

I lean forward on my husband's cock, revelling in the hardness inside me. He has the sense to reach round my hip and rub my clit with his forefinger. I have paused in my story just to get used to the pleasure.

'Tell me more,' he demands.

I jump forward in my story. 'The two lovers have moved to her bedroom. The bedroom she had previously only ever shared with her husband. She is sprawled on her back, legs wickedly thrown apart as she watches her lover undress. She has discovered a wantonness she never knew she possessed. Even with her husband she would not expose her pussy this way. But she wants to lure this man into her. He removes his clothes slowly, clearly confident in himself, and when he removes the last item of clothing – black silk boxer shorts – she is wonderfully impressed. His huge erection is all that she can focus on. He might have been smiling, even scowling, and she would not have known. His muscular thighs, his heavy balls and his hard cock are all that she can see.

'She reaches for him, trying to drag him down on to the bed with her. She wants to hold him tight, to feel his body against hers, crushing her as he enters her sex. He recognises exactly what she craves and holds her tight, kissing her full on the mouth, and she can feel his magnificent hardness pressed against her thigh. His mouth is on her face, her neck, her breasts and he pulls her nipples to exquisite hardness between his strong lips. She holds his face in her hands, stares deep into his eyes. "Fuck me," she moans. She has never used this word before, although she has heard it often enough. But she knows at this moment it is absolutely the right word. He asks her if she is sure and she answers by grabbing his cock and steering it into her.'

My husband started a steady riding motion with his hips as I told him how the wife savours every second of her lover's slow entry into her body – from the moment when the fat head of his prick eases her open, through the gradual easing into her willing body to the moment when he is embedded fully inside her. We both pictured this scene, I could tell. His movements became more energetic and he started to bounce me around. As I moved up and down on his cock, I could feel crackles of excitement travelling through my body. My eyes closed and I was glad that I was facing away from him, as I would not have been able to keep up the pretence of reading.

I continued my story between gasps of pleasure, describing the thrusts of the lover into the wife and how she loved every moment that his cock was inside her. 'Seamlessly, almost without effort, they were making love on the bed, on the floor and even up against the door. Eventually he could not stop himself from coming inside her and she felt every part of his hot discharge.'

My husband was groaning now, his body bucking and twitching beneath me. I continued to ride him but soon the thrusting from below was not enough for him. He pushed me forward on to all fours, and scrambled up and entered me from behind. His thrusting was deep and I arched my back in response. I was still facing away from him so he could not see the wild expression on my face as my body spasmed and triggered his noisy climax.

We collapsed onto the mattress and my husband wrapped his arm around my belly, holding me tight. He was silent, no doubt marvelling at the powerful effect the reader's letter had had on us both. After a while he joked, saying that even I would not be able to resist such a lover.

– Sunita, Leicester, UK

The Nurses' Home

I really shouldn't be admitting to this but it was a while back and it's not like I murdered anybody. Actually I reckon I got what I deserved and it taught me a lesson, sort of.

I was a student at one of what they used to call the redbrick universities and not really any different to anybody else. In my first year I was put in one of the biggest accommodation blocks, a thing like a block of flats with long corridors lined with doors all painted the same dull blue. I was room 314, which meant I was on the third floor at the back and looked out over a lawn and some trees to another block. There was a high wall between us and the other block and if I thought about it at all I suppose I thought it was a block of flats. I soon found out it wasn't.

I'd only been there about three days and I'd been doing all the normal student stuff, like going out to meetings and getting drunk in the Union bar. I came back to my room late, meaning to go to bed, but as I went to close the curtains I could see lights on in the opposite block and people moving about. Most of the curtains were closed, but you could see shadows behind them and it didn't take Einstein to work out that they were female shadows. One was best, a girl close up to the window brushing her hair so her outline showed clearly. I was sure she was in her underwear because I could see the whole of the shape of her breasts and her hips. Two windows had the lights on and the curtains open, one below me a bit so that I could see right in. Two girls were sitting drinking coffee, both in blue-and-white uniforms.

I only looked for a few seconds and I didn't see anything really bad before I moved away. I felt really guilty because I'd never thought of myself as the sort of boy who'd peek in on girls' windows, but just seeing the outline of a shadow against a curtain and realising that she was in nothing but bra and panties had given me a thrill like nothing else. That wasn't something I did. That was the sort of thing dirty old men did and that just wasn't me. Anyway, my light was on and I must have stood out like a sore thumb for any of them to see if they looked out of their own windows.

I closed the curtains and went to bed, feeling really bad and really turned on at the same time. I tried to read my book but I couldn't concentrate for thinking about the shadows in the block opposite and that brief hint of a girl's breasts in her bra. I'm an only child and my parents were very religious and quite strict. I'm shy too and I'd always felt nervous around girls, so the most sexually adventurous thing I'd ever done was kiss my cousin good night after a family party.

The thought of that girl's breasts was like a hot iron down my throat. I could picture her in my head, brushing out her long hair in front of the mirror, never imagining for a moment she was being watched. Her breasts had been quite big, so I'd seen the way they curved underneath and how her bra pushed them out. I imagined how she'd have looked close-up, with all that lovely flesh almost bursting out of her cups, so big and soft and touchable it made me want to cry.

I'd always been taught to respect women, because my mother was a bit of a feminist and used to go on about how I should never forget that women were human beings and not just collections of body parts. I'd always tried to think that way, and be polite and respectful but not condescending, so the more I thought about her body the worse I felt. I kept telling myself it was wrong to think of her that way and imagining how angry she'd be if she knew I'd peeped, and how angry all the girls I'd met in my first few days at university would be if they knew I was a Peeping Tom.

That didn't help. It made it worse, but I didn't understand why. I just couldn't get the image out of my head. Not that it was anything that bad, no worse than what you might get on a magazine cover showing a girl in a bikini and nothing to the sort of porn you get now. That didn't matter. I'd seen and she hadn't meant me to. That did.

I got to sleep in the end but I was tossing and turning all night, imagining that I was watching her undress in my dreams and that I got caught and shouted at. How I managed to stop myself wanking I don't know, but somehow I got through to the morning. I felt bad all the next day, telling myself I'd been really stupid and would never think of doing it again. I might as well have tried to stop breathing.

I spent ages drinking coffee in somebody else's room that evening, and left so late I was sure all the girls opposite would have gone to bed long ago. By then I'd realised that the place was obviously a nurses' home, because there were only women living there and the ones I'd seen had all been in uniform. What I hadn't figured out was that nurses work shifts so they'd be coming and going at all hours of the night and day.

When I got back to my room I left the light off because I was sure that if any of the girls saw me in my room with the curtains open and the lights on they'd realise I was peeping at them and complain about me. I could imagine the disgrace, and the looks I'd get from the female students I knew when it came out that I was a Peeping Tom.

Of course I hadn't really done anything and that was my undoing. I kept telling myself that I was already damned, so I might as well just have a quick glance. It was about one in the morning, but several of the lights were still on, making rectangles of green or orangey-gold light behind the curtains, except for one room where the curtains were half open. A few of them were moving about, but I couldn't really see anything. That was frustrating, but made me want to look even more.

Then came the moment that got me hooked. I was moving my eyes between different windows, not wanting to miss anything, when I caught a movement from the one room with the curtains a bit open. A girl had come to the window. She was small, with blonde hair tied up in a bun, and all she had on was a blouse and a pair of big white knickers. For one instant as she reached up to tug the curtains closed I could see the V shape between her thighs and just a hint of a crease where her knickers had ridden up into her slit.

I'm not even sure that's what I did see, and it was only a moment before she'd tugged the curtains shut, but the image was in my mind as clear as if I'd been in the room with her. I'd only got a rough impression of her face too, but in my head she was very pretty, with small upturned breasts under her half-undone blouse, a little round tummy peeping out underneath as she stretched up and those knickers, tight over her soft woman's flesh, showing every gentle bulge and curve of her hips, her firm little tummy, and her mound with the cotton pulled up into her slit.

I could have died for guilt, but I couldn't stop myself. My cock was so hard I thought I was going to come in my pants and I just had to take it out. I finished myself off right there, standing in front of the window with my eyes closed and my head full of pictures of that beautiful, beautiful girl and what she'd shown. I thought I was in love with her, but even as I came I was imagining how much she'd despise me if she knew, and how utterly unworthy I was of her.

I felt miserable afterwards, so full of guilt you'd have thought I'd at least murdered somebody, and I was sure I'd been seen and that there would be a knock on my door at any moment. I imagined my blonde girl looking at me in fear and disgust as she identified me to the police and the shocked looks of my neighbours as I was led away in handcuffs for being what I'd become, a Peeping Tom.

Of course it didn't happen. There was only one streetlight at the back of my hall and that was not only pretty feeble but cast orange reflections off the windows in such a way that if the light in a room was off it was impossible to see in. I found that out the next evening, during a panic-stricken exploration to discover if she could have seen in. She couldn't, and that really damned me.

I knew I was safe. Sitting in my room with the light off and the door locked I could see across to their block without the slightest risk of being caught. All I had to do was be a bit careful, remembering not to move my armchair into position before I turned my light out and that sort of thing. I stayed up for hours that third night, watching and waiting. Maybe if I'd seen something really good that would have been the end of it, but I didn't and it was the frustration that drove me on. It's like collecting stuff when you're a kid. If you get all the football cards straight away you lose interest, but if you get most of them and can't find those last few players you get the bug and stick with it for ages.

I got the bug all right. I would stay up every night for at least two hours, often a lot more. Often I'd be there from the moment it got dark enough for the girls to put their lights on until I couldn't keep my eyes open any more and fell asleep in my chair. It didn't do much for my studies, or my social life, but I didn't care. I had to watch.

I got what I wanted too, never a lot at once, but always enough to keep me coming back. The girls were cautious, or naturally shy, or maybe they just closed their curtains out of habit, but most of them I only ever saw fully dressed for a few moments before they shut me out, then in silhouette. Not that their silhouettes weren't worth watching, because all the rooms were the same, with a fluorescent light in the middle of the ceiling and the bed to one side near the window. That meant that when a girl undressed for bed she was normally between the light and the window and if she stood close to the curtains I could see a lot.

I quickly became an expert in the way a girl's breasts move when she takes off her bra, from the little pert ones that only jiggle a bit to the real whoppers that flop down even on a young nurse. I learnt a lot about the way girls take down their knickers too, some bending to push them down over their bums first, others doing it straight-legged and wiggling to make their knickers drop, some so shy they'd put on their nighties first. Not that they all slept bare under their nighties, but I'd soon learnt which did and they all had to change their knickers anyway.

I'd soon worked out a grid, with numbers along the side and letters along the top. There were four floors, from A at the top to D at the bottom, and twelve rooms on each floor at my side, from 1 to 12. I couldn't see the higher numbers very well, and some not at all, because of trees and because I could only see in at an angle. Row A was above me, so a bit frustrating as I could only ever see the top half of a girl, if that, but their windows were big; and I could see right into Row B from 2 to 6. Row C was even better, because I was looking a little down and could see just about everything. Row D wasn't so good.

The best were the precious few who left their curtains open. My little blonde was C5 and I soon had her routine worked out. She'd come in from work at midnight unless she was on a different shift, and much the same if it was her day off. When she was in her uniform she'd just slip it off, to leave herself in her bra and knickers. She'd walk around her room like that or, if she'd not been in uniform, in just her blouse and knickers, but that was just as good because while she didn't have much in the way of breasts she had the sweetest little mound and a lovely round bum, both of which stretched out her knickers in a way that used to make me go hard just to think about it.

She was frustrating though, because while she used to take her bra off last thing at night after she'd been to wash, she always did it just before getting into bed, so I never got more than the briefest flash of titties. Her knickers stayed on and she changed them every day in the morning when the sun was on my block and I didn't dare look for fear of getting caught, but I knew because she had pink ones as well as white.

My booby girl was in B3. She was a bit lazy and never tugged her curtains quite hard enough, so there'd be a gap in the middle. She used to go topless too, often walking around in nothing but her knickers so that I'd get tantalising glimpses of her big, round breasts as she passed backwards and forwards in front of the crack in the curtain.

I used to call B7 my dancer. I couldn't see her as well as the others, but she'd often leave her curtains wide open and dance in front of her mirror with her radio on. The way she wiggled her hips used to drive me mad and I could always be sure she'd carry on long enough for me to come, but in a way she was the most frustrating of them all because she'd always get undressed in the bathroom and come back in a long nightie.

They were my three regulars, but the best moments were all one-offs. One of them was watching two girls pillow fighting in C1. Some of them were quite young and used to muck about, like these two: a very pretty girl with long dark hair, and a bit of a tomboy with a short bob cut who used to wear pyjamas. It was her room and they'd often chat together, but I never usually saw much until that night. Maybe they were a bit drunk or something, but I could see them joking about something and then the pretty one whacked her friend with a pillow. They were soon hard at it, grappling together and rolling on the floor and the bed, half the time with the pretty one's nightie up high so her knickers showed, while the shape of the tomboy's bum and tits under her pyjamas would have been enough to get me there alone. I'm glad it didn't, because I was almost there when the tomboy got her friend in a headlock, pulled her nightie, hauled her knickers up tight into her bottom slit and gave her cheeks a couple of quite hard smacks. That was it for me. I'd come and soon after the matron came in and told them to shut up. I was watching that too, and was so far gone on sex that I imagined the matron making them both take their knickers down for spankings, but of course it didn't happen.

Another time the girl in D4 managed to pull one half of her curtains down somehow and I was able to watch her undress properly for three nights before they got fixed. She went all the way too, down to nude before she'd put on a dressing gown and go to the bathroom and I'd get a second flash when she came back and got into her nightie. Only the bad angle spoilt the fun, because I could see her take her knickers off but couldn't get a decent view of what she was showing.

Her neighbour in D5 was gorgeous, tall and busty with a very good body from the exercises she did, always in just her bra and knickers and sometimes with the curtains open enough for me to get a peep, but never a full show. My imagination filled in the details anyway, including how she'd look in the nude with those lovely big breasts bouncing up and down as she did her starjumps.

By the end of the first term I was completely obsessed, and it didn't get any better. All through the holidays I couldn't think of anything except my girls and I came back two days early just so I could watch them. I wanted more too, and that term I joined the Astronomical Society so that I could borrow a telescope and get a closer look. It didn't really work, because while I could get closer in it made it harder to watch all the windows at once and I didn't get to see anything more, only bigger. If anything it spoilt the fun a bit, because without the telescope I couldn't always be sure if a girl was wearing knickers and could enjoy the delicious thrill of thinking she might not be. But I still used it as often as I could without giving myself away.

Things stayed much the same all through my second term, but by the end my need to see a girl completely nude had become desperate. It would probably have stayed that way too, only when I came back after Easter a new girl had moved in, to C8, just where I couldn't see her properly. If the others had been frustrating, she was something else again. She never shut her curtains and I was sure she spent a lot of time fully nude, but I could never quite see. The angle was bad and there was a tree in the way, so that while I could catch tantalising glimpses of soft, honey-gold flesh I could never see properly.

That was what did for me. I just couldn't stand it, night after night, always able to glimpse but never to see properly. In my head she was an angel of perfection, her body straight out of my fantasies, and I just had to see. I knew I could do it too, if I only had the guts, because her room was directly opposite one of the clumps of trees growing against the wall. All I had to do was get in among the trees and up the wall and I'd be able to watch, from less than half the distance and directly into her room.

I tried to put it off, but when my little blonde in C5 left and another girl took her room I just couldn't hold back. It was warm too, and the girls had begun to leave their windows open and wear less at night, making the thought of an expedition even more tempting. So off I went, sneaking out late when I knew my special girl would be coming off shift in an hour and concealing myself carefully among the trees.

My view was perfect, her window just about twenty yards away and directly across from me. I'd be able to see everything, and my cock was hard before she even came home. When she did I was glued to that window. She was just about as gorgeous as I'd imagined, quite a big girl, tall and well built, with big tits and amazingly firm flesh. I could have come just watching her walk about her room in her pretty blue-and-white nurse's uniform but I knew there'd be more to come and contented myself with massaging myself through my trousers.

I had to stop that when she finally started to undress, or I swear I'd have come in my pants. It was so good, after all those months of frustration, to watch the real thing, the way she unzipped her uniform and let it fall open across her shoulders. The way she took off her little white hat and shook out her curly brown hair, the way she pushed her uniform down to show her knickers with just the most beautiful bottom I had ever seen straining out a pair of see-through knickers.

She took her stockings off, seated on her bed and peeling them down her long perfect legs one by one, and by then my cock was in my hand and it was taking all my willpower not to finish myself off before the perfect moment. When her hands went to the catch of her bra I was choking with excitement, but she had her back to me and I only saw the outline of one breast from the side. Then came her knickers, pushed down off that gorgeous bum and off, to leave her in the nude. Then she turned around and I could see it all, those lovely big tits, so firm and big and round, her lovely slim waist and her shapely hips, but best of all the busy triangle of dark curls between her thighs.

I came, all over my hand and on my shirt, making a right mess. I didn't care, too lost in that lovely sight. She was naked and beautiful, and remember, I'd never seen a real live girl in the nude before, let alone such a beauty. I'd have done anything to watch and at that moment I didn't even care about the consequences.

I wish I had, because I fell off the wall. I know that sounds stupid, but you try balancing on top of a brick wall while you're wanking over some gorgeous girl and all you've got to hold onto is a skinny branch. I went down hard, and it hurt, but I was more shocked than anything. Unfortunately one of the few nurses with a car chose that moment to come around the end of the building. I was caught in the headlights, lying on my back with my cock still out, and it couldn't have been much more obvious what I'd been up to. They were furious, every bit as angry as I'd imagined, and there were four of them. The worst was a tiny woman with blonde hair and a shrill voice, who screamed to the others to hold me while she went to ring for the police. I was still on the ground, and they'd caught me before I could get up, pinning me down by my arms and legs and screaming at me, calling me a Peeping Tom and every bastard under the sun.

Then it happened, a moment I'm going to remember for the rest of my life. The biggest of them, a tall black girl who must have weighed twelve stone and had a bum like two bowling balls in a sack, sat on me. She was on my chest, her bum stuck right out at my face, straining her uniform into two fat balls of juicy female flesh. I could feel the softness of her, and her weight as I struggled, utterly helpless beneath them, with my cock still waving around and all three of them yelling their disgust at my behaviour and the state I was in. Then the big girl shifted her weight, just a little, and her bum was right in my face as she took hold of my cock and calmly put it away. And as she did so she called me a dirty little boy.

I've never got over that. I escaped, because she realised she was rubbing her bum in my face and lifted a little. Sheer terror gave me strength and once I was up and running they had no chance. I never got caught either, although I had to suffer the hideous embarrassment of the posters warning of a Peeping Tom stuck up all over the university and listening to my friends' comments. I didn't escape in my head though, because twenty-five years later I can still never come properly unless my wife sits on my face.

– Ken, Dereham, UK

Girl on a Motorbike

They all said that having a baby so young would be the end of my modelling career. But it wasn't. In fact, if anything, I was more in demand, not less. Having an angel on my hip was quite something at castings. Now that Tommy's a six-foot son of a bitch my life is a sunlit field of opportunity.

Except for his love of motorbikes. Oh, I can see the attraction. I rode pillion once. I wore buckled boots and a leather miniskirt and the other bikers whistled and whooped and said I was like Marianne Faithfull. And I actually came. Creamed myself. The throbbing between my legs. A Triumph is low-slung and narrow, you can feel the engine working under that hard narrow seat. And baby, I'm easily pleased.

I was wet when I lifted my leg to get off. They could tell from the way I walked. So why have I never fucked any of them? Because they do everything in a gang, if you get my drift. I'd be up for that, if my son wasn't part of it. I'll take it rough, open air, people watching, the more the merrier.

The other downside is the girls. They're all mad for Tommy. And why not, he's the leader of the pack. But they're the opposite of me. Mostly butch dykes with nothing to say except piston and poke.

So when he phoned me from a Harley trip down Route 66 in the States and told me he'd met a gorgeous girl on the road and she was the one, we had a bust up. I pretended it was because she was older than him. ('Halfway between you and me, Mum, so you'll really get on.') That's when he left home.

So a few weeks later I'm hovering in my own hallway because a girl on a motorbike has roared up and is hammering on the door.

'Where's Tommy?' she's shouting. They all shout, these rough tough girls. I turn from the door. Her voice breaks suddenly. 'The bastard! I need to see him!'

I wrench open the door. 'I'm his mother. How dare you call my son a bastard!'

I'm reflected in the metallic visor. She's my height. I can see my eyes, green, wide apart, long thick lashes – just what the photographers like to see – but flashing furiously, my hair all over the place. Not what the photographers like. And I'm still in my dressing gown. A total harridan, and sounding like one, too.

She bows her head, looking like a kind of weird, weighted flower, helmet bending her neck as if to snap it. 'You're right. I'm sorry.' Her voice is curled, American, and still tearful. 'It's just that I've tried his place and his mobile and he's nowhere. He goes on about you so much. I figured he'd be here.'

I sigh, fold my arms. Realise that makes me look like a fishwife. Unfold them. Realise that loosens my dressing gown, which starts to slide open, silk sliding over my nipples which are stiffening in the fresh morning air. I try not to flinch with sudden pleasure. 'What's he done now?'

'May I? Such a headache.' She lifts her arms. Her leather jacket rises over her leather trousers. I can see a strip of flat brown stomach. She might be slimmer than most but she could still flatten me with one swipe of those businesslike gloves. I step backward as she unbuckles the chinstrap.

'I really haven't got time – sorry.'

'Please, Mrs Jones. I've been driving for hours. He wasn't at the airport to meet me –'

'Rude boy. I wonder where he's got to?' I hesitate, stand aside. Something bitchy uncoils inside me. Perhaps this one won't last long after all. Then the bitchiness merges with a kind of reckless bonhomie. 'Come in, er –'

'Angie. Surely he's told you about me? The bastard! We're *engaged*!'

My son's fiancée. And she really is one. An angel, I mean. She takes off the hideous helmet and it's like one of those Timotei shampoo adverts in slow motion as she tips her head to shake endless silky blonde hair down her back. Her eyes close, her mouth parts, her tongue runs across her obscenely full, wet lower lip – and her leather jacket pops right open, one two three. In the golden sunlight her tits jut under a tiny white vest. Big nipples hard like nuts underneath.

I look away. Since when, in a life of loving and riding men's cocks every which way, have I noticed another woman's breasts? And since when have hard young female nipples, teasing under damp white cotton, looked so, well, edible? Probably fake. I shift my bare feet a little so I can see them out of the corner of my eye. She's like a bunny girl, or one of those perfectly tanned, waxed centrefolds, thrusting their cute butts up at the camera, spreading open their frilly pussies as they poke their long fingers, because that's all there is in the absence of a real man, deep inside. It's been so long since I've been fucked that I take my pleasure on my own, fingering myself hard and fast until I dribble all over my son's soft porn mags.

I try not to stare at her tits again, those incredible nipples. It's like refusing a piece of chocolate. My cunt starts to shiver, melting my knees, prickling dampness on my pussy hairs. She steps nearer. I haven't really noticed the rest of her at all. Her breasts and nipples are stretching her T-shirt taut. Christ, I must be turned on because I'm thinking of those magazines. I want to push her T-shirt up, see them, squeeze her breasts, suck them!

She's looking at me, too, and her hand, wiping sweat off her face, stops on her cheek. I can't remember when someone last looked at me like that. She's incredibly pretty, like a little cat. Probably with the claws to go with. Her eyes are very blue, not baby-blue but sapphire-blue, something a little hard there. Of course. She's not quite as young as she looks. And they are looking me up and down. Right up, from my toes to my bed hair.

'Wow, Mrs Jones. He told me you were a looker. But you know how useless men are. He never said you could be his sister!' She gasps with laughter and smacks her hand over her mouth. 'Even more cool, you could be *my* sister!'

'Then call me Natasha. Sister.' Reckless bonhomie melts into fierce pleasure. I take the helmet out of her hands, thump it down on the hall table. I flush red. Even my mouth feels swollen, aping the lips plumping between my legs. I walk ahead of her into the conservatory. My dressing gown slips off my shoulders. She's close up behind me.

'Coffee?'

She doesn't answer. I turn. She's stopped in the doorway to the kitchen, staring round, and huge great tears are plopping down her cheeks. Her shoulders, and those amazing breasts, are heaving.

'Hey, hey!' I come back and put my arm round her. 'It can't be that bad!'

'He promised he'd be there! I waited for two hours!'

She's exactly my height. Reaching round her is easy. She feels like – my other half. I pull her wet cheek against my face and she sobs some more. I wrap both arms round her and then I get it. A kick deep in my groin as I feel her nipples poking against mine, our breasts squashing against each other. It's like embracing myself. Am I this soft, this warm, this scented? This damp? This goddamn sexy?

All I've ever wanted is a man's hard flat chest pressing mine, stiff cock thrusting up inside me. But right now I want this softness. She's putting her arms round me, not sobbing, sniffing a little, her arms are under the dressing gown, leather squeaking against my skin, and her breath is hot on my shoulder and then oh my God that's her tongue licking across my skin up my throat, a pause, up, and our lips touch.

'Angie. Darling.' I whisper it into her mouth. 'We can't –'

She moves her head and looks down. Such long eyelashes. My insides droop. Why did I have to ruin the moment? I am dizzy with holding my breath. She looks up again, half kitten, half tiger, those eyes and that big wet mouth.

'So? You're not *my* mother, are you?' She pouts so sexily then. 'Just wanted comfort.'

'Let me comfort you then, honey.'

I tangle my fingers in her silky hair and kiss her, part her soft lips with my tongue. She doesn't stop me. No. I'm still older than her, remember? Her tongue flicks out, smaller than a man's, so gentle, less sloppy. I suck on it, kiss her, I can't help it, I want to suck and suck. I wonder if she's done this before, with a woman I mean. As she pushes her tongue in she pulls my gown right off and her hands are all over me.

As we start to breathe faster into each other I do it, I push her little white vest up and feel her tits drop into my hands, no bra, I nearly come just feeling them, did I realise how wet I was already, they are soft and juicy and I want to squeeze them until it hurts and she's fondling mine now and her touch is like an electric shock. I bend to kiss her breasts all over, bite one nipple and suck it in and the knowledge of what I'm doing is so horny, sucking another woman's tits, her smell so sweet, her fingers so sexy fondling me. My nipples are rock hard. It's that mirror image thing. If only we could both suck and fondle at the same time but there's more, isn't there, plenty of time, so we are on the floor now, kneeling face to face, reaching up to kiss, bending down to fondle and suck, and then I push her back on my carpet, right there by the door, we never get any further, I push her back and take a good look before peeling off her clothes. She hitches her hips to help me, I am so determined, and she's moaning now, rubbing and squeezing her breasts, licking her lips like one of those centrefold girls, and I groan too just watching her.

She's waxed to a tiny strip, her pussy lips plump and sweet, a line of moisture between them, and I run my tongue up between them, lick up that moisture. She opens her legs for me, arches her back, rubbing and squeezing her breasts as I take her buttocks and push her into my face, more moisture dripping from her as I lick. I breathe in the sweat and piss and honey of a cunt that's been on a bike seat for hours, roaring down the roads, overtaking cars and lorries, always an inch or so from danger. Now I have it. I part the lips with my fingers, roughly now, and suck on her bright red clit and she screeches and bucks, slamming against the floor, wrapping her thighs round my head as I lick her to climax and with my other hand, just like those centrefold girls, fuck myself with my fingers.

No, we didn't get caught. Tommy arrived a while later, but there we were, squirming admittedly, sitting closer perhaps than we should, but still. Just drinking tea. Angie leapt into his arms, wrapped those same leather thighs round him as his hard flat chest pressed her big juicy breasts.

'You've been crying. Why?'

'I can't remember.'

Tommy kissed her. 'We'll get married soon as Mum can organise it.'

You think I felt something? A tremor of jealousy, maybe? Sure. But over his shoulder, those blue eyes flashed at me. The cat's tongue quivered with promise between those hot lips.

I was more than satisfied, honey. And get this. This gorgeous girl is going to be my daughter-in-law. So how good can it get?

– Natasha, London, UK

Lucy Takes Liberties

I simply could not wait to get married. It's all very well being a single girl about town in one's twenties, but that whole scene (friends, parties, shopping) gets a little tiresome after a while. The same bars, the same faces, the same gossip. 'Did you hear about Tara? She's become a Buddhist!' Yawn.

The decisive moment was my thirtieth birthday. Daddy chose to mark the occasion by getting himself arrested for fraud (so embarrassing), and consequently I found myself a little short of funds. It transpired that my career as a respected literary agent, although resplendent with opportunities for a free lunch, wasn't quite as lucrative in cash terms as I might have hoped. And then there was the little matter of my credit account at Harvey Nics, which exceeded the collective GDP of sub-Saharan Africa.

It would be a tad disingenuous to suggest that the prospect of a lifetime shackled to Ralph set my girlish heart aflutter. He's a decent enough sort, I suppose (pots of money, natch), and he never asks me difficult questions like 'How did you get that bite mark on your thigh?' or 'Weren't you wearing tights when you went out?' But the poor boy has all the sexual charisma of a trout.

However, if life has taught me anything, it is this: now and then a girl has to ask herself some tough questions. Questions like 'How many dangerous-looking rugged types with gruff voices and hard bodies work on the derivatives desk at Schroders?' Answer, none.

So I smiled and I cooed, I sailed and hiked. I was even nice to grandma Ralph and her malevolent little dog. In short, I worked like a bitch to secure my financial future. And once the rock was on my finger and the date was set, my triumphant mood could barely be concealed.

And at first the wedding preparations were very absorbing. Months passed with scarcely a thought for anything other than canapés, seating plans and string quartets. My bedtime fantasies featured holidays in Mauritius and breakfast delivered by Fortnum's. But as the big day approached, some familiar and distracting thoughts started to creep back into my head.

I had decided in advance that I would remain faithful for the length of our engagement, and for a respectable period after the wedding. Six months seemed about right. It was inevitable that I would then take a lover or two, to supplement Ralph's occasional and primitive attempts at 'rogering'. Genuinely satisfying sex is crucial for a woman to maintain the correct balance of hormones; I owed it to my health. But as the engagement dragged on, I started to wonder if abstaining for such a long time was altogether practical. I thought a little treat might be in order, just to tide me over.

The opportunity arose, just two weeks before the wedding. After a morning spent lounging in bed, the ticklish feeling in my clit became so absorbing that I could barely concentrate on my magazine. I thought maybe a quick wank would sort me out, so I rolled onto my tummy and started grinding my pussy lips against my upturned thumbs. It didn't take long, just a few slippery thrusts and my clit was starting to sing. But there was something unsatisfying about it. I didn't look right.

I suppose it must be quite common amongst those with highly developed aesthetic sensibilities, but the truth is that I can't come without tarting myself up. It would be like going to a wedding in sport leisurewear (and yes, I know some people do, but I'm not about to take lifestyle tips from the great unwashed).

First I brushed out my wavy blonde hair and styled it elegantly in a chignon. Then I glossed my full lips with soft coral-pink lipstick and loaded my eyelids with thick liquid liner and shiny black mascara. Finally, I took out the box that held my bridal underwear and slipped it on piece by piece. First, the ivory satin basque which cinched my tiny waist and served up my ample breasts on a taut silky platter. Then my matching satin thong ('a bootlace and a handkerchief' Mummy would have called it). And finally, to top it all off, a pair of whisper-thin ivory RHT stockings with a subtle glassy sheen.

I wriggled my painted toes into strappy heels and crossed the room to survey my handiwork in the mirror. It won't surprise you to hear that I looked sensational. A perfectly presented little slut, hungry for ruination. Just the sight of my own hot and perfumed body made me deliciously horny. Arousal flooded my system and I succumbed to intoxication. My breasts seemed to strain against their sheer cups, my stocking tops brushed deliciously against the soft curves of my bottom. I wanted to act dirty, to do something shocking and depraved.

How nice it would be to have company right now, I thought, some rough type with a filthy mouth who would bark out orders to his posh tart.

'Go on, bitch,' I said to myself, 'let's see your cunt. I want to see you touch yourself.' I parted my legs obligingly and pushed the sodden material of my thong to one side, lifting one foot onto the bed to reveal my pussy in the mirror. 'Open yourself out, slut! I want to see everything,' I continued, and I pushed two fingers deep inside my sex to comply. The sensation was frustrating. I wanted to be really stretched out and filled.

My slender girl-fingers just couldn't produce the right depth and thickness.

I pictured a leering man sitting on the bed. Sitting and stroking his big cock while I stripped and gyrated for his pleasure. I saw his strong hands pumping a thick beating phallus and felt my clit relax into a wave of pleasure as my own fingers pumped in and out of my sex. The imaginary cock continued beating, and now there was pre-come glistening on it. My tongue flicked out to clean it up. I imagined the creamy salty taste. Savoured it on my tongue. And then *ding-dong*, a loud chiming from the hall downstairs disturbed my reverie.

I snatched my fingers out of my puss in surprise and tottered across to the window to take peek outside. On the doorstep were two tall strapping young men dressed in jeans and tight-fitting T-shirts, one red and one black. For a moment, I wondered if I had called them into being by sheer force of lust, but then I noticed their van on the drive, which bore the insignia of the wedding marquee company.

Drunk with arousal and tantalisingly aware of Ralph in his office on the ground floor, I felt an overpowering urge to open the door to them in my half-undressed glory. A little indecent exposure never did anyone any harm, and I was sure that they'd take it in good part. I was convinced it would make their day, in fact, and I knew that the act of revealing myself would make my eventual orgasm a thousand times stronger. Who could resist?

Concealing most of my body behind a curtain, I gestured out of the window, indicating that they should climb the fire escape that led to my en suite bathroom. I don't think I have ever seen two men move so quickly. On reflection, I think the curtain material may have been rather more diaphanous than I thought.

Up close, I could see that they were both a little younger than me – nineteen or early twenties maybe. The one in the black T-shirt was just to my taste, with long brown hair, smoky grey eyes and the body of a marine. He was confidently looking me up and down with a broad grin on his face. Red was less striking, and seemed nervous. Perhaps because his semi hard-on was visible beneath his jeans.

'Can I help you?' I asked, leaning elegantly against the doorframe and absentmindedly stroking my barely concealed breast.

'I don't know,' Black said, apparently taking my state of *déshabillé* in his stride. 'You could do some starjumps. That would be nice.'

Red just gaped.

'I assume you came here to discuss the arrangements for my wedding reception,' I said, playing it straight.

Red nodded, glad to be on safe ground. 'Yes, we've got various options for you to consider, Madam, with regard to lighting effects and . . . um . . . there are things we ought to measure . . .' He trailed off and I followed his eyes down to the visibly wet sliver of satin between my legs. I parted them a little to show him just how ineffectual a covering it was. He flushed.

'You don't look like the sort of chaps who like to hang up fairy lights and fool about with measuring tape,' I said, my green eyes appraising their hard young bodies. 'Those things require an artistic eye, a sensitive temperament. You'd be more suited to basic tasks surely . . . like hammering marquee poles in with your heads!' I suppressed a giggle and locked eyes with Black. He had the look of one of those domesticated tigers you see in nature films. His expression seemed to say: *I'm just play-fighting now, but pull my tail one more time and I'll have your arm off.*

Turning my back on them, the better to display my pert behind, I mentally rehearsed another witty put-down. But before I could deliver it, I felt the shock of cold hands on my body. Black had gripped me under my arms and lifted me clean off my feet. It happened so quickly that I didn't have the presence of mind to kick, and in moments he had manoeuvred me through the door and into my bedroom, dumping me face down on my bed. The impertinence! It was really too much to have the help manhandling one in one's own home. I could hear Red following behind us, protesting but with excitement in his voice. 'Shit, Mark, what are you doing!'

I wriggled ineffectually but Black's body was pressed against mine, his lips brushing my ear. 'Stop your silliness,' he ordered. 'I've heard enough from your smart mouth today. It's time you shut up and let me have a good look at you.' His tone was firm, but gentle and somehow reassuring. I knew I ought to be irate but for some reason my clit was singing louder than ever. His sharp masculine scent was invading my senses. My mind became a scramble of half-thoughts and flashing impressions and I found myself unable to speak. I simply lay, prone, under his heavy male frame.

'I think you want to be fucked today,' he continued, 'and I'd be more than happy to fuck your posh little cunt as hard as you like. But first you've got to ask nicely.'

I could hardly believe my ears. And I was ready to tell him just how presumptuous an oik he was, but for some reason when I opened my mouth I actually said, 'OK, but you'll have to be very quiet. My fiancé's downstairs.' Damn it! Where was my self-control? Black must have found this highly amusing because he began to convulse with laughter. I felt him release his pressure on me and he sat up on the end of the bed. I took the opportunity to roll over and sit up as well. I tried to regain some composure.

I couldn't believe I was about to fuck some upstart menial in the middle of the afternoon, and with Ralph downstairs to boot. I'd always been a fast worker but this was a new high, or low, depending on your perspective. Still, I couldn't deny the urgency in my pussy. I could barely sit still, the urge to move and grind it against something was so strong.

After a brief tussle with his belt, Black pushed his jeans down and his impressive length sprung up and out at me from his lap. I'm sure some girls can take the sight of a gloriously thick, smooth and stiff erection in their stride. I, however, am not one of them. Whenever I am in the presence of a hard cock, I go into a trance. The urge to prostrate myself before it and fulfil its every desire becomes overwhelming. My head sank down of its own accord until the few free strands of hair around my face were tickling his smooth purplish head.

'Oh yeah, that's where you need to be,' he said, a more tender tone in his voice. 'Someone woke up a bit horny today, didn't she?'

I answered his question with a moan, all semblance of linguistic ability seeming to have deserted me. He laughed and gave my head an affectionate stroke.

'You've got me too hard now, sweetheart,' he continued, gently but firmly. 'I'm going to have to fuck that pretty mouth. I'm just going to have to, understand?'

I nodded my assent, leant over and pulled his thighs wide apart, pushing my nose into the base of his cock and lapping hungrily at his balls.

His musty male scent, laced with a reassuring hint of soap, was delicious. I savoured the salty taste of his skin as my tongue travelled slowly up his member, leaving a trail of coral-pink gloss in its wake.

'Oh you're a special one!' he exclaimed, as I painstakingly licked and sucked it clean of pre-come.

While he lay back to enjoy the ride, my brain shut down every area not actively engaged in sucking cock. My only sensations were the aching in my puss and the feeling of cock-skin against my lips. I resisted the urge to gobble it down straight away, pacing myself with little pecks and licks. Every touch of my mouth seemed to make him longer, harder and more insistent. His breathing came in fast pulses. I knew he wanted harder contact but I refused to comply, I didn't care if it pushed him over the edge.

As I made another long slow sweep of my tongue around the base of his phallus, he finally lost control, fisted the hair at the back of my head with one strong hand and started pumping his cock into my face. Although welcome, his urgency was a little more than I'd bargained for. I lost my balance, falling ungracefully backwards onto my bottom.

Before I had time to recover my composure, he was above me, his thighs straddling my upturned face. Moments later his cock was pushing at my lips, sinking deeper and deeper into my throat. I felt a little shiver of fear as he pushed himself in. I couldn't imagine how I was going to accommodate something so thick. But there was no time to think. He was already powering in and out. I relaxed my jaw and gave way to the rhythm, my mouth and nose saturated with cock taste and cock smell.

Soon it began to beat and I could almost feel the come inside trying to boil its way out. My clit pulsed too in anticipation of the hot mouthful of cream that was just moments away. But suddenly the motion was gone, my mouth was empty. I opened my eyes, and in my woozy cock-drunk state I propped myself up on my elbows to see what was going on. He was on his feet, breathing heavily and staring at me with a serious expression.

'What's wrong?' I asked, suddenly feeling rather silly, all spread-eagled and disarranged.

'Nothing, sweetheart. I'm just thinking that you're the most beautiful slut I've ever seen.'

I knew full well that my mascara was streaked down my cheeks and I could feel little wisps of hair sticking to my perspiring forehead, but I didn't doubt that I was a glorious sight.

'Well, of course, I am,' I said, and let my head fall back on to the pillow with a triumphant beaming smile.

'You're almost too good to fuck,' he said, beating his cock absentmindedly with his right hand. 'I think I'd rather watch someone else do it.' He looked over at Red, whose presence I had completely overlooked, and raised his eyebrow with a smirk. Red was standing over by the mirror, cock still tenting out the material of his jeans. Despite a slightly apologetic expression, I could tell his desire for me was no less powerful than Black's. He was quite cute, I realised, now that I looked at him properly. With a shaved head and piercing brown eyes, he had the look of a man who was good with his hands and his mouth.

My clit pulsed as I imagined those rough working-man's hands on my soft body and my cunt ached desperately with the need for penetration. He seemed to need some encouragement though, obviously still intimidated by my superior social status, so I rolled on to my tummy and parted my legs invitingly. With satisfaction, I noticed his eyes fixate on the narrow strip of material bisecting my bottom and glossy labia.

'Go on, mate,' said Black, 'she must be desperate for a fuck by now.' He wasn't wrong, my cock-sucking session had made me so wet, my pussy was pink, hot and tender. I couldn't resist slipping a hand beneath me and grinding my swollen clit against it. As I did so, I flashed my best come-hither eyes at Red before lowering them to the floor in a gesture of submission.

That did the trick. The next thing I felt was strong hands yanking my thong down over my bottom and the firm pressure of a tongue probing deep inside my bare sex, licking and sucking at the walls of my cunt and massaging my clit with masterful technique. I really couldn't deny that the boy knew what he was doing. Every thrust had me teetering on the verge of orgasm. But before I could really get into my stride, I felt more hands, this time tugging at my basque to expose my breasts. I looked up from the duvet in surprise and found myself staring into Black's parted thighs, his cock looming over me, still wet with my saliva. If it had been a box of Godiva chocolates, it couldn't have been much more tempting.

I struggled forwards eagerly, unable to take my hungry eyes off the target. Red gave my bottom a helpful push from behind, and I pulled myself into sucking position in Black's lap. But as I settled into another bout of deep throating, I noticed to my annoyance that Red and his delicious tongue were slacking. My bare and tingling puss was wide open for business, but business came there none. I gave a little squeal-cum-choke to register my irritation and hoicked myself on to my knees to make my pussy even more accessible. But still my furiously beating clit had nothing to grind against but thin air. I attempted to lift my head up and complain but Black was once again fisting the back of my head and I had no choice but to follow his rhythm up and down.

'Nice one, mate!' I heard him say eventually. 'That'll keep her quiet.'

About time too, I thought, relaxing my pelvic floor in the assumption that penetration was now imminent. Red's hands swept up my legs and took hold of my suspender straps like reins.

You can imagine my surprise when the next sensation I felt was something akin to reverse defecation. An eager pressure against my anus, followed by a painful stretching that reminded me of losing my virginity. I mouthed an 'Oh!' but the sound was muffled by Black's cock, which still filled my throat.

Thankfully the pain was soon replaced by an odd burning sensation, as he continued to slide himself deeper and deeper inside me. He moved desperately slowly, but still every millimetre felt like a mile in my rectum. When he'd gone in as far as he could, he stopped and held me there. His hands pulled my bottom snuggly into his lap while his thighs pushed forwards to keep his cock at maximum depth.

'You like it in your ass, babe?' he whispered. Black helpfully withdrew his cock from my mouth to let me answer.

'Yes, I . . . I think I do. It's a bit sore though.'

'I know, sweetheart, just try to relax. I won't hurt you.'

Too late, I thought. Still, the longer he held himself inside me, the more comfortable it felt. As the pain ebbed away, I became more intensely aware of the two pairs of eyes studying me in my compromised state. Against my nature, I felt more than a little embarrassed.

'Um . . .?'

'What is it, babe? Still hurting?'

'No, it's not that . . . it's just that I'm worried it might look ugly.'

'What?'

'My . . . You know . . . Bum. What if it looks ugly all opened up like that?' I heard Red smile and then felt his hands move up to my cheeks and spread them even further apart. I wriggled with discomfort.

'It's the prettiest thing I've ever seen,' he whispered. 'It was made to take my cock, and if you were marrying me and not that fat tosser downstairs, I'd spear it three times a day.' Saying that, he slammed his body into me from above, forcing me back down on to my tummy. His full weight compressed my slender frame into the bed, whilst his muscular buttocks pumped the base of his nine-inch cock relentlessly in and out of me. The speed of his onslaught winded me at first. Every muscle seemed to contract with shock and my heart beat fit to burst. But it was impossible to maneouvre myself into a more powerful position, and eventually I became limp and allowed myself to be mastered by his cock.

He acknowledged my submission with a soft kiss on the back of my ear and moved his rough hands underneath my body to pull me even closer into him. I shivered as his fingers brushed the tender skin of my nipples, and then bucked with surprise when the sensation in my breasts took hold between my legs. I became aware of a new and strange urgency inside me. Some mysterious network of nerves in my tummy had somehow started to connect with my clit, and the feeling was thrilling and scary.

'You want it now, don't you?' Red whispered.

I groaned in response.

'It takes a while the first time, but I knew you'd take to it,' he continued. 'You were made for fucking, you know that?'

I heard a noise somewhere in the room, like an animal keening, and realised that it was coming from me. Red had slowed his pace and was powering his full length in and out of me, setting off waves of pleasure that flowed from my tummy down to my toes. I found myself crying out for him to go deeper and deeper, and hot sticky juices started to flood out of my puss and soak my thighs and stocking tops. As I started to come, I felt a sudden rush of warm liquid cascading onto my cheek. I looked up as far as I could and saw the fuzzy impression of Black's cock releasing the last few droplets of come from where he stood over my head. It trickled down my cheek and into my open mouth, and as it touched my tongue I finally gave way and came with a ferocity that almost made me faint.

I'm not sure exactly what happened after that. I suspect I fell asleep for a moment (I tend to get a bit woozy after I come). My next memory is of being woken up by the sound of hurrying feet, followed by Black's voice whispering urgently in my ear.

'Wake up!'

'Mmph?'

'Your husband just called for you!'

Fuck! Ralph! My tummy convulsed like a pump, releasing a sickening wave of adrenaline. I struggled to my feet, but blacked out with dizziness almost instantly (damn, low blood-pressure, runs in the family). For a few seconds, everything seemed to be happening underwater. Black hauled me back onto the bed whilst Red smothered my crumpled form up to the neck with the duvet. As the bubbles in my vision cleared, I could see both of their faces hovering nervously over my head.

'There's two of us, mate, he can't knock us both out.'

'That's not what I'm worried about, I just don't want him calling the boss and getting our asses sacked.'

'Bollocks, yeah . . . look at the state of her though, she's got spunk all over her fucking face.'

There was a pause, and then two outbursts of muffled laughter.

'I'm OK, I'm OK' I whispered, my powerful instinct for self-preservation finally kicking in. I shooed them away with my hand. 'I'll look after myself, just get yourselves out and try not to make so much bloody noise.'

Their chests still heaving with silent laughter, they hurried over to the en suite where the door to the fire escape was still open. Black's flies were undone and Red was trying to do up his belt as he went.

'He's on the stairs, Mark, I can hear him whistling some jazz shit!'

'He'll hear you too if you don't shut the fuck up.'

Red blew me a kiss before easing the door shut behind him. He must still have the taste of me in his mouth, I thought, and my clit gave a little pulse. Then, remembering what he'd said, I reached out a hand and plucked a tissue from my bedside cabinet. It wasn't much use but it did get the worst of the spunk off my face. I screwed it up, and as I pitched it into the bin there was a tentative rapping at the bedroom door.

'Darling? Are you awake? I heard such a commotion up here a moment ago.' Ralph's voice had an edge to it that made me worried.

'Just about,' I murmured, scouring the room with my eyes for anything that might give me away. He was already halfway through the door before I noticed my sodden thong lying limply on the shag pile. Shit!

'Poor sleepy thing!' he said and sat down on the edge of the bed. I smiled weakly as he beamed down at me and planted a gentle kiss on my forehead. 'Blimey, you feel ever so hot. Almost feverish. Are you feeling quite well?' He made as if to peel back the corner of the duvet and I tensed.

'Oh I'm all right really, just a little hot and bothered.' But it was too late, the sheets were off and my nylon-clad legs, bare pussy and dishevelled basque were on display. His eyes widened, drank me in slowly from painted toes to smudged lips, and then fixed on my face with a bewildered expression.

'What do we have here?'

'Mmm . . . well . . . you see . . .'

He put a finger to my lips to silence me. I sighed and contemplated a bleak future with no husband and, more importantly, no joint account.

'Don't try to explain yourself,' he said. 'It's quite clear to me what's been going on.' He took my hand and continued earnestly, eyes downcast. 'I always knew that you had a very strong sex drive, and I've done my best to keep you satisfied, even though I'm a bit of a duffer in that department. But even though I'm clearly still failing in my duty, I just don't believe that locking yourself away in a frenzy of masturbation is the answer.'

A frenzy of masturbation? The first green shoots of hope began to germinate in my mind. Ralph walked thoughtfully to the bathroom, and returned with a warm wet sponge. I decided that the best policy was to keep schtum, and so I meekly allowed him to rub away the remains of my make-up. And I put up no resistance when he parted my thighs to soap away the stickiness between my legs. It was actually rather a pleasant feeling, especially after the morning's exertions. I spread my legs nice and wide for him, encouraging him to continue.

He clambered onto the bed next to me, still soaping, and curled up with his head on my tummy. 'Tomorrow I'll take you shopping and we'll get you a little toy, something to keep you busy when I'm not around.'

'Thank you, darling,' I whispered, 'that's terribly sweet of you.' I couldn't believe my luck, how did he not hear the boys on the stairs?

'It's the least I can do,' he said, and we lay still for a while. I sensed that some new thought had entered his head, but I couldn't work out what it was.

Then he discarded the sponge and began probing my pussy with slippery fingers, his breath coming in short bursts.

'Do you want to go inside there?' I asked, stroking his hair. It couldn't do any harm. And anyway, I was feeling warmly disposed towards him now that I'd had my fill of fresh cock.

He nodded enthusiastically and wrestled his trousers down to half-mast. As he clambered on, I lifted my knees and wrapped my calves around his back, clamping him into place. I was so wet that I barely noticed the semi-flaccid cock slide into me (it never got that hard, even on special occasions). But the gentle friction of his fucking was soft and reassuring. He had such an excitable cock, if I gave so much as a squeeze it would usually shoot its load.

With my eyes closed, I found myself playing back the morning's events in my head. The sensation of cock in my mouth, those rough hands on my nipples, that thick phallus mastering my anus. To my surprise, my clit began to throb and hum, the first time it had ever happened with Ralph pumping away on top of me. 'Mmm,' I said, screwing my eyes tighter shut. Ralph responded by pumping away ever harder, and his cock seemed to get longer and bigger.

As I relaxed into the first stages of climax, I wondered if this was the key to married life with Ralph. Fresh blood every now and then to warm me up, and then Ralph's gentle and reliable humping to see me through to the finishing line. The idea made me wriggle with excitement. Could I possibly get away with it?

'You wicked, wicked girl!' he yelled, and shuddered violently inside me.

Poor darling, I thought, you really don't know the half of it.

– Lucy, Hertfordshire, UK

Win-Win

After getting hired by a large international accounting firm, the first thing that the company did with me, and the other new recruits from the surrounding states, was to ship us all off to a country retreat for a week of orientation. The prospect of five days at a luxury resort in the woods was what had made me decide to accept the firm's job offer over the three other offers I'd received upon graduating from high school.

So, bright and early one Sunday morning, I piled into one of a number of chartered buses with my fellow trainees and headed for the hills. I sat next to another girl, Morgan, and we got to talking and eventually decided to share a room together at the hotel-resort complex. She was a hot-looking babe, with long, straight, black hair, a pale, fresh-faced complexion, crystal-clear blue eyes, and, most importantly to an avowed tit-woman like me, she sported a pair of jugs that would've put Jayne Mansfield to shame. She sort of looked like Jennifer Connelly, with Pamela Anderson's tits.

'This place is gorgeous!' Morgan squealed after we checked into our five-star accommodations.

The resort was on the sandy shores of Oak Lake, and comprised a huge main lodge and a hundred or so separate cabins, all made from polished cedar logs. The cabins were large, with each one containing a kitchen, living room and bedroom, and a hot tub built onto an outside deck. The deck provided a fantastic view of the big blue lake and the surrounding pristine forest.

'Yeah, it's great,' I agreed, sucking some pure, pine-scented wilderness into my lungs. I walked into the bedroom and plopped my suitcase down on a bed and yelled, 'Why don't we go for a swim?' Our formal orientation programme didn't start until the next day.

'Sounds great, Katy!' Morgan hollered back, then bounded into the bedroom, her huge boobs bouncing happily.

She tossed her bag on her bed, and then popped it open and took out a skimpy blue swimsuit. I held my breath and prayed to the ghost of Marilyn Monroe that she wouldn't go hide herself in the bathroom to change, and, indeed, she proceeded to pull off her T-shirt and unzip her tight jeans right then and there. 'Aren't you getting changed?' she asked, catching me staring at the pale twin globes that were putting a heavy, heavy strain on her pink satiny bra.

'Huh?' I responded, my throat gone dry with all the breath caught in there. 'Uh, yeah, sure.' I fumbled my own yellow bikini out of my suitcase.

I gripped the flimsy beachwear in my trembling sweaty hands and pretended to do something with it while Morgan broke open her bulging bra and her huge tits tumbled out into the open. Holy shit! I almost fell to my knees and fanned my arms in exultation at the big-breasted goddess. Instead, I licked my desert-dry lips with a wooden tongue and gazed in awe at the bodacious girl's wicked titties. They were massive – huge and heavy and snow-white, firm and round and peaked by ultra-pink nipples that seemed to swell to erection right before my bedazzled eyes. Her tits were larger than any tits I'd ever seen, or handled, in my short but exciting eighteen years.

'Like what you see, Katy?' she asked suddenly, blushing and lowering her head.

I swallowed hard and my throat clicked. 'I-I-I . . . I love what I see.'

She lifted her baby-blues out of the inch-long shag and looked directly at me. 'Since I've shown you my boobs, why don't you show me those long legs of yours?'

So, she was a leg-lover. What a well-matched couple we were proving to be, because my secret weapon with the guys and gals was a pair of lithe honey-dipped legs that would've made a ballerina proud. I fumbled my jeans open and slid them down my legs, never taking my astonished pupils off Morgan's magnificent mammaries. I stepped out of the form-fitting jeans and strutted around the bed so that she could get a good eyeful of my slender legs. I'd spent a lot of time playing beach volleyball that summer, and my legs were sun-kissed a golden-brown, smooth and supple.

'Ohmigod,' she breathed, her eyes widening with excitement, 'you're beautiful.'

I grinned at her. My T-shirt hung down over my panties, so my slim legs were nicely showcased for her appreciative eyes. I turned my back to her and bent over so that she could get a nice view of my taut round ass. I heard her gasp.

I paraded around the room some more, her eyes tracking me like a pussycat tracks a mouse, and then I sauntered over to her where she stood next to her bed in just her low-rider jeans, her over-ripe titties bare and bold and begging for attention. I was only two feet away from her, and my body shook gently and my brazen legs sprouted goosebumps as the air grew thick with anticipation. I jerkily breathed in the sweet scent of her body spray.

She looked up from my legs and murmured, 'What are you waiting for?' And she cupped her humungous hooters in invitation.

Now, normally I like to enjoy a few sensuous minutes of kissing and frenching before I get down to the soul-searing business of tit-groping and sucking, making love to a girl, but there was nothing normal about

Morgan's chest. So, I grabbed as much of her boobs in my worshipful hands as I could and started fondling. They felt even better than they looked – firm and hot and smooth and heavy. I lovingly caressed the babe's massive mounds, brushing my twitching fingers over their immenseness, swirling my silver-painted fingertips around her huge pink aureoles, her engorged, half-inch nipples.

'God, that feels good,' she groaned, closing her eyes and throwing her head back, her lustrous jet-black hair cascading down her naked back.

My body caught fire from the incredible heat of her hooters, and I exploded with passion. I clutched her mammoth mams and desperately squeezed and kneaded them, my small brown hands barely beginning to cover her awesome feminine charms. I cupped their weighty masses and bent my head down and flicked my tongue across her nipples, teased the underside of her lust-hardened, rosy-red nips with my warm wet tongue.

'Yeah, suck my tits, Katy,' she moaned, gripping my shoulders and pulling me close.

I swirled my tongue all around first one luscious nipple and then the other, recklessly slathering them with my saliva. I hefted her tremendous tits, pushed them together, and bounced my head back and forth between her obscenely swollen nipples, lashing her nips with my slimy pink pleasure tool. Then I latched onto her left tit with my pouty lips and hungrily sucked on it.

'Fuck, yeah!' she screamed, her eyes popping open. She stared down at me as I stared up at her, her eyes wild, my mouth full of glorious rubbery nipple.

Her tits were obviously as sensitive as they were huge, because she grabbed my head and held on tight, her lush body quivering as I sucked and sucked, tugged on her flowered nipple with my mouth. She ran her fingers through my long blonde hair, then pulled me hard up against her tit as I greedily chewed her nipple, almost suffocated on her giant titty.

She bit her plush lower lip and whimpered, and I suddenly realised that the extremely well-endowed hottie was almost ready to come. My tit-worship was bringing her off, big-time. I quickly unmouthed her left breast and swallowed as much of her right as I could. I groped her terrific ta-ta's while I torqued up the mouth-suction. I flattened out my tongue and painted her inflamed nipple with my hot spit, urgently scrubbing her nub even harder and longer.

'God almighty!' she shrieked, and her voluptuous body seemed to dissolve in my hands and mouth. She shook like a fig leaf in a sexual hurricane, and then her twin-peaked torso was jolted with orgasm, again and again and again, until she collapsed backwards onto the bed with me riding her tits all the way down.

'I want to make love to your legs,' she gasped eventually, as I fondled her splayed mounds, lightly bit and twisted her fat nipples.

'Sure,' I responded, tearing my hands and mouth off her boobs, standing up and stripping away my T and bra. My titties are small at the best of times, but they were positively minuscule in the shadow of Morgan's mountainous mammaries. But Morgan didn't care; she wanted my legs and feet, wanted them bad. I spun around and gently slid my panties over my firm sun-burnished butt cheeks, then all the way down my glistening bronze legs.

She sat up on the edge of the bed and eye-fucked my dancer's legs, her huge chest heaving with excitement. I poured it on for her, standing on my tippy-toes to daintily and seductively step out of my panties, my brown legs flashing in the hot afternoon sun that streamed in through the window. I picked up my crumpled panties with my slender toes and flung the sexy cotton garment her way.

She caught the piece of intimate-wear, rubbed it all over her face, and then stood up and peeled off her own jeans and panties. Her pussy was slick with desire, brazenly bare except for a small tuft of black fur just above her clit. She rushed over and captured me in her arms and mashed her mouth against mine, her gigantic jugs flattening my over-matched hooters as we heatedly embraced. We kissed long and hard, then frenched ferociously, our slippery pink tongues slapping together in an orgy of eroticism.

She broke away from my gaping mouth and pushed me down onto the bed. I lay flat on my back, and she quickly grabbed up my supple sun-kissed legs and started fondling them. I reached down to my sopping pussy and buffed my electrified clit as Morgan caressed my legs. She raked her purple fingernails up and down the soft shiny lengths of my legs, then encircled my ankles with her fingers and placed my left foot on her right tit, brought my other foot up to her mouth and teased my wriggling toes with her outstretched tongue.

'Good girl,' I groaned. 'Suck on my toes.'

She brushed the underside of my arched foot with her moist tongue, then lapped in earnest at the tender, ticklish foot-bottom. My leg jerked in her hand as she tongued my sensitive sole, but she held on tight to my slim ankle. She'd obviously had a lot of practice with women's feet and legs, because she knew all the hot spots to hit in order to make a girl's pussy tingle with sensual delight.

I frantically frigged myself as Morgan licked and licked at the sole of my foot, then naughtily probed the space between each toe before swallowing my big toe in her warm wet mouth. I moaned my approval and fondled her tit with my other foot, rolled her engorged nipple between my dexterous toes, as the busty young Miss sucked and sucked on my big toe. She tugged on it with her red full-bodied lips, swirled her tongue all around it, bathing it in saliva. Then she finally disgorged my toe and ran her tongue slowly and sensuously over the top of my foot, across my ankle, down the side of my fleshy calf. She kissed and bit my calf, and tongued the vulnerable underside of my knee.

I couldn't take any more. 'I'm gonna come!' I cried out, my hand a blur on my swollen button.

'Let me help,' she responded, dropping to her knees and shoving two of her fingers into my drenched pussy. She shouldered my legs and hammered away at my cunny as I frenziedly polished my clit, her mouth-watering jugs jouncing in rhythm to the finger-fucking she was providing.

And when she kissed and licked the super-sensitive golden flesh of my inner thigh, it all became way too much for me and my body burst into flame and was consumed by orgasm. 'Yes!' I screamed at the top of my lungs, almost bringing the sturdy log walls down on top of us as I was jolted with ecstasy. My body convulsed in orgasmic shock, and I whipped my head back and forth and clung onto my clitty as Morgan relentlessly plundered my pussy. Orgasm after orgasm thundered through my stoked, sweat-dappled body, and my cunt gushed super-heated girl juice as I came and came and came. Until finally, my body and soul wasted, a last orgasm tore me apart, and then I lay still and exhausted.

Morgan pulled her dripping fingers out of my smoldering snatch, licked them clean, and then lapped at my steaming cunny as I gently stroked her silky hair. 'This is going to be one fun week,' she quipped from between my legs, her lips and chin shiny with honey.

From then on, the fun for Morgan and me began around four o'clock every day. After grinding through courses in the morning and team-building activities in the afternoon, we would get the rest of the day, and night, off to enjoy ourselves – and each other. We fucked to the wee hours of the morning, every morning, the two of us never getting tired of each other and our chosen fetishes – her beautiful bountiful boobs for me, and my lovely long legs for her. It was a match made in sexual heaven. And just to put the figurative cherry on top of our supremely sweet week of erotic enjoyment, on the final day of training we discovered another girl who shared our own particular orientation – Anita.

Anita combined the very best of both worlds; she had large over-ripe melons and long slender legs. She was a sultry girl a year older than Morgan and I, with shoulder-length brunette hair, flashing green eyes, pouty lips and those aforementioned much-admired breasts and legs. The two of us wasted no time in trying to indoctrinate the busty leggy Latina into our lusty world, with Friday night finding all three of us sharing a blanket on a secluded section of the twilight beach.

Anita was barely wearing a lime-green bikini with a thong bottom, her gigantic jugs straining the thin fabric of her top to breaking point. Morgan and I were similarly clad, finally getting into the flimsy beach apparel that had first touched off our passion upon arrival at the resort. We quickly shed our swimwear, however, when Anita confessed that she had caught us savaging each other in our hot tub and wanted to join in on our recreational activities.

'There's always room for one more,' I assured the Hispanic hottie. Then I pushed her down onto the blanket, slid my eager hands under her top, and started caressing her bronze bumpers. Her jutting nipples were an even darker brown than her boobs, and they grew longer and harder as I teased them with my fingertips.

'*Si*, Katy, *si*,' she mumbled, closing her eyes as I bent down to wetly kiss her thick lips.

'I want in, too,' Morgan exclaimed, kneeling down behind me.

I straddled the stranded Latina, sat on her stomach and fondled her boobs while Morgan scooped up her legs. She joyfully rubbed Anita's luscious legs, then encircled the hard-breathing, heavy-breasted girl's tapered ankles with her fingers and steered one of the sweet babe's feet up to her mouth. She crammed all of Anita's wiggling toes into her mouth and sucked on them.

'Ay yi yi,' Anita gasped, as I gripped and squeezed her golden casabas, and Morgan tugged on her slender toes.

I kneaded her breasts, revelling in the firm, hot and heavy feel of them, the spectacular size and weight of them, and then I toyed with her rigid nips with my flicking tongue. I tongued up and down and all around Anita's inflamed chocolate nipples, as Morgan sucked and licked the girl's toes, lapped at the soles of her feet. I pushed the writhing vixen's massive mams together and dragged my slimy tongue across both of her hardened buds at once, then tried to jam the two of them into my greedy mouth. I savaged her blessed burnished hooters with my hands and mouth, while Morgan licked and kissed and bit her slim ankles, her muscled calves, and finally ran her paintbrush tongue down the overwhelmed girl's soft inner thighs.

'Sweet Jesus!' Anita yelped, her senses shattered by what was probably her first girlie threesome. She frantically twisted her head from side to side, her hair flying across her lust-contorted face, her jade eyes wide and wild.

Morgan cranked up the sexual heat yet another notch by sliding her big toe into the total-package wet dream, foot-fucking the poor overwrought girl while I swallowed as much of her right tit as I could and tugged on the firm sopping flesh with my mouth. Morgan pounded her big toe into Anita's pussy, at the same time sucking and sucking on the squirming girl's own outstretched toes – toe-fucking and toe-sucking the increasingly desperate babe as I pulled on her tits with my lips, bit down on her rock-hard nipples, and painted her jugs with my tongue.

It was way too much for Anita to withstand for long. 'Heaven help me!' she screamed, her throaty voice blasting across the placid water, shattering the peaceful evening air into a thousand jagged pieces.

And just as the fiery red sun sank into the tree-lined horizon, Anita's fiery body quivered like a sexual tuning fork and the superheated tit and leg goddess came over and over. 'Mother of Mercy!' she hollered, then bit down hard on her lower lip as her body trembled uncontrollably, as she was devastated by orgasm.

It took a while for Anita to recover sufficiently for us to resume our sensual activities, but when she did, she attacked Morgan and me with a vengeance, with an uninhibited animalistic passion. And, as it happily turned out, the three of us all ended up working in the same office, and putting to excellent use the things we had learnt during our company orientation.

– Katy, Austin, TX, USA

A Financial Arrangement

We first made the arrangement as a private joke between us. Larry would pay me £100 for each sexual service I provided. As we had been married for five years by that point it added a kinky new twist to our sex life. The sex seemed to improve when he realised he was giving me something I wanted and I realised I could enjoy myself in the bedroom and profit from the experience.

Also, and I have to admit this was the best part, I always felt wonderfully dirty when Larry paid me afterwards. Watching him thumb through his wallet, having him hand over a fistful of grubby fivers and tenners, made me feel cheap and extremely satisfied. It reminded me of all those seedy things you see on TV about prostitutes and their customers and it made me feel as though I was one of those brazen women who would do anything for cash.

Larry got bolder with his requests. Our tame sex life got kinkier as he would ask me for a blowjob or anal or suggest watersports or something equally deviant. Because I was getting paid I was happy to go along with whatever he wanted. If I liked it, I'd often suggest that we do it again. If I didn't particularly enjoy the experience I'd still be £100 better off and I'd know not to try whatever it was in the future.

But the biggest thrill for me always came when I was getting paid.

One night, when we were travelling back home from a restaurant, Larry said he wanted me to suck his dick while he was driving. I told him it would be £100 and he said that wasn't a problem. He pulled out a roll of notes, counted off my hundred, and then pushed the money into the right cup of my bra. Feeling the scratch of the notes against my nipple and breathing in the dirty scent of the money was a bigger aphrodisiac than anything chemical. I got really turned on, unzipped him and sucked him to climax as he drove us home. While I was swallowing his come I was also frigging myself to orgasm and scrunching the notes hard against my nipple.

Eventually I changed my pricing structure. Larry had developed an appetite for anal and, while I also found it pleasurable, I was missing the sensation of having his cock fill my pussy. So I told him anal had become £200, while regular sex remained a bargain at £100. Larry accepted this and I made a small fortune from him the following month as he continued to fuck my arse and then pay me in full for the pleasure.

But I'd always thought our arrangement was a secret. I hadn't told my sister or any of my friends about the way Larry paid me for my services and I'd assumed he hadn't told any of his friends. I discovered I was wrong when we were entertaining one of his business colleagues.

Larry had told me to expect Jonathan for dinner that evening and I was happy that we'd be having the company. I'd met Jonathan before on a couple of occasions – usually related to Larry's work – and he'd struck me as being personable. I'd gone to the trouble of preparing a three-course meal, and everything seemed to be going well. We were eating dessert when Larry suddenly said, 'Jonathan thinks your prices are too low.'

I didn't know what he was talking about at first. It was only when Larry explained that he'd told Jonathan about our arrangement that I realised he'd been discussing the intimate details of our sex life with his friend at work.

I was blushing as though my head was on fire. Trying not to appear fazed by this development I glanced at Jonathan and said, 'Why do you think my prices are too low?'

He gave me a look of appreciation and said, 'I'd happily pay double what you're charging Larry for your services.'

I don't think I've ever before been in a situation where I've been so suddenly and totally aroused. It was almost as though Jonathan had flipped a switch on my body that instantly made my pussy wet. Larry was grinning broadly and I could see that he was desperate for something to happen. Trying to appear cool I shrugged and went back to finishing my meal. Without looking at either of them I said, 'I'd charge a full grand to do a double-header with you both. I'd expect the money in cash and up front. And, for that grand, you could expect to have me at your disposal for the entire evening.' With that said, I took my empty plate and disappeared into the kitchen.

When I came back there was a pile of money in front of my seat.

My heart was hammering as I counted it. I could see Larry and Jonathan were both watching me and had forgotten about the remainder of their meals. I concentrated on counting the bundle of fives and tens while my pussy got wetter and wetter.

'There's a fiver missing,' I told them.

Jonathan grinned. 'I kept that in my pocket,' he said. 'Do you want to come and get it?'

I glanced at Larry, just to make sure he was OK with what we were doing, but I think I would have gone ahead with it regardless of whether he minded or not. He was the one who had shared the secret of our arrangement with Jonathan so I figured he could just go along with whatever I decided. However, since he was grinning from ear to ear, it seemed fairly obvious that he was a hundred percent behind the idea of my doing a double-header.

'Which pocket?' I asked Jonathan.

He shifted in his seat and pointed to his left trouser pocket. He was looking at me and smiling and I knew he was trying to find out how far I would dare to go. I reached into his pocket and felt the fiver straight away. I also felt the thickness of his semi-hard cock, loose beneath the fabric of his pocket. Encircling my fingers around him I kept my expression poker-faced so that Larry had no idea what I was doing. Slowly, I wanked my wrist back and forth for him before pulling my hand out of his pocket. I had the fiver in my hand and I went and added it to the rest of the money.

I have never felt more like a prostitute in my entire life. My pussy was sopping and I could have come while I was handling the notes.

'What do we get for our money?' Larry asked.

I glared at him. 'You get full value,' I promised. Still looking at Larry I said, 'You get to watch your wife sucking on Jonathan's cock. Then you're going to get sucked inside out while Jonathan licks and fingers me. If you can both get hard after that I'll expect you each to fuck me. I don't mind if it's one after the other, or if you fancy squeezing both your cocks together and sliding into my pussy at the same time. After that, if you can manage a third time, I'm up for doing whatever you want.'

While I was talking I had been unfastening my blouse. That was dropped onto the floor and I stepped out of my skirt a moment later. I was standing in front of both men wearing only my bra and knickers. Stuffing the thousand pounds into the right cup of my bra I shivered when the paper pressed hard against my nipple. I told Larry and Jonathan, 'When I say we can do whatever you want, I mean you can do anything to me for the third time. Do you understand what I'm saying?'

Larry was almost coming in his pants. Jonathan was wide-eyed and I could see the considerable bulge in his pants was now more than semi-hard and standing proudly to attention. As soon as I unzipped his flies I knew his thick hard cock would be exposed and ready for me to suck.

Both men pushed their plates aside. Jonathan shifted his seat away from the table. I got down on my knees, ignored my husband, and started to unzip Jonathan's fly.

'Are you sure you want to do this?' Jonathan asked. He looked a little nervous and I knew the question was directed to me and Larry.

Releasing his cock I wrapped my fist around the nine-inch monster he was carrying and pulled downwards so his foreskin was away from his glans. Licking my lips, and moving my face closer to him, I patted my right breast and said, 'I want to earn this money. Sit back and let me show you that I'm worth it.'

Patting my breast, scrunching the notes hard against my stiff nipple, I almost came. Pushing my mouth quickly over Jonathan's cock, licking, sucking and finally swallowing, I spent the first half hour of the night quivering on the verge of orgasm.

I didn't come when he exploded in my mouth. I didn't even come when I was sucking Larry. Jonathan had his fingers in me then, and his tongue was chasing incredible circles around my clit. But, for some reason, I just wasn't able to get past the point of orgasm. My first orgasm only came when I was straddling Larry's cock with my pussy and Jonathan was trying to squeeze his monstrous erection into the same hole. The combination of pain and arousal was an intoxicating blend. I was really horny from the fact that I was being sandwiched and fucked by two men. And the pressure of the money against my right breast was a constant reminder that they'd paid for my services and I was giving them value for money. I think it was that thought that got me wet enough to accept Jonathan's cock. And I'm sure it was the pressure of his huge dick in my pussy that finally forced me to have my first climax.

Larry came at the same time as me. I felt his sticky load spurt into my pussy and leave me feeling beautifully wet and soiled. Larry pulled out and left Jonathan's cock inside me.

Jonathan didn't seem to mind that he was sliding into me on a lubricant of my husband's cream. He began to ride me and pound me with so much vigour I was having another orgasm by the time he eventually came.

'What do you want to do to finish off the evening?' I asked.

Larry said nothing, and I knew that he was going to have difficulty getting another hard-on that night. Jonathan looked at me and said, 'You said we could do whatever we wanted?'

I agreed that I had said that.

He said he wanted to ride my arse.

I have to admit I came close to saying no. My pussy was sore from having Jonathan ride me so hard and vigorously. My anus, I knew, would have difficulty accepting his big thick cock. But since he and Larry had paid £1,000 between them I felt obliged to give it a try. And, if the truth be known, the idea of having his huge tool inside my rear was getting me very excited.

The three of us finished the night with me on my knees, sucking on Larry's semi-erect dick, and taking all nine inches of Jonathan's big cock up my backside. I was the first one to come in that position. Jonathan came a close second, shooting a dollop of his hot load into my rectum. When Larry saw me moaning through a climax, and realised Jonathan had just shot a load up my arse, his semi-erect cock came up with enough life to spurt at the back of my throat.

I brought the night to a close shortly after that. I was exhausted, I'd given them both good value for money, and I wanted to go to bed and count the notes that were still stuffed inside my bra. Jonathan said it would be great if we could all do it again some time but I could sense that Larry wasn't too keen on that happening. I don't know if it was because Larry felt small next to Jonathan's big size, or if he felt inadequate because Jonathan had been easily able to get it up for me three times in the space of a couple of hours.

So I said nothing at the time. And I've said nothing to Larry about my Wednesday night visits to Jonathan where I earn a regular £400.

– Sally, Bristol, UK

A Night at the Opera

Three years ago I had the most inappropriate relationship of my life, also the most intense. I'd like to tell you about it, but first, a little background. I am now twenty-eight, and come from what I suppose many people would regard as a privileged background. My father was a senior civil servant, now retired. My mother was the daughter of a Conservative MP and did as little as she possibly could. I went to fee-paying schools, spent most of my gap year in Europe and studied Politics, Philosophy and Economics at university. Having got an MA in Management I took a job at one of the oldest and best known city companies, which will remain nameless.

I'm not a conventional person. I never follow the pack, and you definitely won't catch me wearing something or going somewhere merely because it happens to be fashionable. Unfortunately my relationships were conventional, at least until I met Christopher. I don't know why it should be, but men either seem to find me intimidating or want me as a trophy. The first sort I can't abide anyway and the second sort never last long.

Christopher was different. For one thing he was almost thirty years older than me, and for another he belonged to a very different world. Excepting a few old friends, everybody I know is in professional work and has an appropriate lifestyle. Christopher had the same background, but he'd made his money in the 'eighties and retired.

I was fascinated from the start. Here was a man who treated me as an equal, and without taking my job or who my parents were into account. He was far more interested in who I was, in my opinions on art or philosophy, and in me as a woman. He was also very open about his sexuality, unashamedly so, even aggressive. Up until then I'd thought of myself as modern and uninhibited, much like the women from *Sex and the City* I suppose, looking back, but there had always been something unsatisfying, something I couldn't define.

Christopher could. He explained to me how modern life has eroded the biological dynamic between men and women, so that while the physical sensations of lovemaking remain the same, much of the mental aspect has been lost. Tepid is the word he used to describe modern romance, and I felt he was right. He also had the answer.

Equality, he explained, is for day to day life. Mutual respect should be the norm, and no one individual has the right to claim superiority over another, and control only within the context of making an organisation run efficiently. Unfortunately we have allowed the same concepts to enter our sex lives, with the result that we are unable to reach the highest levels of pleasure. For that, a woman must surrender herself to her man, the naturally dominant partner in a primitive sense.

I found the concept hard to accept, despite his insistence on detaching submission in real life from sexual submission, but just to think about what he was suggesting made me react deep inside myself, not on an intellectual level at all, but as something visceral, something animal. Within a few days of meeting him I had realised that he had something to offer far beyond anything I had experienced before.

What he was suggesting was that I surrender control of my body to him, subject only to the limits of common sense. He didn't put me under pressure, or I think I'd have backed off, but made it very clear that the option was there if I wanted to take it up. I did, but I was very aware that my friends and, more importantly, my business associates would see what I was doing as inappropriate, which within the context of our society it is. Not that there was any difficulty in my being with him, despite the difference in our ages. He was wealthy and that made it acceptable. The difficulty was in me and him becoming a couple within my social set, because he refused to compromise his principles by pretending to believe in the normal sexual conventions when he came into contact with other people.

If we were to be together it would have to be a clandestine affair. I admit that appealed to me, and for him it was familiar territory. He suggested a trip to Italy, and there, in an opera house that must remain nameless in a city that must also remain nameless, I was given my first experience of how it feels to be under a man's control. It was a simple thing, presented to me as an experiment to test whether my feelings were genuine, whether I was capable of that essential surrender, or whether I was too deeply tainted by modernity to explore the darker areas of my femininity. He made me wear a collar, but no ordinary collar.

It was steel, a simple elegant loop, thick at the back and tapering to the front, where both sides curved back to allow it to be fastened with a small but effective padlock of the same bright metal. The moment it was clipped around my neck I felt owned, his property, to do with as he pleased. It was an extraordinarily powerful feeling, so strong it left me weak at the knees, and that from merely standing in our hotel room with nothing that ordinary people might have considered sexual contact at all.

To a casual glance my collar might have been a fashion accessory, the sort of *faux* expression that has been popular on and off since Madonna hijacked sadomasochistic imagery in order to give her flagging career a boost. People might wonder, and as I was in a low-cut evening gown they couldn't help but see. I knew.

He had added the key to the same ring that held his car key, and that was important to me. For the evening I would be one of the beautiful things he owned, cherished, and yet no less his property. Simply leaving the hotel was an overwhelming experience, leaving me flushed hot and aroused to a level I had never before experienced. Attending the opera was stronger still, standing among the crowds in the brightly-lit vestibule, collared for all to see, seated and lost in the music save for a tiny part of me that remained painfully aware of my status from start to finish. By the end I was walking on air, so detached from the mundane world around me that I would have done whatever he told me to, then and there. Fortunately he had perfect self-control, remaining calm and firmly in charge all evening until we returned to our room. There, he fucked me.

That sounds so crude, and yet that harsh word best expresses the raw, primitive act. There was nothing contrived about it, no carefully phrased questions or testing caresses. He simply told me to kneel on the bed, to bare myself to him. I did and he took me from behind, rough and hard, and I came. I've never come like that before, simply from having a man inside me, and most of the pleasure was not physical at all, but in my head, exactly as he had told me it would be.

After that evening I was lost to the pleasure he alone could provide. I had never experienced anything of the sort, and he outshone my previous lovers as the sun outshines a candle. There were still issues: my friends, my work, my difficulty in overcoming what I logically knew to be a phoney concept – that a woman who surrenders control of her sexual being to a man diminishes herself. They call it self-respect, but really it's just a moral prop for those who haven't the courage to let themselves go.

I told Christopher that I needed to overcome that feeling. He understood and agreed, telling me that the best thing to do was to push my limits. I agreed, and there's a paradox there, because not to have done so would have been to give in to the very thing I was trying to overcome.

London was out of the question, so once more we went under the Channel, to one of the old European capitals, which he assured me would be exactly right for what he had in mind. As always, he was right. The sense of ancient, lost grandeur that the city conveys was perfect for my mood, enabling me to detach myself from all that is mundane long before I was even put in my collar. Once I had been, the evening became a dream, and a dream that will live in my head for the rest of my life. He took me to the opera house, a wonderful place of faded gilt and old crimson velvet, with here and there a double-headed eagle worked in among the ornaments. There were boxes, three tiers of them, hidden in a multitude of subtle shadows so that while a member of the audience might glance in and gain a hint of something, he would never be sure.

Christopher took me in my collar, a cape, a beautiful evening dress in rich blue silk, heels, and nothing besides. My legs were bare, I had no panties, no bra, no bag, no money, no phone, no keys. I felt utterly and wonderfully naked. We drank Champagne, enough to allow me to conquer those final reservations I was so desperate to shed. If he had ordered it I would have stepped from my dress there and then, to go naked at his will, and without thought for the consequences.

He held back, in control as ever, waiting until we were seated in our box. There, in the shadows of the second row of seats, he laid my breasts bare. I could see out from the box, full across the stalls, where several hundred people were gathered, and I was naked, naked because Christopher had chosen to have me naked. Yet I had never felt so free, nor so aroused.

One beauty of being under the control of a man like Christopher is that sex is never hurried. Altogether too many men see everything that goes before as no more than a rather tedious prelude to their orgasm. Not Christopher. He would allow my feelings to build up slowly, for hours, always patient, slowly lifting me to greater heights, until the act itself became the final, perfect note of a performance.

This time he allowed my feelings to build to a peak, judging me perfectly, and when the time was right he leant close to my ear and gave me a single, calm command, to urinate. I simply let go, breaking what must be one of the most forceful taboos of our culture, too lost to his control even to think of resistance. Simply to feel the warm urine running down my thighs and soaking into the silk of my dress brought me close to absolute surrender, but to know that I'd done it because he had ordered me to was too much.

I did it then and there, lifting my dress as my stream dried to a trickle and spreading my thighs wide to the auditorium. He could see, and I wanted him to, to know how completely he had conquered me, until I could no more refuse his command than stop myself breathing. I was in heaven, my head thrown back, my naked breasts pushed out, my thighs wide, completely vulnerable, while he watched with his wry, knowing smile, watched me masturbate in a puddle of my own urine as we sat together in a crowded theatre.

Never, ever, could I have imagined I was capable of something so utterly inappropriate, so primitive, so blatantly sensual. Yet I did, and as I came I was crying tears of joy, and of release. Once again Christopher had lifted me beyond not only what I'd experienced before, but beyond anything I'd even believed could be experienced.

Unfortunately that was the high point of our relationship. For all his talk of equality, he really wanted me to be his unconditionally. That meant giving up my work, my friends, everything. I nearly did, but there was a always a tiny spark at the back of my mind; asking what would happen if her grew bored of me, or when I grew older. When I was offered promotion and a move to our New York office I took it, and that was that. It didn't work, but I like to think that in different circumstances it could have done, and that maybe, one day, it will.

– Cordelia, Richmond, UK

Couple Cruising

I signed up to a swingers website recently. I'm not sure how I came across it. I think I just pulled up Google or some other similar search engine and typed in the words 'casual', 'sex' and 'London' in the hope that it would bring up something interesting. I mean, how else am I going to find it? It's not something you ask your friends, is it? 'Hey Sarah, where do you go when you wanna get screwed?' – or a query that I could bring up with my much older sister, who is in her late forties now. She would have been mortified at the idea of her newly divorced younger sister's eager ambitions to get laid. It was hard enough for her hearing I was getting divorced. It was a cardinal sin in her rule book and she cried down the phone when I told her. I remember neglecting to add to this wave of emotional grief that I was actually OK about it and wanted to move on. That very morning I had fucked Alex, a guy from another department in my office building who had been giving me the eye for weeks. It was a symbolic fuck marking the end of my old life and the beginning of my new one.

Alex's favourite trick was to wait until I was in the copying room and then appear behind me. There wasn't much room in there so the element of brushing past another was not uncommon. He'd like to rest as his crotch touched my bottom, with nothing but the skirt material between us. I slammed the cover on the machine down hard as I felt his cock position itself between my ass cheeks. I could still feel the heat from the machine and the warm smell of the toner filled my lungs as I breathed hard with a frustrated lust.

I didn't really go in for younger men – well, not ten years my junior like Alex – but something compelled me to react and see how he would respond to me putting down the copies of the previous year's forecast sheets and reach behind me for the crotch of his trousers. I was pleasantly surprised. He turned me round and whispered, 'How about it, babe, you and me?'

His arrogance and corny swagger offended me but he had a nice erection growing in my hand. I wanted to test this kid's bravado and was seriously in need of some rebound shagging.

'Women's toilets on the fifth floor,' I said. 'Know it?'

'Not intimately, but I know where you mean.'

'Ten minutes?'

'Sure.'

Of course he was there. He probably went straight up and hid in one of the stalls because by the time I had got up there, after a machine-granulated Nescafé and a good gossip with my mate Lorraine about the previous night's *American Idol*, there he was naked in the stall and erect.

'So, could you have made it any more obvious how much you wanted me, do you think?' I asked, naughtily. I grabbed his shaft hard and squeezed it making him whimper as he started to laugh.

I stepped back and peeled off my cotton blouse and pushed my boobs together, just to see the glee on his face.

Generally, I was in the position for some unabashed, no-strings sex, there were no two ways about it. Sure, I could have gone to a bar and waited to see what happened, but there is never any guarantee you will find what you want. More often than not you go to a place and can't shake off the first guy that approaches you so you end up sat at the bar nodding politely as much nicer men you would like to chat to come and go through your peripheral vision. So the website acted as a buffer between all of those opportunities wasted. To say that it has now got to the point where I have struck up a relationship with the website, not unlike the one an all-night trucker has with Little Chef, wouldn't be so far removed from the truth.

So, a few months after my thirty-fifth birthday, with my marriage over and still deep in the period of stressful negotiation that is dividing up all your joint assets, I decided to spend the evening with a bottle of Merlot and flirt away with some people in the chat room.

I watched the random banter and salutations appear on the screen while Ant and Dec's *Saturday Night Takeaway* played in the background out of sight. I had changed from my sweat pants and T-shirt into my best twin-set and fishnet hold-ups for the occasion. I flicked away at my little love button through my favourite silky French knickers, smelling the warm rose oil floating up my body that I had rubbed into my crotch and stomach, and waited for someone to strike up a conversation.

I get a good reception from this. I'm not gym fit but I think I have a great figure (shoulder-length blonde curls and a hefty bosom) along with a healthy dress size. I realise that I am no supermodel and the couture labels will not be knocking on my door, but I still get my fair share of compliments and glances out in the real world. Plus, I get plenty of adoring comments from both men and women when I'm online, which pleases me and does nothing but great things for my previously battered self-confidence.

I'd met guys from the site for a drink a few times and third time lucky, I'd bagged myself a lovely man called Tom, fresh from his office job in Canary Wharf. When the evening turned the right way and when I felt comfortable enough, I suggested driving back to my place. I got the flat (thanks to my husband's infidelity and being a crap liar) and I fully intended to use it for my casual desires. Tom screwed me in my kitchen for half an hour while I was making two cups of Gold Blend. He came up from behind and hunched my skirt up over my ass, gave my suspenders a ping in an almost childlike way and then bent me over the oak table my husband and I occasionally had dinner on.

The sex with the likes of Tom and Alex was illicit and exciting and they'd made me feel desired and certainly pleasured, but I was looking for something more. I had always felt bisexual, something I had broached with my husband and suppressed in myself when he got both rather offended and threatened by the notion, so this night, Merlot in hand, I brought up my new favourite bookmark on Internet Explorer, the one for likeminded partnerships who wanted to share an evening with another woman. The adverts section was by far the largest on the site, and I felt a surge of admiration for all those couples proud and confident enough to let another into their sacred union.

In the chat room, a few couples sat fully clothed and staring into the space beyond their computer screens, taking in my graphic display of self-pleasure. I carried on with my flirting and what they call in the media 'social networking'. What I really love about this website most of all is the lovely large-cocked men who are also doing the same. Watching me, watching them. One of them was a tall attractive black guy called Michael.

I warmed to him because unlike a lot of the other cams, which just showed men's cocks, I got to see the whole of Michael in all his fit glory. Admittedly, the main reason I was straying to his camera more than to any of the others (you can only watch one at a time) was because of the sheer size of his cock. It was huge. Long and thick and hanging off the front of the chair in front of him, almost itching to touch the carpet beneath him. I was quite in awe at the sight. But despite this, I actually enjoyed the fact that I could see the rest of him. He had a lovely smile and was dressed in just a crisp, open shirt that was resting on his shoulders. I wanted to say hi, but I didn't have to as soon enough, just as all the other men in the room already had, he sent me a message.

'Hi there, I'm Michael. You are just down the road from the two of us . . .'

I thought that was a lovely subtle way of pointing out that they were a couple and they were possibly interested in me. Straight away it made me pull up his profile and check them out. He knew we were so close because when you click on a possible suitor's name, it quite cleverly tells you exactly how many miles you are away from them, which seems to me to be the ideal application, perfectly tailored to the most important swinger's need, i.e., to quickly decide whether they are within your 'tube ride/drive to' range.

I was on the site as a single woman and had a couple of pictures up that my ex had taken of me and a quite clear message on my profile for what I wanted: a couple for friendship and fun. I also hinted that if they were of a different race (and by that I meant 'I'd like my first black cock'), this would be welcome too. Michael and his wife, Lavinia, were both mid-thirties, like myself, and both of Caribbean descent. The idea of being with a black couple both beguiled and excited me.

I found it quite ironic that the pictures my husband had obsessively taken of me posing fourteen different ways in the very expensive lingerie he'd bought (probably out of guilt from fucking that 24-year-old estate agent from Catford) were now being displayed for thousands of like-minded perverts to both ogle and admire. It seemed both liberating and apt, considering he was something of a bitter and uncomfortable prude himself.

Michael needn't have bothered going to the trouble of approaching me though. I had already spotted the sexy half-naked girl in the background, pottering about doing chores while he jerked himself off for me, and was wondering at the possibility of slipping in between them. I was quite impressed at the nonchalance Lavinia displayed at Michael's activities that Saturday evening. She clearly knew what he was doing and that the people he was chatting to could probably also see her trotting around half dressed. In fact, she occasionally wandered over and either snuggled up to him to snag a few thrusts on his huge erection with her hand, or stared at my private messages on the screen and blew kisses towards the folk who admired her from all around the country.

I pored over their pictures and began referring quite playfully to some of their graphic shots. They had clearly met someone in the past who was quite handy with a camera and happy to sit back and chronicle their fun by the looks of it, as I was faced with many detailed examples of their exploits. Lavinia seemed to have something of a penchant for groups of men as there were more than a few shots of her surrounded by hairy legs and bottoms of all colours, shapes and sizes, with the occasional appearance of her basque or a stockinged leg poking through the array of flesh.

The fact that she appeared briefly in her set in stockings and heels pleased me immensely. Her beautiful chocolate skin blended in with the dark mesh of the silk material on her legs. She had cute kitten heels in one shot and her legs were wrapped around Michael's neck while a young white guy fed his small penis into her mouth. I wanted to be there with them and make it a four. In another she was welcoming two black cocks into her mouth from either side, but the crowning glory had to be the final picture of her with a face messy with man-juice.

I knew right then I wanted to meet these guys. After some to and fro in the room, I directed them towards my MSN, where it's a lot easier to have a one-on-one chat. Instantly, they signed out of the room with their cam and invited me to watch via messenger instead.

This sign of commitment is always encouraging and exciting. Michael seemed to signal to his wife who came over and flopped down on the couch, intrigued.

'Hello, sexy,' I enthused to the cutie in her bra.

'Hi, I'm Lavinia,' she replied.

We chatted for about an hour, like girlfriends do over a bottle of wine and a Working Title film. I didn't tell her everything at once, deciding to keep relationships and all that awkward stuff for when we met in person, but we did cover sexuality, what she liked and what I liked etc, etc. She told me about him and what they enjoyed together: he liked for the girls to get in a squelchy 69 so he could feel free to apply himself to whatever end or orifice he chose, and she desired both the touch of a woman and the sight of her husband pounding mercilessly upon some willing languid piece of scented and trussed flesh.

The couple both spoke to me on the phone later that night, insisting on vocal contact as I do not have a cam at home. This was fine with me and we continued our chat for a few more sexy minutes. I loved Lavinia's soothing tones and the sound of her husband kissing her neck and boobs as she chatted to me.

'Is he getting naughty with you?' I giggled.

'Yeah,' she sighed. 'But I'm getting naughty too. I'm only in my robe and I am rubbing my pussy, which he loves to watch.'

'Sounds good. How would he like me sitting next to you and joining in on the show?'

She giggled. 'Yeah, he would love that.'

'Well, I will leave that thought in the air. Let me know if you want to meet?'

'Sure, we will pick out a date for later in the week and let you know.'

Five minutes after I hung up, my phone buzzed.

'Free midweek?' the text from them read.

Despite this new-found bravado I had discovered, I was quite shocked at how quickly things were moving.

Gosh, I thought. I could actually get to meet them soon and 'midweek' was only a few days away. I nibbled at the thumbnail on my left hand, a nervous habit I haven't been able to shake since uni. I stumbled over the clicking buttons on my phone as I texted them in return.

'Sure thing, let me know when and where you want me?'

I agreed to meet Michael and Lavinia at a bar on Hammersmith Broadway with the idea hanging in the air that if things went well, we could then go back to their place, which was a five-minute walk. I got a cab over from Richmond because of the killer heels and the tiny little skirt I had decided upon. It showed off my ass perfectly and I knew that both of them would appreciate the style I had adopted for them. I certainly had a butt fit for a rap video, as one lecherous chav told me in a bar recently.

I instantly recognised them sat in the corner of the bar, him smartly dressed in a well-cut suit and her in this tiny little cotton dress. It was orange and barely the length of a T-shirt, with matching killer heels. She had done her hair in seventies layers and looked like a black Farah Fawcett. A pang of excitement ripped through my stomach as I paused at the bar and gave them a polite little wave to let them know I knew them.

I much prefer breaking the ice from a distance. It gives the people you meet for the first time a chance to relax, safe in the knowledge that you have turned up, while also giving them a chance to check you out and, if necessary, bolt for the door.

Because it happens to us all.

I tottered over in my heels and plonked myself down on the chair opposite, holding out a hand to Lavinia. She seemed surprised at my confidence. She raised an eyebrow and checked out the tiny skirt that was riding up my ass on the chair.

'Where on earth did you find this little diamond, honey? Girlfriend is smokin'.'

I lifted up my glass to them and thanked them.

Should I try and go further? Yeah, why not. I'm feeling exceptionally naughty now.

'So . . . do I get to pleasure the both of you tonight?'

The two of them reached for their drinks at the same time, embarrassed. I laughed and tried to break the ice further.

'I take it you are pleased with what you see, then?'

Lavinia turned to her husband and pursed her lips in thought. She looked back at me and laughed.

'Yeah, girl, you all right . . .'

I got the sense that there was absolutely no need to stay for more than one drink. Michael had gulped most of his pint in about ten minutes and his goddess of a wife was gently stroking my leg (and vice versa) under the table as we chatted enthusiastically to one another.

The skirt I wore is one of my favorite micro-minis as it rides up far too much once you sit anywhere. That was certainly the impression I got from the table of builders across the way anyway. They looked like they had just knocked off from the site and were all dusty and covered in plaster. I sat there daydreaming what it would be like to be manhandled on a site and have them get me all dirty as Lavinia chatted to me about her work.

As she did this I stroked a finger up her leg and across her chocolate skin. I have a penchant for black girls. It must be a phase. Most of the porn I watch online involves a black girl. I love their big juicy lips and how their pussies taste. It's just different, I guess, and that's always good once in a while. A black girl broke my cherry back when I'd first moved to London, fresh from university and before I'd even met my ex.

Her name was Mary and she was from Kenya. We both worked in this hotel reception and went on lunch together. Once, when we were short of a clean room from the housekeeping handover, an important client turned up out of the blue. The front office manager apologised profusely to him, saying they were fully booked, but when this guy kicked off, threatening never to grace our establishment again, we were both sent up to straighten this dirty room. We got quite excitable and playful and, as we were trying to remember how to do our hospital corners and falling over laughing, Mary quipped that she really fancied me. I kissed her there and then. I have no idea what came over me. I think it was the hotel room. Hotel rooms just breed an illicit naughty streak in people. It was probably that or the half-drunk bottle of Moët, I can't be sure.

Anyway, it wasn't very long until we were pulling our starch-pressed cotton jackets from one another and frantically kneading each other's chests underneath our work blouses. The main thing on my mind at the time was that I hoped Dave hadn't cut the guest a key already but had sat him in the bar with a free glass of the thirty-quid-a-shot Rémy Martin XO.

We eventually came to and realised where we were and ran around the room, collecting together stained coffee cups and emptying the bin with the thought of completing the other task later on at her place.

Lavinia responded well to the stroking and put her hand up my skirt to finger my clit. One of the builders could clearly see what I was doing but decided not to share it with the others, enjoying what he thought was a secret show. For this, I was actually grateful and rewarded him with a horny look and a slightly better view as I moved around in our corner booth a little to enjoy her caress while Michael took his cue to tell me all about himself. To be honest, I wasn't really listening as I felt the urge inside me to come and this I eventually did after a few minutes. I creased up in giggles and thanked her with a peck on the lips.

'Can I take your man downstairs for a quick blowjob? I'd love to see his cock,' I announced to her, referring to where the toilets were.

'Sure, honey.'

I turned to Michael. 'Meet me in the men's in a few minutes.'

Five minutes later and we are in a little private stall and I have his lovely length in my hand, wanking him off. He takes my head in both of his big hands and I sink my mouth onto him. I pull away and spit on it.

It's like a fucking baby's arm, I wanted to say. *I'm going to have fun getting that into me*.

But there wasn't time.

'We should be quick, darling,' I said, massaging his balls.

'Take off that top and rub your tits and play with yourself too. Give me a show, honey, and I'll soon end this.'

'Cool,' I replied. I pulled up the front of my skirt and lifted up my top. I knew there was a reason I hadn't worn a bra today. Within a couple of minutes, he'd come into my mouth. I let it drip off my chin onto the tiled floor. We both laughed. I swallowed some of it and licked my lips before reaching for something to clean myself. We straightened each other and went back to his wife, who was happily flicking through a discarded *London Lite*.

'You'll both be spent now,' she tutted on our return.

I patted her leg gently.

'Starters, darling, starters.'

Within half an hour of Michael giving me a facial in the bathroom of a bar in Shepherd's Bush, I was on all fours on the black silk sheets of their bed as they both took turns at licking my arsehole. I'd suggested this myself as they gave me the tour which ended where we were to romp. As the great hosts they were, they'd courteously obliged and took one of my hands each to lead me into their sacred sanctuary.

As soon as I saw the shiny sheets and the white, ribbed butt-plug on the dresser, I insisted that they indulged in what was clearly a favourite pastime of theirs.

'Is it OK if I just strip here?' I asked them. I didn't want to worry about inhibitions and I wanted to get home at some point, not too late.

'Go ahead,' Michael said as he took the coat I was wearing.

'Great, I've been dying for a fuck all day.'

'Mmmm, this is a girl after our own heart,' grinned Lavinia.

'She is pretty insatiable . . .' answered her partner.

'Insatiable?' I chuckled, walking over to him. 'You've come already.'

'She does have a point,' Lavinia agreed. 'Hope you are not too tired, darling.'

We'd both made him blush and, to give him a little break, we decided he could indulge me while I backed onto his tongue, while his wife crawled around to the head of the bed and leaned against the steel railings of the headboard. She offered me her pussy for the first time and Michael tongued my hole with vigour and curiosity, getting it nice and wet with saliva and then working in a few fingers, preparing me for their toy.

Meanwhile I nibbled at his wife's clit and fondled her mounds. I grabbed her wide hips tight and lapped at her juices, which were flowing at the sight of her husband stuffing what was likely to be her pride and joy most nights into their new friend, still practically a complete stranger to them.

I noticed the leather cuffs and begged Lavinia to strap me up with them to their headboard. I lay on my back as the couple continued to feed on my flesh, so pale and white in comparison to theirs.

I threw my head back and imagined myself in a world of submission and desire, where young white girls like me are taken captive and forced to be the willing subjects of strapping men and Amazonian women just like the two gorgeous people I had here at the foot of this bed, their faces between my legs in their own passionate clinch.

They both used one of their hands to rub me to a joyful conclusion, my anus still gripped tightly around their toy. I rattled my bonds as my groin buckled at their forceful touching and the pleasure from their tool of intimacy, the sign of their implicit and simple union. The leather felt oh so good as I pulled my arms into their tight grasp.

I am fixed. I am caught. I am torn.

They both alternated fingers into me and massaged me to my ultimate goal. Michael was rock hard at the sight of this. This may have had a lot to do with Lavinia diving down there as they both knelt either side of me. She reached over and let him fuck her mouth, one hand punishing me.

'Give me your pussy, hun,' I begged, still strapped up and helpless.

'What do you think, darling?' she asked her husband, ignoring me.

'I think you should hover over her face and make her work for you . . .'

I purred at the sound of this while he continued.

'. . . then as you do that, I'm going to fuck her until she screams the place down and then I am going to finish myself off with you, my darling wife . . .'

We both gasped at this demand and immediately snuggled into the romp. Lavinia knelt above my head and turned to face her husband. She took hold of my ankles and spread them for him, while I pulled on my restraints in desperation to cross those vital inches above me so I could taste the pleasure oozing from the slight stubble on her pubis and clit.

Michael got distracted by this sight and eased back so he could compose himself for the task ahead. Lavinia took this as her chance and fell forward to eat my pussy for the first time. She had already given me so much pleasure with so few digits and now she was taking my clit and my hood and sucking it between those gorgeous big red lips, lightly flicking it with her tongue-piercing.

While she worked my desire, Michael pulled on what I hoped to be an extra large (and extra strong) condom, pouring on some water-based lube in the process. I was pretty much helpless in the unforgiving leather cuffs and covered by the body of Lavinia. For the first time in a long time I felt myself completely submit to someone's control, their every whim and instruction. As soon as Michael eased that cock into me and secured the butt plug with his hand, I felt that there was absolutely nothing I could do.

Lavinia sat up and ground her face down on my face, grabbing hard on my boobs as she gave her husband the wiggle room, and the force from the three of us gyrating rocked the bed back and forth.

Michael made a special effort and managed to get all of himself inside me once he'd released the toy from my arse. I started gasping for breath and Lavinia jumped off me, straddling my boobs and facing my head, tugging at my hair. She pulled at the bars in my nipples and let me catch myself up. She took a long deep kiss from me as she lay next to me.

'Would you like me to take off the cuffs?'

I nodded, panting, and as soon as my wrists were released I threw them around her husband's waist and scratched at his butt cheeks as he cried out with pain and pleasure, taking the prompt to fuck me harder.

He flipped me over on all fours and grabbed my hair. With his other arm around my belly, he lifted me and nodded for his wife to return to her initial position in front of me, with her legs apart. He forced my head into her groin and I licked her again while she rubbed herself to a climax.

Michael couldn't take much more of me gripping his huge cock with my pussy and eventually he pulled back, ripped the rubber skin off and ejaculated onto my bum. Lavinia crawled around and licked his juices from the sunken arch of my spine before she asked me to suck him clean.

I lay between their two bodies just as I had fantasised when I first saw them on their camera and grabbed myself a butt cheek in each hand, taking in the smell of sweat and pleasure.

'Nice to meet you both . . .' I gasped.

We lay and chatted for a few minutes and I rubbed his balls and his length until he got hard again. I wanted to prep him so he could fuck his wife before I left, and he more than rose to the occasion. He mounted her as she lay on her back and I nuzzled into her neck on her left side.

I lay facing them, a hand between my legs as I watched this beautiful couple make love to one another. They moved together and wrapped themselves around each other with familiarity. She reached across and held my free hand as he brought her to a bone-shaking climax once more.

I gathered my clothing from around the room and dressed as they lay, exhausted, well fucked and happy.

'Hey, I'll see you soon, yeah?' I suggested.

'Yeah, we would love that. Keep in touch.'

I knew that I'd probably be invited back very soon.

– Judith, Richmond, UK

The Tent

I've never told anybody this and I'm never going to, certainly not my mates. I'd never live it down. Not that it's wrong or anything, but you know what people are like. You see, I sucked another guy's cock.

I'm not gay, I'm absolutely not, and I bet any money that in the same position you'd have done the same as me, just as long as you could be sure nobody would ever find out.

It was like this. I went straight out of school into a job with a local company. The pay was OK, for an eighteen-year-old, but there were people working there who'd done the same as me only thirty years before and I could see myself turning into them. So after a few months I quit and set off around Europe with nothing but what I could get in my back-pack and the money I'd saved. It was a great life, and I'd do it again like a shot. Maybe I will one day.

I was planning to spend the winter in the south of France or maybe Spain, so I made my way down through France, sleeping in cheap hostels or under the stars, as free as a bird. I'd got to the Pyrenees before long and climbed well up into the mountains. What I hadn't realised was how bloody cold it could get at night, and how sparse the population is. The first night was so miserable I felt homesick for the first time since I'd left, and in the morning I started back down.

At least I thought I'd started back down, but I managed to lose my way and by the time it started to get dark I was walking along a high valley with even less shelter than the night before. I couldn't work out where I was on my map because I hadn't seen a signpost in ages, so you can imagine how pleased I was to see a neat little tent set up beside the stream I was following, with two people sat outside cooking their meal over a gas burner.

They were German, and really friendly. Maybe rather too friendly, but I didn't realise at the time. Come on, I was nineteen. They were brother and sister, both big and fair-haired, maybe in their mid-twenties, and she was gorgeous. Christa she was called, and if you picture her you'll understand. She had the longest legs you can possibly imagine, slender yet very feminine and leading up to perfectly formed hips and a belly and bottom like something out of a fantasy, a tiny waist and great, heavy breasts. She was also beautiful, with long silky blonde hair in a plait that went right down to her bum. Not only that, but she was in tiny shorts and a jumper so tight I could see every little jiggle of her breasts.

I tried hard to keep my eyes off her, but after they'd let me share their dinner and a bottle of wine it wasn't easy, especially when she so obviously found my attention flattering. They were very open too, the way Germans often can be, expressing a frank if rather clinical admiration for my own looks. Looking back I think they'd been planning it, maybe from the moment they saw me coming, but at the time I was just glad of their company and the prospect of sharing their warm tent next to Christa.

I was soon beginning to wonder if I'd be sharing rather more of Christa, because I could see the mischief in her eyes and the way she kept glancing at my crotch. Guthrie, the brother, had opened a bottle of some local brandy, pretty rough but effective, and with Christa openly showing off I was getting bold and psyching myself up to make my move. She made it first, coming to my side of the fire and putting her arm around me. I could feel the swell of her breast against me and smell her scent, which had me hard, which is probably why I didn't realise there was anything odd about the way she kept telling her brother how handsome I was, or the way they'd occasionally pass a laughing remark in German instead of English.

They just reeled me in. Soon I was kissing Christa, and she didn't waste any time in putting a hand to my crotch and giving me a squeeze. I'd never known a girl like her. I was no virgin, but I was used to girls who expected me to make the running, at least at first, while I hadn't had any sex at all for months. Not only that, but Guthrie obviously didn't mind, and while I was wishing he'd go away so that we could get down to it properly I was so heated up I'd have had her in front of him.

He waited until I had my hand up her jumper before he made his move. I was lost in her, kissing and cuddling, not watching him at all, when he called out for my attention. I turned to find him sitting cross-legged on the far side of the fire we'd built, just as before, only with the most enormous pale pink erection sticking out of his trousers. I'm not badly endowed, but he was huge, and very hard, not that it would have been much less of a shock if he'd been like a cocktail stick.

I didn't know what to say, especially as I still had my hand up his sister's jumper, but she knew exactly what she was doing. Her hand went to my crotch, taking hold of my cock again, and as she began to rub me through my trousers she came straight out with it. I could fuck her if I'd let Guthrie take me into the tent and suck him off. He grinned and nodded as she spoke, flourishing his enormous cock at me.

Of course I refused, and I was going to leave, but she held onto me, stroking me and telling me it wasn't important and that it didn't make me gay just because I did another man a favour, and telling me all the things I could do to her if I gave in. She also pointed out that nobody else ever need know, and that was what swung it. I have never, ever felt so embarrassed in my life as when I said I'd do it, but they applauded me, saying how liberated I was and all sorts.

Maybe I was, maybe not, but I felt sick to the stomach at the thought of taking that huge pink cock in my mouth, never mind what was going to happen at the end. I didn't trust them either, and they didn't trust me. There followed the most bizarre conversation, with me trying to persuade them that I should go with Christa first and them telling me I'd only get what I wanted once I'd sucked Guthrie off. All the time Christa was massaging my cock and whispering dirty suggestions in my ear, and in the end I just couldn't hold back.

I'm not going to go into detail. Let's just say he took me into that tent and I let him put his big pink cock in my mouth. I had my eyes closed all the time, and I was hideously ashamed of myself, but he was telling me how to do it and I couldn't help but follow his instructions, not well though, and in the end he just fucked my mouth. And he made me swallow.

I have to say, it was worth it. Maybe it was knowing what I'd done. Maybe it was because she wanted to give me a good deal, but afterwards Christa was like an animal. I've never had a woman like it, before or since. She took me into the tent and turned a light on so that I could watch as she undressed, very slowly, baring her beautiful body a bit at a time and pausing occasionally to tease my cock.

She took me out when she was down to her bra and panties, and she stayed like that as she tongued me, licking ever so gently and using her fingers on my balls and shaft until I thought I was going to come then and there. By the time she knelt up again I was rock hard, and I didn't dare touch myself for fear of coming while she stripped me. Then I watched her take her bra off, revealing a pair of breasts the size and shape of small melons. She put them in my face, feeding me her nipples and stroking my hair, all the while straddled over me so that the soft moist gusset of her panties was rubbing on my cock.

That was too much for me. I came all over my belly, and to my amazement she not only didn't mind but licked up what I'd done, all the while with her eyes locked to mine as her tongue flicked in and out to lap up my mess. That wasn't the end either. She made a show of taking off her panties, very slowly and turning around twice to make sure I got a good view of everything, and I do mean everything.

She asked if I'd make her come and I could hardly refuse, so ended up licking her while she squatted over my face and played with her breasts. By the time she'd got there I was getting stiff again, so she took me back in her mouth, and this time I managed to hold off long enough to get inside her. That was when she went crazy, demanding that I fuck her harder and making me take her in one position after another until I finally came a second time while taking her from behind.

There was a third time, late that night in the snug warmth of their tent, when she mounted me and brought me back to erection between her breasts and in her mouth. Guthrie was awake and I knew he was listening, but I no longer cared. She had me completely. A little later, with her mounted on me and wriggling herself on my erection I felt something hot and firm press to my face. It was Guthrie's cock, and I'm afraid to say I didn't put up much resistance about letting him into my mouth.

– Danny, Liverpool, UK

Female Bonding

This is a confession from my teenage years and features another girl who had a major influence on my life. I met Ursula while I was working in a Kensington department store back in the late 1980s. She was three months and a hundred light years older than me. We were both on holiday jobs during the long vacation from university, stuck together in the electrical goods section. We were told that 'You need to have brains to sell this stuff', but knowing how to turn a piece of equipment on and off was all it boiled down to. Still, we were left alone and could watch what we wanted on TV or listen to vinyl records and CDs on the expensive stereos. And talk. Oh, how we talked.

She had done everything I had dreamed of. Holidayed on her own in the Far East. Smoked dope. Got drunk in pubs at fifteen. Slept with everyone – boys, girls, older men, sort-of-famous musicians. She even claimed to have been at an orgy and done it with several people at once. Me, I had struggled through what Ursula called 'the inevitable let-down first fuck' (she spoke like that all the time, even in the shop) and then I'd slept with a couple of 'nice boys' before my first 'Oh my God' orgasm. Ursula always wanted details. Was he big? Did I scream? How many positions? While I tried to summon nerve enough to reply, she would launch into explicit memoirs of her own.

Ursula. Always smiling. Always loud. Always cheeky. Constantly raising the stakes of what she would make me do. She introduced me to *serious* clubbing. It was still the 80s and we would go out dressed in coloured bras, straps on show, and revealing inches of teasing cleavage. Our skirts were so short that even my daughters would be shocked if they knew. I had great legs and Ursula always paid me compliments. She seemed to enjoy dressing me up, showing off little innocent me.

And shocking people. How often had we flashed our bright knickers at staid passers-by, before running off giggling down some alleyway, leaning on each other for support while we got our breath back? Once, in the middle of a club, she deterred an over-attentive boy by grabbing me, kissing me deep and wriggling her tongue around inside my mouth. That may not seem so daring now in these days of lipstick lesbians, but we felt truly cutting edge that night. Outside I remember complaining that she tasted of lager but by then our night of notoriety was sealed.

The next day at work, I wasn't sure if I was buzzing with excitement or hung over. Ursula, as ever, was irrepressible. Turning up Human League as loud as we dared without censure, she grabbed my arms and started dancing me round the showroom.

'*Don't you want me baby . . .*' she sang until the track stopped. 'Well, don't you?'

'What?'

'Don't you want me?'

'But –'

'But nothing. Never fancied a woman? Never wanted to do it with a woman?'

'I haven't really thought . . . '

'Aw, go on, Yasmina. Doesn't Annie Lennox get you wet down there?' She seemed to be getting rather loud now.

'But she looks a bit like a man,' I stated unsurely.

'So what? Come on, imagine that tongue between your legs. Imagine it lapping away. Bet you'd come in no time.' I was almost trying to back away from her now. There were customers on the floor and I didn't really want this discussion to be overheard. And I'm sure Ursula knew this. At the time I took this as part of Ursula winding me up. Shocking me. Then she waggled her tongue at me over the back of a customer I was serving.

When the holiday job ended, we each had to return to our respective universities. Me to Sussex, Ursula to Newcastle. We promised each other we would write and phone. And we did at first. A lot. She came to see me in the New Year and we blitzed Brighton before falling asleep, totally out of it, wrapped round each other in my single bed. We both woke twisted and hung over and had to brave the bracing air of the stony beach to wake up properly. Then she had to return north.

We kept in touch for the rest of the year, but less frequently. Ursula was much better than me and she often scolded me for leaving too long between calls. She always planned to come down again but something always got in the way. Not until the long summer break, when we both managed to get the same jobs again, were we in frequent contact again. It was like we hadn't been apart. We were closer friends. Occasionally Ursula would touch my arm when directing me towards a customer, like we were sharing something. Or lean against me while we made awful coffee in the tiny kitchen.

We were going out again, chasing the bright lights. As Ursula lived nearer, we went back to hers to change into our clubbing clothes. Once, after I had showered and was sitting on her bed towelling my hair dry, she came up behind me and started to dry it for me. She worked far more slowly and thoroughly than I had, stroking the water from my hair. I had almost fallen into a trance under the regular stroking when she touched my bare shoulders. I started into consciousness and jerked upwards.

'I love it when you do that.'

'What?'

'Just jerk like that. Your boobs bounced. So gorgeous.' I looked up and Ursula was staring at the wardrobe mirror before us, intent on the image.

'Oh, you mean like this?' I deliberately jerked again, trying to make light of things. I saw my boobs lift pertly then settle. 'Some boy will love that.'

'Not just some boy . . .' Ursula's gaze seemed to almost burn through the mirror. Then she shook herself. 'Some man too. These are so gorgeous!' She reached round me and put her hands over my dressing gown, cupping my breasts. 'I could just eat them!' Then, she lifted her hands away and turned back to her preparations. Even though she no longer touched me, I could still feel the presence of her hands on me while I dressed. Something somehow made me turn away when I dropped my dressing gown and pulled on my bra and knickers. Not shyness. Nothing tangible. Almost a fear of what might have happened next perhaps.

As we had the previous year, we dazzled London with our presence. Still dressed unsuitably. As likely to have a red bra strap showing as white. Big hair. We were wicked sisters. We teased the boys and left them frustrated when we ran off hand in hand. We artlessly revealed our bodies each night but kept hands off. It was dizzying to play this way. We could not have been closer.

My back was always killing me from standing all day. I was constantly flexing it to try to get comfortable. Deep into our second summer as work buddies, I was bending awkwardly when Ursula offered to massage my back. She had done a course in Thailand, she said. While she prepared oils and lit candles, I stripped to my pants and lay face down on her bed. At first it was strange having her hands pushing down on me. But then the smell of the oils and the subtle pressure of the fluid stroking movements made me relax. Up and down my back her skilful hands went, easing away the pain, calming, soothing and sensual. Was it something in the oils that made her touch so warming?

Ursula leant over me, easing the last vestiges of tension from my back. She returned to my upper torso to rub my shoulder blades and gradually found the outer sides of my breasts. Her fingers began to knead them and I winced at the sheer guilty pleasure she was stirring up inside me. Her hands then slid down to my waist and across my bum. It seemed just convenient to slip my pants down so she could manipulate the oil into my buttocks and then on down the backs of my thighs. I swear I was floating inches above the bed I was so comfortable. Even now I can remember the precise moment when her thumbs slid along the sensitive inside of my thighs, just lightly rolling the muscle. For a moment I was aware of every millimetre of their progress. Then my whole body was bathed in warmth and pleasure.

It felt somehow exactly right when Ursula's fingers, almost feather light, brushed against my sex. It could have been accidental. But we both knew it wasn't. We could have moved on, shifted awkwardly and coughed. But we didn't. Afraid to move a muscle at first, for fear of losing the moment, I ever so slowly allowed my thighs to part. Ursula was responsive to my unspoken wishes. One of her hands eased forward, the leading finger just breaching my sensitised sex-lips before the tip grazed my clitoris. Even now, almost twenty years later, I can recall exactly the effect that Ursula was having on me.

I was cowardly, I admit it. As soon as she touched me, I knew I wanted to experiment, to feel this experience fully. But I lay there, resolutely face down, just occasionally moving my hips to allow her greater access to my sex. Ursula was not so reticent. She teased and she probed and she rubbed. Still pretending that it wasn't really happening, I pushed my face into the pillow as she began to make me moan and cry out.

Then there was no pretence. Her arm went round me and pulled my shoulders. I turned to her, my nipples hard with excitement as she bent down to mouth them. My breasts were smaller back in those days and as round and pert as half-lemons; she could take almost the whole of each one into her mouth. She sucked them hard, swirling her tongue over the plump flesh and even bit down on them gently. The sensation made my legs part and my sex open up to her. I could feel myself wet and excited, swollen and demanding her attention. This was far better than having a boy touching me.

We both began pulling her clothes off and soon the pair of us were naked on the bed. We explored and compared each other's breasts, nipples and open wet pussies, as if we had never seen such things before. Even with her boasted sexual experience, there was an appreciative glow in Ursula's eyes as she stroked my body with her hand.

We kissed, deep and full, our tongues dancing around each other. I groaned into her mouth when she used her hand on my sex. She seemed to know exactly what I wanted and touched all the right places. I felt my body leap in climax as she teased me with thumb and finger until I cried out. Then she held me tight to her, trapping the glorious feelings between us.

I allowed her to steer my hand where she wanted it. We both teased and stroked pleasure out of each other. Ursula's head was thrown back and her mouth wide open when the sound of her own cries filled my ears. I was so excited to have made her moan like this. For long moments we lay in each other's arms, almost as if we were pretending this had not happened.

Then I noticed a bead of sweat drip down her collar bone and across her right breast. She saw me watching and together we followed the path of the tiny drop as it rolled down the smoothness of her belly and into the blonde hair of her groin. Something gripped me. I could not resist. Leaning over her I traced the path of the tiny drop with my tongue, feeling her boobs heaving below me and the hardness of her nipple. I could not resist a swirl round her navel before proceeding downwards. I had never done anything like this before and was guided by instinct alone.

As I moved down towards her crotch, I could smell her. That spicy, slightly feral perfume that I had smelt on myself after vigorous sex. I felt that her scent was just for me. I had caused it. Tentatively, I dabbed at her sex with my tongue, just easing the tip across the puffy reddish lips. She groaned and I pushed harder, parting them and feeling the warmth inside. I flicked upwards and felt my tongue catch on the hard little bud of her clitoris. I teased it, darting my tongue snakelike, pushing and swirling it. Having come already, Ursula was sensitive to my every move. Her hips jerked and rolled and she grabbed at my head.

'Oh my God, Yasmina, that's sooo good.'

In a very short time, she was pressing me hard against her groin while she ground her clitoris against my tongue. I merely had to remain still to bring her howling to completion.

'My turn.' She pushed me back and dove straight into the junction of my thighs. I almost panicked, worried that she might do things that affected me for ever. Then I relaxed and allowed my body to accept whatever she had planned. Although I had made her cry out in ecstasy just moments before, I still felt shy and vulnerable. It was more intimate, more revealing to receive oral sex than to give it. I trembled at the sensation of her lips on my sex and ripples of pleasure ran through me, making me arch up my back. My scissoring legs almost crushed her head as I came with a suppressed groan.

Why did we stop seeing each other? I don't truly know. Was I too prudish to accept the exquisite pleasure? The remaining couple of weeks of our vacation had been hedonistic. We could hardly wait to leave work and rush to her bed, instantly naked, hands all over each other. I can sit here now, in a sensible jumper, and vividly recall Ursula's tongue on me, in me, our hot young bodies intertwined.

But we had to part for our respective colleges again. We called every day at first, describing all the filthy things we would do when we were next together. I even thought of Ursula as my lover, not just my friend. I wrote, pouring out visions of entwined and thoroughly sexualised women. She responded and even added her own drawings. And yet it was Ursula who first, almost casually, mentioned a man. Not just chatting with a man or having a drink, but full-on sex with a man. I still called and I listened to her stories of how he'd fucked her in a nightclub toilet or made her blow him off while he drove his car, and I pretended to be happy for her.

Then, I too started seeing a man. It just seemed to happen. Evolution. It wasn't better sex or more natural sex, just different sex. Later Ursula wrote and told me she was off to the States with a guy named Rob. And within a year they were married and still are, as far as I know. I didn't fly out for the wedding but I was pleased for her. By then I had met Bruce.

Yes, Ursula is my secret, part of my wild past. I enjoyed writing this confession and reliving those wonderful days and nights again.

– Yasmina, Enfield, UK

Male Chambermaid

It all started when they made cutbacks at the post office. I'd worked at the sorting office every holiday since I was in the sixth form. Now I'm in the middle of an MA and my bank balance is permanently in the red so I couldn't afford to be choosy.

When people find out I'm working as a chambermaid at one of London's most expensive hotels their first reaction is to laugh and their second is to make jokes about frilly aprons and black stockings. I stopped laughing ages ago.

Thankfully, I don't have to wear an apron, just black trousers and a white shirt. Plus I have to tie my long hair back in a ponytail. They asked me to cut it but even I have limits on what I'm prepared to do for money.

The work's deadly boring and never ending. You make a room sparkle and the next morning you've got to do it all over again. One day I was cleaning the suite where a well-known actress was staying. You get pretty blasé about celebrities after a while. They're so used to being looked after that they're usually terrible slobs and it's hard to be starry-eyed about someone who leaves a filthy ring around the bath and food stains all over the sheets. But once in a while, someone does still get to me.

Obviously I can't reveal her identity, but you would recognise her instantly if you saw her picture. She is a genuine A-list American actress, with sultry Latina looks, who specialises in playing feisty, ass-kicking heroines. She had just come over from LA where she'd attended the Oscars as a nominee and was using the hotel as a base while she promoted her latest film. I'd finished cleaning her bathroom when I went into her bedroom and spotted her scarlet Oscar gown hanging outside of the wardrobe. Made of sensuous red velvet, the dress was stunning with a corseted bodice and a long skirt cut to make it flow as she moved. I'd watched her on TV, gliding up the red carpet in that spectacular dress with a dinner-jacketed escort on her arm and wished it could have been me beside her.

Seeing the dress for real made my heart beat a little faster and there was a distinct tingle inside my underwear. I walked over and reached out a trembling hand to touch the dress and the tingle became a throb.

I could hardly breathe. I took the dress down, wrapping one arm around the waist and using the other to support the back, as if she were inside it and I were her dancing partner. I bent down and smothered my face in the bodice. I inhaled deeply. Was it my imagination, or could I smell a hint of her perfume and, beneath it, the ghost of something more womanly?

My cock was rigid now and, without thinking, I reached down and unzipped my trousers to give it more room. The relief was enormous and knowing that she was at some press junket miles away, I decided on the spur of the moment to take off my clothes and finish what the dress had started.

I ran over and made sure the door was locked, then I carried the gown over to the bed and quickly got out of my clothes. I climbed between her rumpled sheets, burying my nose in her pillow, seeking out her scent.

It was unbelievably exciting lying in the bed where she had slept and, if I closed my eyes, I could almost imagine that she was lying beside me, waiting to see what I would do next. I reached for the dress, pulling it up the bed until the skirt was spread out over my naked legs and the bodice lay against my chest. It felt soft and sensuous and my already stiff cock seemed to grow a little harder. I rocked my hips, rubbing my crotch against the warm velvet.

I couldn't tell you exactly when I decided to put the dress on, it was a gradual process rather than a conscious choice. It was so good against my skin and I felt so close to her that it just seemed to make sense. If I was inside the dress, in some perverse and deep way I'd be inside her. And, let's face it, for a penniless student working as a chambermaid that was as close as I was ever likely to get to fucking a Hollywood star.

I scrambled off the bed and stood in front of the mirror. I slowly unzipped the dress and stepped into it. The satin lining was fantastic against my skin, silky and soft. I struggled to get it zipped all the way up and I felt the corseted bodice gripping me around the ribs like a lover's eager embrace.

I gazed at myself in the mirror. I actually didn't look half bad. I'd always been slender and didn't have much body hair, so in a bad light I might have been able to pass for a woman. I freed my hair and let it fall in soft waves around my face. The front of the dress was tented by my erection and I was pretty sure that I was leaving little wet stains on the lining.

I was beside myself; torn by a desire to lift the front of the gown and wank until I came in long splashes on the mirror and never wanting it to end. I spotted the shoes she had worn to the ceremony and I picked them up and turned them over. Size 8. They'd actually fit me. I put them on, fastening the delicate rhinestone-covered strap around my ankles, and then straightened up and looked at myself.

I was six inches taller and somehow more feminine. The high heels did something to my centre of gravity that gave me a more womanly stance with the hips thrust forward and the shoulders back. I attempted a few tottery steps and, after a little practice, was able to glide in the shoes. The dress seemed to flow as I moved and the lining gave a faint rustle.

My cock was rock hard, standing out beneath the dress, ruining the line. I looked around the room for something I could put on to strap it down and I spotted some discarded underwear in a corner. I went over and selected a pair of red lace panties and I put them on. It wasn't easy to arrange my erection inside them but I managed to push my cock to one side where they were held in place by the tight fabric of the panties.

I fluffed up my hair and smiled. 'I'm ready for my close-up, Mr De Mille,' I murmured, in my best siren voice. I stroked the tip of my cock through the dress.

'Well, don't you look gorgeous?' someone said.

I turned to see a figure standing in the open bedroom doorway. There she was, the sex goddess herself, looking twice as perfect in the flesh than she ever had on-screen with a look of amusement and surprise on her beautiful face. I was ashamed, excited, aroused and utterly humiliated. I could only gaze at her.

She closed the door behind her and began to walk over to me then stopped and let out a gasp of shock. 'Oh my God! I've just realised. You're a boy.' She laughed. 'Though I must say you look pretty damn good in that gown. I'm far too busty for it. Every time I moved I risked spilling my boobs over the top.'

In spite of my shame I felt an irrational sense of pride at her compliment and the image of her overflowing boobs made my cock tingle. 'Er . . . I suppose you're wondering why I'm wearing your clothes . . .' I didn't know how to go on.

'Well, it did cross my mind.' She came up behind me and looked at us both in the mirror. She began to primp my hair and a bolt of cold excitement shot down my spine. 'You've got gorgeous hair, haven't you? I'm not surprised you keep it long.'

I didn't know what to say so I said nothing. I just looked at us both in the mirror as she handled my hair. Shivery tingles crept up my nape and over my scalp. When she seemed satisfied with her hairdressing I saw her looking down at my body and when she saw the bulge at my crotch I heard her take a sharp intake of breath. Then she began to smile.

She stepped aside and laid a hand on my cheek. Gently she turned my face towards her and kissed me. Her scent engulfed me, every bit as intoxicating as the hint of it I had smelled on her bed but twice as arousing. My cock grew half an inch and, when she laid her hand over it a moment later, it did it again.

She broke the kiss and took my hand, pulling me towards the bed.

'Aren't you just a little bit curious about why I'm wearing your clothes?' I allowed her to lead me and didn't protest when her firm hands pushed me down on the bed.

She shrugged. 'It was there . . . you were curious . . . these things happen. So you're a transvestite? Who cares? All I can see is a beautiful man who looks gorgeous in my dress and that I want to fuck him.' She began pulling up the hem of the dress, uncovering my legs.

'You want to fuck me? An Oscar-nominated actress wants to fuck a male chambermaid in a dress?' The dress was up around my thighs by now and I helped her to push it back out of the way, revealing my erection stretching the fabric of her lace panties.

'Stranger things have happened.' She stroked my cock through the lace and I gasped. 'Slide over into the middle of the bed,' she said, 'while I undress.'

I didn't need telling twice. I moved over and watched as she threw off her clothes. In seconds she was naked and she climbed on to the mattress and straddled me. She freed my cock from its lace prison and pushed back the foreskin. She ran her finger across the glistening tip then raised herself up on her knees and positioned it.

In seconds I was inside her. I watched her eyes narrow as she lowered herself on to me. She was tight and hot and slippery and by the time it was all the way in she was smiling.

'Can you feel how wet I am? I don't know why but the sight of you in my drcss has got me all worked up. Stick your thumb on my clit and fuck me.' I slipped my hand between us and fingered her. I saw her body quiver as I touched her and my cock twitched inside her.

She began to move, slowly raising and lowering herself on my cock. I brought my hips up to meet her on every thrust, matching her rhythm. Her magnificent tits bounced as she rode me. I brought up my free hand and teased her nipples and was rewarded with a long moan of pleasure.

Sweat was beginning to form beneath the bodice of the dress which gripped my ribs so hard it was difficult to breathe but I couldn't have cared less. I dug my heels into the mattress and rocked my hips. I moved my thumb, working her clit, as my other hand stroked her boobs.

Her face had grown pink and sweat glowed on her upper lip. A red rash of arousal speckled her throat and chest. 'I'm going to come. Don't stop.'

I felt her clit growing tense and her cunt muscles seemed to turn solid, gripping my cock like an iron vice. She bent her head back and her long hair flowed down her back like a waterfall. She was coming. Her breathing was rapid and noisy. She moaned and sobbed.

I gripped her hips and began to pump hard. She fell forward onto her hands and started to kiss me. I gave one final, deep thrust and I came. I could feel her slippery cunt grinding against me as she rode my cock. Her nipples grazed my chest. Her mouth devoured me.

I pumped out hot spunk inside her. The dress gripped my body in its rigid embrace. And all the time she kissed me, covering my face and mouth with hot wet hungry kisses as I came.

When it was finished she didn't move. She lay on top of me for what seemed like ages, stroking me and kissing me until my cock softened and slipped out and she gave a little disappointed sigh.

'Next time, maybe you could put on some stockings and a bra.' She rolled off me.

'Next time? Aren't you going to report me to the housekeeper?'

She laughed. 'I wasn't planning to.' She bent and kissed my cock. 'After all, it's not as though I have any complaints.'

– Graham, Isle of Man, UK

Dirty Girl

I like to sunbathe. I like to sunbathe naked in my garden. I like to sunbathe naked in my garden to tease my neighbour. Last weekend I sunbathed as usual.

I know he watches me from his kitchen window because I always watch *him* through my big dark sunglasses. So I set out my sun lounger, facing the house, wearing just my sage-green bikini, and lay down with my book. Sometimes I take a dirty book and spread my legs and play with myself. Other times I just touch my clit as I watch him watching me.

I wonder how often Eddie strokes his cock while watching me? He usually watches for quite a while – unless his wife is about, of course. The pixie-like redhead is cute, but the few times I've met her, she's seemed like a bit of a prude.

I wonder if he knows I 'perform' for him? Knowing he is there watching me makes me feel so exposed, and I love it. Sometimes I even fantasised about him knocking on my door.

I held out hope for that weekend. Having signed my garden up for the town open gardens, people were free to wander in and out of it for the whole of Saturday and Sunday. Maybe he would pop over for a quick peek too. If he asked nicely, I certainly wouldn't mind giving him an eyeful. I could just imagine it – showing him around the small wooded area at the bottom of my garden; him leaning me against a tree and just looking at me. Exposing my wet pussy to the cool air and examining it. Maybe he would fuck me in the potting shed, bent over the workbench. I'd be so wet my juices would drip down the inside of my thighs.

Thursday was sunny, so naturally I sunbathed. I spread my legs on the sun lounger, knowing full well I had a damp patch in the crotch of my bikini bottoms where I was already wet, just from thinking about what he might do to me.

I could see him watching from the house. His bright blond hair looked striking against the dark interior of his kitchen. He was tall and had a commanding presence that I could feel just by looking at him. I untied my top from behind my neck and pulled it up and off, almost dislodging my all-important sunglasses. My skin shimmered from the baby oil I had applied earlier. Could he see how hard my nipples were? One of my hands tweaked my nubs, and the other pushed my bikini bottoms aside. My dark strip of trimmed hair stood out against my golden skin, and my moist pussy glistened in the sun. I wondered if he could see from his house just how wet I was. My skin was warm under the gaze of the sun – or was it Eddie's gaze?

I put on a darn good show. I licked my fingers and played with my nipples, dipped my fingers inside my wet hole and then licked them slowly. It was an exaggerated little performance to say the least, but I enjoyed every second of it. I silently willed him to climb over the fence and take me hard on the grass, to push me down on to my hands and knees and fuck me mercilessly. Or even better, for him to watch me fuck someone else, his hand stroking his stiff cock as he took in the scene. Perhaps he would he push me down across his lap and spank my bare backside until my eyes stung with tears? Maybe he would use the garden trowel as a paddle? He seemed like the kind of man who didn't mind getting a little dirty.

I jumped when my mobile vibrated against my leg. I answered it, flicking a glance up towards Eddie who still stood at the window, now with a phone to his ear.

'Hello?' I said cautiously.

'You have gorgeous tits.'

I grinned. *He wants to play*. 'You like thcm, eh?'

'Squeeze them,' he said huskily.

I pinched the nipples, circled them softly. Then, holding the phone against my shoulder, I pushed my tits together, and gave them a good squeeze. I heard his breath hitch.

'Are you hard for me?' I asked, watching him.

'I'm always hard for you.'

'I'm so wet.' My voice was a whisper and I imagined him stroking his thick cock.

'Rub yourself for me. Slide a couple of fingers into your tight little hole.'

I grunted lightly as my fingers plunged into my pussy, my thumb brushing my clit with every stroke. 'Stroke your cock. Imagine my mouth on you as I suck and lick.' I licked my lips, as I spoke. My fingers moved furiously, my orgasm creeping up on me.

'Are you almost there, babe?'

'Almost. Squeeze your cock. Come for me. I'm so close,' I urged. I heard his grunts and groans and my body arched against the sun bed as I came. I moaned loudly as the walls of my sex clenched around my fingers.

The phone went dead.

I looked up at Eddie through the window, but he was still on the phone. I frowned, confused. I checked the phone, but the call had finished. My eyes shot back up, but he was still talking. Then a movement in another window caught my attention. My other neighbour, a forty-something businessman called Andy, was standing at his upstairs window, staring at me.

Oh fuck. How could that have happened? Mistaking Andy for Eddie? Fuck.

* * *

Sunday morning dragged on and by three I was more than a little fed up and frustrated. Thankfully, I hadn't seen hide nor hair of Andy. God knows how many people asked me about trees and flowers in the garden. It was tough work playing hostess! The day wasn't through, though. Unfortunately, Eddie hadn't shown up the whole weekend, which disappointed me. I hadn't seen him at the window either – although, to be fair, with so many people around I hadn't had much chance to sunbathe.

I was explaining to Mrs Morris from down the street just how often the garden needed weeding, when I spotted Eddie in his customary position at the kitchen window. He must have seen me look over at him, because seconds later he disappeared from view.

'Well, now there's no chance of him coming over,' I mumbled to myself, confusing poor Mrs Morris.

I left Mrs Morris to admire my hanging baskets up by the house and made my way down the garden to pick up the jumper I had left in the wooded area earlier that day. Secluded by the leafy trees and bushy hedges, I snuck a peek at Eddie's house and saw that he was still at the window. He was peering down the garden to see where I had gone. On the other side of my house, Andy was nowhere to be seen.

A grin stretched across my face and I walked into a small clearing where Eddie could easily see me. The garden was empty. I stroked my breasts through my thin top and squeezed my arse through my blue jeans.

I'm a dirty girl. I'm a dirty girl who likes getting what she wants. I'm a dirty girl and I wanted Eddie. When I looked up again, he had disappeared. *Fuck.* I sighed in defeat and struggled with my jumper. I decided to go back into the house and make a start on dinner, but then I heard the sound of metal squeaking. It was my garden gate opening.

'Sorry, the garden isn't open any more,' I shouted.

'Good.'

A gasp escaped my lips when I turned to find Eddie staring at me with a predatory look in his eyes. Strong features and a healthy smattering of stubble graced his face and blond spiky hair gave him a roguish air. I remember licking my lips at the sight of the large bulge straining the front of his trousers.

'Eddie!'

'You're a dirty girl.' He stepped towards me. 'You're a dirty little exhibitionist, aren't you?' Another step. 'You know I watch you.'

I nodded, not quite believing he was actually there in my garden after all those months.

The leaves crackled loudly under his feet as he stepped even closer. 'I'm fed up of watching.'

My breath caught in my throat. Trembling with excitement, I crooked my finger and motioned for him to follow me as I shuffled backwards. I reached up, snapped a small branch off a beech tree, and handed it to him. His look was one of puzzlement, until I turned around, pushed my jeans down around my knees, and bent over against the beech.

'Dirty bitch. Dirty little fucking whore,' he mumbled.

I shuddered. Being called those names turned me on. Made me feel dirty. I could feel my thong sliding against my wet pussy lips. I was drenched. Suddenly I felt the branch strike the soft sensitive flesh of my bottom.

'I knew you were up to no good, sunbathing and teasing me.'

I bit my lip in an effort not to cry out at the stinging that slowly crept its way down my thighs. But I let out a yelp as the tip of the branch caught my swollen sex lips.

'Quiet,' he snapped. 'You're a bad girl for teasing me, you know that?'

I was silent.

Crack.

'Yes! Yes!' I whimpered. 'I'm a bad, bad girl.'

'And are you going to tease me like that again?'

'No, I promise!'

Crack.

'Yes! Yes!'

A smile settled on his lips, and he stopped and ordered me to take off my shirt. His eyes widened in delight when he saw my peephole bra. The looks you get from men walking down the street with one of those on – priceless. Nope, not peanuts in the bra, guys – those were my own dusky-pink rock-hard nipples.

'I love seeing you finger your holes,' he said, tugging his gaze away from my tits. 'But you know what I like best?'

I shook my head.

'When you lick your fingers clean.' He wriggled two long fingers inside me and then held them up against my lips, as if offering me food. I sucked them slowly, while his eyes bored into mine. My tongue swirled around his fingers, just as it would move against a cock. I do love sucking a handsome cock and couldn't wait to get my lips around his.

He unzipped his trousers and his stiff flesh sprung from its confines, standing proudly to attention.

My expectations were exceeded. His cock was just beautiful – straight, thick and the perfect length. The bulging purple head glistened like a jewel. I trailed my fingers along its length. 'Fuck my arse,' I said, batting my eyelashes and smiling girlishly.

'Get on your hands and knees, then.'

I did as I was told, tingling with anticipation at being filled with the cock of a man I had been teasing for months. He was bound to be one horny fucker after the way I'd provoked him. My guess was right. He pushed my thong to the side, parted my cheeks, spat on my tightest hole, and pushed a finger in.

'Please, put it inside me,' I whimpered as he stretched my opening with the head of his meaty prick.

'That's it, you dirty bitch!' he said and bit his lip as my tightness gripped his glans. He wrapped his arm around my waist, pulled me back against him and drove home his entire length with a long, slow and deliciously painful thrust. Then we fucked like animals, hard and loud. His balls slapped against me with each ecstatic thrust and I would have climaxed had a voice not interrupted us.

'Why was I not invited?'

'Andy!' I certainly wasn't expecting *him* to turn up.

He stood there in a blue shirt and tie, his square jaw line clean-shaven and his grey suit trousers making him look way too overdressed for the situation. Suddenly, the thought of being penetrated by two men excited me.

'Well, don't just stand there and watch.' I winked. He didn't need any more encouragement and I admired his body as he hurriedly stripped off his clothes.

He was certainly in shape, with a taut stomach and muscled thighs. His cock stood straight out from a nest of dark curls, his balls dangling tantalisingly. What he did next surprised me. He lay himself down on the ground on his back and gestured for me to come over.

'Sit on my face,' he grunted.

Turned on by the idea, I slid off Eddie's still-hard cock and stepped over to Andy. Placing a foot at each broad shoulder and facing his twitching erection, I squatted down over his face. He was obviously desperate for me and greedily spread my pussy lips with his fingers and ran the flat his tongue all over my cunt. It had been way too long since anyone had given me such a treat and I moaned with pleasure. Eddie picked up the tie that Andy had discarded, which was still knotted, and slipped it around my neck. He pulled it tight and kept hold of the longest end like a leash.

Suddenly we heard voices – latecomers to the open garden. Eddie quickly loosened the tie, only to move it up to my mouth and pull it tight again, making it serve as a gag. He passed the leash-end to Andy, who gripped it firmly, while continuing to service my oozing pussy with his mouth and free hand.

Eddie disappeared for a few seconds and I couldn't turn my head to see where he had gone. But moments later he reappeared with the mini garden fork I had left down the end of the garden. A feeling of excitement filled me as I realised what he was going to do with it. The handle was short and hard and made from smooth plastic. A perfect synthetic cock. Eddie stroked it teasingly and winked at me. I leant forward, so that I was resting on my hands and my bottom was raised towards him. I wanted to feel that tool buried inside me.

'What would everyone think, babe? What would people think if they saw you on your hands and knees in the dirt, with a trowel handle up your tight, juicy little snatch?'

His words made me shudder – and not from disgust.

Andy's fingers slid from my pussy, leaving me with a brief empty feeling, before something cold and hard replaced them. I could feel myself clenching around the handle as he slid it in and out. I moaned through the gag, but the sounds were muffled. Eddie came and stood in front of me, stroking his solid cock. The temptation was just too much and I pulled the gag from my mouth.

'I want to suck your cock, Eddie. I've waited so long,' I begged, thrusting my hips back. The trowel handle was replaced by Andy's fingers. They curled up inside me, thrumming against that delicious spot that makes me squirm.

Eddie waved his hard cock in front of my face, a cheeky smile on his lips. 'Come on then,' he said, 'if you want it, reach for it.'

I stretched forward and ran my tongue slowly up the veins on the underside of his masterful cock. Then I swirled it around the bulging head, savouring his saltiness. Would he like to splash his come all over my tits? I wondered. He moaned as I squeezed his balls tightly in my hand.

'Suck harder,' he gasped.

'Say please,' I teased. I felt his hand grip my hair forcefully, and his whole length slid to the back of my throat. At that moment, Andy's tongue lathered my sensitive nub, and I almost choked on Eddie's cock as I gasped with joy. My nails scraped over Eddie's stomach and he bucked when I pinched his nipple lightly.

By this point, I can honestly say that I didn't realise what was happening. Suddenly, Andy wasn't between my legs any more and Eddie slid from my mouth. I found myself straddling Andy's cock, which was impatiently probing my pussy.

'I've waited so long to fuck you,' said Andy. He pulled my head down, and our lips met in a fight for dominance. Our tongues writhed together, plunging into the other's mouth until we were both gasping for air. Meanwhile Eddie pressed his cock against my tight little puckered opening, and squeezed inside. My hands scrambled for purchase on the ground, as I pushed back against him, wanting him in up to the hilt. Andy slowly guided my hips as I slid down on to him.

I panted, trying to catch my breath; the sensation of having both holes filled was overwhelming. I let out a loud guttural moan as both men started to move inside me, each with his own unique force and rhythm. I didn't know what to do with myself. My mouth was wide open, my chest heaved and sweat trickled between my shoulder blades. My hands scrambled for purchase on something – anything. My stuffed pussy and ass felt like they couldn't be stretched a millimetre more without splitting. It was the most exquisite sensation I have ever experienced. Andy and Eddie must have been enjoying themselves too, judging from the wild noises they were making.

Strangely, it was not until I felt a droplet of sweat fall

from Eddie on to my shoulder that the full strangeness of the situation occurred to me. We were three neighbours who, through misread signals, had ended up in a hot sweaty threesome in the bushes at the end of my garden. *Thank fuck for mishaps!* I thought. My hands and knees were sore and covered in dirt and I felt thoroughly fucked.

I snaked my hand down between our bodies and, with what little conscious thought I could muster, I rubbed my pulsing clit. I was so wet, it felt like we'd used up a whole tube of lube, but it was all my juices.

Eddie left bite marks along my shoulder and down my back and Andy played with my bobbing tits. All the while they moved their cocks inside me, front and rear, and I could feel myself starting to come. I scratched my nails along Andy's sides and dipped my head to nibble on his nipples, making him arch, and thrust harder and faster.

Now, I'm not quiet in bed by any means, but that day, in the bushes of my own back garden, I actually screamed. When the delicious pressure that those two men built inside me reached its peak, I howled out my orgasm, mindless of the fact that I could be heard by the people milling about my garden, and probably streets away. My body shuddered. My pussy spasmed and I clenched around each of the diligently thrusting cocks, and I gave in to a deafening, mind-blowing orgasm.

I watched Andy's eyes roll back in his head. He let himself go and thrust a few more times into me, roaring my name as he filled my cunt with his hot cream. Eddie pulled out moments later and, with a yell, shot hot come down the back of my thighs. I didn't move. Still on my hand and knees, Andy's tie dangling from my neck, I panted, trying to catch my breath.

Then I heard the ground crunch underfoot. With dreadful apprehension I turned my head towards the bushes. My operatic orgasm certainly had grabbed the attention of the visitors to my garden.

Half a dozen of them stood just beyond the bushes, watching us through a gap in the leaves, their mouths wide open. There was a look of utter horror on the face of one woman – a petite blonde with pixie features.

– Anthea, Darlington, UK

TV Bitch

I'll be honest and admit I wanted Cheryl to catch me wearing her clothes. It was a Saturday afternoon, she'd gone out shopping with her best friend, Sharon, and I was left alone at home. As soon as her car had disappeared from the driveway I was in the bedroom and rummaging through Cheryl's knicker-drawer. I kicked off my jeans and T-shirt as fast as I could and tried to decide between matching sets of bra and pants in black or blue. I was already hard, just with the thought of wearing her underwear, and my modest erection flopped around as I vacillated over which set to wear.

I think most men find women's clothes arousing. I just don't think there are many who ever dare admit it. Stockings feel gorgeous when they're sliding over your freshly shaved legs. Bras are so tight and restrictive you can't take a single breath without remembering you're wearing women's underwear. Silk panties feel gorgeous as they caress your balls and whisper against your stiff length. I keep my cock and balls shaved, specifically so I can enjoy the sensation of Cheryl's silk panties sliding against my smooth flesh.

I find Cheryl's clothes infinitely exciting.

And that Saturday I intended to let her know just how exciting I thought they were. I picked the black set. I put on a pair of heels I'd bought for myself because Cheryl's shoes are the only items in her wardrobe that I can't squeeze into. And then I went to admire myself in the bedroom mirror.

And I don't mind admitting that I looked pretty good.

The combination of heels and black stockings made my legs look feminine, slender and yet shapely. The silk panties bulged with my erection, but from behind the way they clung to my buttocks looked wonderful. The bra was a little loose with me not having anything to fill the cups, but the lacy black fabric did look beautiful against the pale smoothness of my skin.

I was already hard, and tempted to relieve myself. But I thought that pleasure would best be saved to share with Cheryl. I figured she would get a small shock when she caught me dressed in her underwear, but I thought we could overcome that shock together with a mutually satisfying romp.

However, when Cheryl came home, I was the one who got the biggest shock. Cheryl didn't come home alone.

I watched the front door open, saw my wife's familiar figure step into the doorway. And then she rushed up the stairs without noticing me. I was left alone in the hall with Cheryl's best friend, Sharon.

I had no idea what to do. I didn't want to run away and hide because that would be tantamount to admitting I was in the wrong. But I didn't want to make Sharon uncomfortable either – that had never been part of my plan.

Sharon stood and stared at me. Her eyes were wide, her mouth hung open, and she didn't move for a full three minutes – until the upstairs toilet had flushed and Cheryl had come down the stairs and seen me.

'What the hell are you doing?' Cheryl demanded.

'I'm wearing your clothes,' I explained. 'I wanted to show you that I enjoy wearing your clothes and I wanted you to see I'm not ashamed.' Struggling to make my explanation satisfactory I added, 'I wanted you to see how much this excites me.'

She was quiet for a moment and then said, 'Did you also want Sharon to see all this?'

I admitted that hadn't been part of the plan and said we could continue the conversation once Sharon had left but Cheryl wore her wickedest grin and I could see she was in a mood to tease me. 'What do you think, Sharon?' she asked. 'Do you think he looks good wearing my clothes? Or do you think he looks like a pathetic TV who needs humiliating?'

I wanted to protest but Sharon was clearly up for playing Cheryl's game and stepped closer. It was shocking to feel her gaze on my scantily clad body. She was smiling and invading my personal space as she stepped very close and started to touch the bra and panties I wore.

'I don't understand why he's wearing a bra,' she complained. Her fingers squeezed at my chest through the lacy fabric. 'He's not got any boobs to go into the bra. That doesn't make sense.'

Cheryl followed Sharon's lead and stepped closer. 'You're right,' she declared, fondling the other empty cup of my bra. Cheryl's caress was crueller than Sharon's. I could feel her nails biting at my flesh as she squeezed through the fabric. I wanted to flinch from the punishment but I didn't dare show such a cowardly response. I thought about telling them to stop but I could see they were enjoying their game and I didn't want to suffer the embarrassing laughter that I knew would come if I pushed past them and fled to the sanctuary of the bedroom.

'Do you think he should be wearing knickers?' Cheryl asked nastily. 'It's not like he's got anything to put in those.'

Sharon chuckled at that line, and then her fingers snaked down to my black silk panties. Her fingers moved softly over the shape of my erection and she gripped it tightly for a moment. I glanced at her and, when our eyes met, I was almost on the verge of coming.

'I wouldn't say he's not got anything there,' she told Cheryl. 'Although it doesn't feel like much of a cock to me.'

The crushing comment pushed me close to orgasm.

'Should we play with him?' Cheryl asked Sharon.

Sharon's fingers remained around my cock. 'That might be fun,' she admitted. Cheryl didn't bother asking what I wanted. She led us upstairs to the bedroom and proceeded to undress. Glancing at Sharon she said, 'Strip down to your bra and pants. Let's show this pathetic TV what real women look like in their underwear.'

I watched in amazement as my wife and her best friend removed their clothes. Because I was only wearing skimpy silk knickers it was impossible to hide my excitement. But neither Cheryl nor Sharon were looking at me. And, as Sharon had already pointed out, my excitement wasn't particularly noticeable.

'That's a nice set,' Cheryl said, stroking Sharon's lacy red bra and then touching the front panel of her matching thong. 'The colour suits you.'

I noticed that her fingers lingered against Sharon.

My erection throbbed with the renewed urge to come.

Sharon didn't seem to mind Cheryl's caress. She was grinning at Cheryl and holding her waist. My erection was so hard it hurt. When Sharon cupped Cheryl's left breast, eased it out of the bra, and then lowered her mouth to Cheryl's nipple, I moaned.

Cheryl's breathing deepened. She waited until Sharon had finished suckling against her and then said, 'That felt good.' Slowly, she returned the favour to Sharon. Watching my wife suck another woman's breast, seeing the pair of them stand before me in their underwear while I was dressed as a woman, was almost more excitement than I could bear. My erection leaked a steady stream of pre-come that formed a glossy wet circle on the front panel of my panties.

Cheryl lifted her head and glared at me. 'You can't

play this game,' she said meanly. 'You don't have breasts so we can't do this for you.'

She then got to her knees and began to slide the lacy red thong from Sharon's hips. I watched in awe as Cheryl exposed the bare flesh of Sharon's pussy. I had never thought that Sharon would be the sort of woman who shaved her bush. That idea had never crossed my mind. And when I saw the hairless split of her cleft I was mesmerised. Even more exciting was watching my wife's mouth slip closer to Sharon's pussy. Her tongue was pushed out and I watched as Cheryl licked against the folds of Sharon's labia. She spent a good five minutes tonguing her, and Sharon simply remained standing, her smile growing broader and her gasps growing louder and more urgent.

Eventually Cheryl moved away, wiped her mouth with the back of her hand and went to lie down on the bed. Sharon followed when Cheryl said, 'It's your turn to do me. I want you to lick me until I come.' She glared at me while Sharon was between her legs and said, 'You can't play this game either because you haven't got a pussy for us to lick.'

The frustration and humiliation were enormous. I was in desperate need for release and Cheryl was making it clear that I wasn't allowed to participate in any of the lewd games with her and her best friend. I wanted to drive my fists against my groin but I knew that the slightest pressure on my erection would cause me to spurt in a triumphant climax. And I could see Cheryl would not be happy if I climaxed without her permission.

Sharon licked Cheryl's pussy until my wife came.

I stood and watched, loving the scene and hating the frustration.

Cheryl recovered from her climax with her grin seeming even crueller. She winked at Sharon and then reached into the bedside drawer where she keeps her sex toys. Taking out three vibrators from her collection she gave us one each and told me I could join them on the bed.

'We'll have to use vibrators because there's no man available to us right now,' Cheryl said loudly. She sneered at me and said, 'I know you're not a man because you're dressed in stockings, bra and panties. However, I'll let you play this game with me and Sharon because I figure you're girl enough to take a cock like thc rest of us.'

My erection was an agony as it pushed against the silk panties. I watched as Cheryl took her vibrator and pushed it against the sopping centre of her pussy. Sharon had clearly licked her to a frenzy because the vibrator started sliding inside as soon as she touched it to her labia. Equally exciting was the sight of Sharon pushing a vibrator between the flushed pink lips of her hole. I gaped and squirmed and watched as my wife and her best friend impaled themselves on thick dildos.

'Come on,' Cheryl growled. She had half her vibrator inside and was sliding it slowly back and forth. The length was glossy with her pussy juice. 'We want to see you taking your vibrator, don't we, Sharon?'

Sharon looked as though she was about to come. She managed to say she wanted to see exactly that, and then I realised Cheryl was pulling my silk panties off so I could use the dildo on myself.

'Oh! Look!' Sharon shouted. 'He must be a man. He's got a cock.'

I blushed when Cheryl snorted in my direction and said, 'He's not a man. That cock is barely larger than my clitty.' And then she and Sharon were both laughing at me as I tried to guide the vibrator toward my rectum.

It was a humiliating experience. Cheryl made me take all the length of the vibrator and warned me I wasn't permitted to climax until she said so. She made me watch Sharon frig herself to orgasm, and then told me to use my tongue to lick Sharon's pussy clean. Cheryl then pushed me down on the bed and got me to tongue her labia while she pushed her own vibrator in and out and brought herself to a shuddering, wet climax. I was pinned beneath her, my own vibrator thrust inside my rectum, and its constant buzzing made my excitement unbearable.

Sharon was the one who took pity on me. She had showered after her orgasm and came back to the bedroom to see me sprawled on the bed, writhing on the brink of climax. Cheryl was retrieving her clothes and ignoring me.

'We have to let him come,' Sharon insisted.

Cheryl looked like she was going to argue, and then seemed to think better of it. She reached over to me and placed her hand around my balls. Squeezing with a painful tightness, she pulled on my sac and said, 'Do you like dressing up as a woman? Did you enjoy being our bitch?'

I struggled to spit the words out, but I managed to say I had loved every second.

She asked if I wanted to do it again and I said that would be a dream come true. Cheryl squeezed harder on my balls and said I would be allowed to dress as a woman in the future, but only when she and Sharon wanted a TV bitch to abuse. I came when Sharon said she'd be happy to call round frequently to help abuse Cheryl's TV bitch.

– Tony, Milton Keynes, UK

Designing Women

When the managing partner of the public accounting firm I work for decided to renovate the office, my job suddenly got both a whole lot busier and a whole lot more exciting. I'm the office manager, so I was put in charge of the project, coordinating the tradespeople and the staff requests regarding colours, furnishings, lighting, window coverings, etc., and deciding on about a thousand other small but significant details. Fortunately, I was provided with the services of a pair of interior design specialists, and that made all the difference – for everyone concerned.

Their names were Britta and Inez, and they were two of the leggiest ladies I've ever had the pleasure of getting personally acquainted with. Britta was tall and blonde, eyes blue as a Norwegian glacier, with a slim sensuous figure and a set of legs that seemed to flow on forever from beneath the short form-fitting skirts she favoured. And Inez was the mirror image of her colleague, only in a darker shade. Whereas Britta was pale, Inez was golden-brown, her hair black and shiny, eyes a sparkling brown, caramel legs every bit as long and lithe and lovely as Britta's.

The interior design company the women worked for was owned by one of the managing partner's clients, so I hadn't had the opportunity to choose it, but it was like someone had read my leg-addled mind and delivered me a limbsome present gift-wrapped in silk and tethered with pink-bowed garters. I first met the pair, and their pair, in the boardroom, at the beginning of the project. And when they strolled into that staid place of business I lit up like a Christmas tree, my quim going all warm and gooey in a most unprofessional manner.

Britta came first, dressed in a red satin blouse and tight black skirt, platinum hair loose about her shoulders, legs sheathed in sheer black stockings that accentuated every smooth muscle and delicate curve, feet poured into a pair of spike-heeled black pumps. She smiled as we shook hands, crimson lips shining wet and soft, hand warm and strong. 'I'm Britta Sorenson,' she said, setting an attaché case and a book of swatches down on the gleaming surface of the boardroom table. 'And this is my partner, Inez.'

I reluctantly peeled my eyes off the shiny lower limbs of the blonde princess to let them embrace Inez. This twenty-something girl was clothed in a midnight-blue jacket and skirt combination and a cobalt-blue blouse, her glossy dark hair pulled back in a ponytail, her sleek legs clad in a pair of dark-blue stockings, arched feet in a pair of dark-blue high heels. I could hear her legs swishing together as she advanced on me, drowning out her greeting – to my ears, at least.

I blinked my eyeballs almost back into place and we sat down at the conference table and got down to business. Or rather, they got down to business. Inez outlined their overall plan for the decidedly utilitarian audit, accounting and tax office, while Britta flashed colour and carpet and furniture samples, and I pushed my chair back from the head of the table to get a better view of the women's legs.

I'm not exactly sure of the precise date when I first fell in love with ladies' legs, but I know it dates back to the time when Jennifer Lopez was a 'fly girl' on the television show *In Living Color*, and my first exposure to the movie *Flashdance*. (And when the two came incandescently together in that J-Lo *Flashdance* take-off video, in support of her single 'I'm Glad', I creamed for weeks, my VCR popping sprockets and smoking in protest.) To me, there's just nothing more beautiful in this oftentimes ugly world than a pair of elegantly sculpted legs, with a pair of high-arched peds dangling from impossibly slender ankles.

All those thoughts, and ones much, much wickeder, were flashing through my mind as I half-listened to what Britta and Inez were telling me, as I flat-out stared at their spectacular legs. Britta would lean back and cross her limbs as Inez spoke, the rustling silk music to my hyper-sensitive ears. Then she'd uncross her legs in a blinding swirl of silk, as she leaned forward to make a point. Inez, on the other hand, kept her shimmering limbs crossed the entire time, hands in her lap. She perched on the edge of her chair like she was riding sidesaddle, her legs daintily folded and fully on display.

Needless to say, I bought whatever they were selling, and the two women went to work putting their vision into paint and particle board.

I only saw them sporadically over the next month, unfortunately, as they surveyed the work results of the tradespeople, supervised the placing of this and the hanging of that. They usually came individually, their luscious legs always out in the open and catching my eye, and fancy. Their visits always ended the same way for me – with a quick trip to the washroom to relieve the tension and relive the experience.

The men on the staff ogled the flamboyantly dressed design professionals almost as rapturously as I did. They found excuses to hang around the office when they should have been out with clients performing audits and providing accounting and tax advice. Until, that is, Mr Kleiner, the managing partner, finally put a stop to it. He wanted to make budget on his share of the partnership earnings for the year, after all, and that meant staff in the field, racking up chargeable hours. Plus, he wanted to get an uncontested eyeful himself.

By the end of the one-month period, with visions of delectable legs dancing constantly in my head, and with the project nearing completion, I knew I just had to do something or miss out on the opportunity of a lifetime. So I arranged an after-hours tour of the office with the two women. Supposedly, it was so I could inspect the reno's, note any problems that needed following up – a final 'walkthrough', if you will.

'Ready to start?' Inez asked me when she and her colleague arrived at the deserted office right on time, and in style, as usual.

The raven-haired beauty was not-so-casually dressed in a burnt-orange vest and skirt, a big black belt buckled around her slim waist, her legs stretch-wrapped in a pair of ultra-sexy black striped stockings, her feet strapped into a pair of patent-leather pumps. Blonde Britta was equally outrageously attired, in a sleeveless white blouse and pink bum-hugging skirt, a pair of dazzling snow-white stockings and pink stilettos.

'Al-ready,' I gulped, blinded by the erotic sight, and lust. I dampened one set of lips with my tongue, the other already being moist. 'Sh-shall we get started?'

Britta and Inez smiled at each other, then at me, the room and my life lighting up. Then we went on a tour of the transformed office, the women making notes, asking my opinion, answering my gargled questions. I lagged a few steps behind so I could fully capture the thrilling twin pairs of legs in my own personal vision of the newly renovated workspace.

And when we finally arrived at Mr Kleiner's office – the office with the big black leather couch and spacious expanse of high-polish desktop – I at last worked up the nerve to make my move. I dropped my pen on the carpet, in behind Inez, at her feet, and bent down to pick it up.

I'd had the taped razor blade in my sweaty hand for the last five minutes, my 'plan' being to surreptitiously slice an opening in the girl's sexy leg covering which would, hopefully, serve as my opening to getting even better acquainted with the two women's legs. The Marshall Plan it wasn't, and I so hated to vandalise such a gorgeous garment, but desperate girls call for desperate measures.

So, as Inez and Britta debated the aesthetic merits of Mr Kleiner's couch, I knelt down at Inez's five-inch heels, hands shaking, and got ready to try to cut myself in on some action – until I noticed the small tear in Inez's stocking, on the inward side of her ankle. Somehow, I had missed it before, but then again, I'd been observing things from the rear most of the time.

I stared at the tiny slit, at the gleaming bronze skin winking through, and the razor blade tumbled out of my hand and my forefinger dove into the opening. I touched skin – smooth, warm skin – and I brushed it with my twitching fingertip. Then I gripped the sensuous stocking material between my forefinger and thumb and started reverentially rubbing.

'Oh, I see you've noticed the little run in my stocking,' Inez said from on high. 'Look, Britta, Amanda's noticed the little run in my stocking.'

'I see,' Britta responded, legs flashing closer. 'She's a very observant girl.'

I hardly heard what they said, so enthralled was I with sliding that slick see-through fabric between my fingers, breathing in the sweet scent of that legsome woman. My mouth had gone dry and my pussy very, very wet.

But when Britta laughed and moved her vanilla-slick legs even closer, I slowly raised my eyes up from Inez's slim, tendon-cleaved ankle, up the rounded curve of her calf, the bend in the knee and the vulnerable soft spot back there, up her fleshy, perfectly shaped thigh to where it disappeared into the hem of her skirt and merged into rounded buttock.

I looked up at Inez and Britta, looking down at me. They had smiles on their pretty faces, knowing smiles. Like they could plainly read what was written on my hopeful face and in my glazed eyes. Like they'd been able to read me like a dog-eared leg fetish book from the get-go.

'I was hoping you were going to notice,' Inez said. She wet her scarlet lips with the tip of her pink tongue. 'It would've been a waste of a perfectly good pair of stockings otherwise.'

I pushed my finger and thumb inside the rent in the fabric, tearing the material further, encircling the woman's exquisitely constructed ankle and smiling shakily up at her.

'Rip it,' she hissed.

I jerked my hand up, the silk tearing in a straight line. I grabbed onto Inez's knee, tore at the ruptured garment with my other hand, ripping it apart, exposing hot brown skin, hot leg. Inez glared at me, eyes flashing. Then Britta seized her by the neck, grabbing her attention, roughly pressing her mouth against Inez's mouth.

I watched the two women passionately kiss, both my hands on Inez's bared limb now, squeezing and rubbing. I saw their tongues flash together, felt their kisses getting deeper and hungrier. I kissed Inez's leg, her knee, her thigh, licked at her taut skin. I dropped down and ran my tongue all the way from her naked ankle up to her naked thigh, tracing the wicked contours of her leg, her stocking and all pretensions of business hanging in tatters.

Inez's leg trembled under my mouth and hands as I gripped her clenched calf and licked at her thigh, bit into her sweet flesh. I anxiously felt up her golden limb, caressing her ankle, clutching her knee and pressing my thumbs into her soft spot, running my fingernails up and down her shin as I kissed and licked and nipped at her thigh. She moaned into Britta's mouth, the three of us striking just the right nerve.

Then the pair of women broke apart and grabbed me by the arms and pulled me to my feet, away from theirs. 'But-but your legs . . .' I mumbled, before Inez smothered my protests with her lips.

She darted her tongue into my mouth, and I frenched with the black-haired lovely, then with Britta, then all of us together. My head spun and my body flooded with heat as our tongues swirled joyously together, as I felt the naughty women unbuttoning my blouse and unhooking my skirt.

I was soon flat on my bum on the boss's couch, in only my lacy black panties and lace-topped black stockings, a gorgeous girl on the end of each of my legs. They cradled my stockinged feet in their hands, admiring my stockinged legs, the red-bowed garter straps that dangled from my red-bowed garter. Then they went to work as a team, unhooking and rolling down my stockings, baring my legs and feet.

'Yes,' I murmured, as they rubbed and caressed my nude peds, squeezed and massaged them, tickled the tender bottoms of them with their thumbs and fingernails. I slid a hand into my damp panties, grabbed onto a breast and fingered a swollen nipple.

Inez pulled my foot up to her mouth, sending me sliding down the couch. She stuck out her tongue and pressed the tip of it against my exposed sole, sending sexual electricity arcing all through me. Britta did the same, and I rubbed even quicker, squeezed even harder. And when Inez stroked the arched bottom of my foot with her warm wet tongue, I just about liquefied.

Inez lapped at my left sole from heel to toes, Britta my right, as I urgently polished my puffed-up clit and anxiously rolled nipples gone rock hard with excitement. They licked and licked at my sensitive soles, dragging their tongues across my tender skin over and over, my legs jerking and my feet jumping in their hands. Then Britta slithered her tongue in between my toes, and Inez followed suit.

Shivers of sheer delight raced through my body, my finger-buffed clit the epicentre, as the two wicked women tongued in between my outstretched toes, their hands all over my ankles and calves. 'Jesus, yes,' I moaned, on fire.

Inez tilted my ped downward and vacuumed all five of my foot-digits into her mouth, sucking on them. Britta did the same, the two hotties tugging on my foot-tips, their tongues scouring the underside of my toes. I rubbed faster and pinched and pulled more ruthlessly, boiling with imminent release.

'God,' I yelped, quivering with ecstasy. Orgasm swept through me with tidal-wave ferocity, the women sucking on my feet, groping my legs, my fingers flying on my button.

It took me a solid minute or so to clear my head and drag my dampened hand out of my sopping panties. And in that short time, Inez and Britta dealt with the matter of their clothes, stripping off the fashionable garments and leaving themselves stark, blazing naked – aside from their sexy stockings and shoes, of course.

They grabbed a hand each and yanked me to my feet, helped me over to Mr Kleiner's huge desk. And while I struggled to fully regain my footing in reality, Britta swept the mundane business minutiae off the solid slab of mahogany and climbed atop the desk. She turned her back on the two of us, standing up there on her high heels with her head in the clouds, like an erotic work of art on a pedestal; a stunning, statuesque blonde goddess with gleaming ivory body and peach-contoured bottom, white-stockinged limbs stretching on forever.

'I-I want to worship your legs,' I breathed, extending a shaky hand, touching the seam on one of Britta's exquisite stems.

'Will mine do?' Inez asked, grinning.

I looked at her and nodded, and she kissed me. Then she carefully scooched onto the desk herself, bum-first, so that she was in between Britta's skyscraper legs, facing me, facing Britta's shaven pussy. I dropped to my knees at the feet of Inez's dangling striped legs, grasping onto them as she tilted her head back and jabbed her tongue into Britta's pussy.

I ran my nervous hands up and down Inez's silky limbs, marvelling at their strength and their softness, their limitless warmth. Inez held onto Britta's legs, supporting the backs of the woman's trembling knees while she poked at the woman's sex. Britta put her hands on her ass and ground her pussy into Inez's mouth, urging her girlfriend on.

It was a breathtaking sight, but I had eyes and hands and mouth only for Inez's legs. I carefully pulled off her high heels and gathered her stockinged feet together, tongued the darker, reinforced material that covered her shapely toes. And when I had her foot-ends all nice and wet, the fabric glistening and clotted with saliva, I opened up wide and eased all ten of her toes into my mouth. I sucked on both of her tapered ped-tips at once, a technique I'd perfected over hours and hours of arousing practice.

Inez pulled her face away from Britta's pussy to look at me, at what I was doing to her, her lips and chin shiny with Britta's joy. She watched me tug on her two feet with my mouth, then stuck her head back in between Britta's legs and resumed lapping at the anxious woman. Britta cupped and squeezed her breasts, undulated her bum on Inez's face.

I pulled Inez's feet out of my mouth and smeared the deliciously damp silk all over my face. Then I spread the woman's limbs apart, shouldered them, began kissing and licking and biting my way down her long legs, headed for the slick fur-tufted apex of her sexuality.

I bit into her thighs where pitch-black stocking top gave way to golden skin, and Inez moaned, jolting Britta with the sensual vibration. I speared my tongue into Inez's pussy, digging into her slit, and the woman just about strangled me with her thighs. I could've blacked out and gone to leg-heaven right then and there, but I kept on plugging, fucking Inez with my tongue.

And then Britta suddenly screamed, gushed all over Inez's upturned face, her legs quivering like live wires. I tickled Inez's clit with the tip of my tongue and the girl went orgasmic, flooding me with her own tangy juices.

I got plenty of compliments on the redesign of the office – even from Mr Kleiner himself. But the real reward I received from the whole experience was the warm, wet, wonderful memories of the leg-beautiful designing women Britta and Inez. Their services were second to none.

– Amanda, Florida, USA

Tango

'There's an old saying in Buenos Aires,' Tomás said, as he held me, 'the Tango is a sad thought you can dance.'

Our chests were pressed so closely together that I could feel his heart beating. My head was turned to the side as if he were about to whisper a secret. I could feel his warm breath on my neck.

'The dance is powerful and intimate,' he whispered. 'It's not necessarily sexual.' He brought his mouth closer to my ear. 'Though sometimes of course . . .'

A long slow delicious thrill slid up my spine as he spoke.

'Now . . . lean closer. Press against me with your –' he paused '– breastbone.'

I instantly obeyed and found my centre of gravity shifting forward and my weight transferring to the balls of my feet.

'Keep your chest parallel to mine at all times.' He began to move and I tried to keep up. 'I will lead and you must follow. Our arms form what is called the frame. It is our legs that will dance.'

I'd always loved the Tango. Let's face it, if there ever was a dance that really is the vertical expression of a horizontal desire then the Tango is it. It's powerful yet tender; it can be simple and restrained or fiercely grandiose, and those who dance it say it is somewhere between a prayer and making love. There's something about the sinuous, elegant, controlled and yet utterly sensuous way the dancers move that hits you right between the legs.

Tomás, my new teacher, had the dark brooding looks of Joaquin Cortés and intense dark eyes beneath heavy black brows that any Mills & Boon hero would have been proud of.

He began to move and I struggled to follow. I felt clumsy and awkward. 'Your legs must dance alone, stop using your brain to control them. Let them follow me,' he whispered.

My heart was beating so hard I was sure it must be rattling his ribs. Around us, elegant couples were dancing to the melancholy music, their feet moving in unison with seeming effortlessness. I felt like a carthorse amongst a stable of Arab stallions.

'I'll never learn.'

'Stop for a moment.' Tomás's feet stopped moving but he continued to hold me. 'Now relax. Allow me to move your body.' His voice against my ear felt like an intimate caress. I could hardly breathe. He leaned forward, supporting my back tenderly with the hot palm of his left hand and I bent backwards. He straightened up and my body followed. He twisted to the right and then the left and I twisted at the hips, matching his movements.

'In the Tango, the man directs the dance with his hands and the movement of his torso. The woman responds to him, allowing herself to be led. This is the balance of power that is at the heart of Tango.' Was it my imagination or was there a slight quiver in his voice – the way a man sounds when he's just finished making love to you? 'To dance it properly the woman must learn to surrender . . .' He drew out the *s*, elongating it so that the word sounded like a sibilant promise. 'Do you think you can surrender to me, Louise?' But we both knew I already had.

I learned slowly, gradually mastering the rhythm which mimicked the throb of sex, and the gliding synchronised movements. I grew used to the feel of Tomás's strong sensitive hand in the small of my back and only felt truly alive when my stiff nipples were brushing against his chest.

When I buckled on my dancing shoes with their strap around the ankle designed to stop them from flying off when you execute the *gancho* (when the woman hooks her leg behind the man's knee with a sliding backwards kick) I felt a warm rush of blood to my face and a corresponding, much bigger one, to my crotch.

I became an obedient student, surrendering myself to Tomás and allowing him to control my body as thoroughly as he already controlled my nightly dreams. I learned how to shift my weight from one foot to the other as he gave me subtle signals with his hands and body. How to stand straight and tall during the *ocho* as I swivelled in a close figure of eight by his side.

But, though I'd seldom felt closer to a man or more nakedly vulnerable than when we danced, the moment the lesson was over, Tomás would nod formally then move on to his next client.

After about a year I began to have an extra private lesson on Friday nights. Alone in the studio, we watched our reflection in the huge mirror as he handled and manipulated my body with the skill and sensitivity of the most sensitive lover. I spent most of the hour with my crotch hot and slippery and my nipples rigid. I slowly grew in confidence and suppleness. I began to receive the occasional compliment from him and the approval made me blush with pride. Dancing with him became a pleasure and a torment, satisfying my desire for closeness but always leaving me ravenous for more.

One night, we seemed to dance like a single body. I responded to his subtle movements and direction almost by telepathy. It was exciting, beautiful and I never wanted it to end. When the music drew to a close, we stopped moving but I remained in his arms, breathless, hot and trembling.

Tomás let go of my hand and brought his fingers up to my face. He looked into my eyes. 'Finally . . .' he whispered, '. . . you can Tango.'

Before I could respond he kissed me. His mouth was hot and hungry and he pulled me closer and I felt the bulge of his erection against the curve of my belly.

I ran my hands up and down his back, slid them under his sweater. I pushed them down the back of his trousers and cupped his buttocks. My crotch ached.

I felt him sliding down the zip on my dress. I heard him gasp in surprise and delight as he slid his hands down my body and discovered I was naked. 'I should have known that you would wear nothing underneath your dress.' He cupped my breasts and ran his thumbs across my taut nipples. 'You Tango as though you would prefer to be fucking than dancing.' His fingers snaked between my legs and I gasped.

'That's because I would. I've wanted to fuck you from the first moment I saw you.'

His thumb found my clit and my legs trembled so hard I almost fell over.

'I know that, of course.' He began to tear off his clothes. As he removed each piece he threw it to the side of the room, then did the same with his socks and shoes. His cock stood to attention, its tip purple and swollen. He held out his arms, inviting me to dance. I stepped into his embrace and we began to Tango.

The sound of my high-heeled shoes against the wooden floor was our only music. His erection bobbed between us. My heart thumped, my crotch tingled.

Our upper bodies were pressed together and I could feel the slick warmth of his skin against my nipples. I whirled elegantly around him then arched my back as I executed the *gancho* until my long hair swept the floor.

I don't know how long we danced, but I'd seldom felt so alive or so excited. We whirled around the room, our feet in perfect synchronisation accompanied only by the sound of clip-clopping heels and our own excited breathing.

He steered me towards the edge of the room and stopped. He placed each of my hands on the ballet rail. I watched our reflections in the mirror as he stepped up behind me and placed a hand on each of my hips. His cock was hard and hot and thick and I squeezed my muscles as he pushed it into me, relishing the sensation of it sliding past my excited nerve endings. I saw my own eyes narrow in delight as he entered me and watched his mouth curl into a smile as he slid all the way in.

He slid out again and I sighed in disappointment. For a moment, he remained still, tantalising me with just the tip of his erection inside me then he pulled on my hips and thrust forward, pushing inside me to the balls. He circled his hips slowly and I felt his scratchy pubes rubbing against my lips.

Tomás began to fuck me, pumping his hips back and forth. He reached around and his fingers found my clit. His other hand stroked my breasts.

In the mirror, I could see that my cheeks were flushed and my lips were swollen and dark. Tomás's eyes glistened as they met mine and the front of his hair fell across his forehead in a damp curl.

His hips pumped. His fingers worked my clit. I was moaning and gasping. After months of excitement and frustration I knew it wouldn't take long for me to reach my peak.

Tomás was grunting, breathing noisily between parted lips. His face glistened with sweat. He squeezed my nipple and I moaned. His cock stretched and filled me as his expert fingers brought me ever closer to the edge. My nipples burned and throbbed. Tension and excitement coiled in my belly.

His thrusts grew quicker and shorter. In the mirror, I watched as his eyes widened and he began to moan. I knew he was about to come and the thought was all it took to push me over the brink. Orgasm exploded inside me like a volcano blast. I cried out. I held onto the ballet bar, my knuckles white and my body trembling.

I felt Tomás's body quiver and then stiffen. His cock twitched inside me as he pumped out hot seed. He let out a long low moan of satisfaction and release. I watched as his chest heaved and his legs shook. And all the time his eyes gazed into mine in the mirror shining with triumph and satisfaction and surrender.

He never fucked me again after that, though we continued to have our lesson every week, and I could never quite pluck up the courage to ask for a repeat performance. I think both of us knew that we'd come together in one perfect moment when the dance and the music had moved us and that we'd never be able to capture that magic again.

But our dance was perfect; tender, sensuous, and full of passion, and gradually I understood that what Tomás had really wanted to teach me was that the Tango is a dance of perpetual arousal and unfulfilled desire.

All I know is that I've never felt more alive or more utterly myself when I'm in a man's arms giving myself up to the music and surrendering to the power of the Tango.

– Louise, Cannes, France

Mercy

I don't know if this counts as a confession, but I've always been a sucker for mercy sex. I suppose it's just that I'm too soft, and maybe a bit because I could never see what the big deal was about doing sexy things. I mean, I know people go on about how you should save yourself for marriage, but that's really just propaganda from a bunch of selfish old gits who aren't getting it any more and don't want anyone else to either. Which is another good reason for mercy sex, because if everybody got off more often there'd be a lot less misery in the world. It's true.

So that's my excuse, but I've always felt guilty about it. I mean, it's not the sort of thing good girls do, is it? It's not the sort of thing bad girls do either. Good girls don't do it at all. Bad girls do it with the attractive boys. That's why I'm confessing here instead of telling my friends, because I don't dare!

Anyway, I'm sure that what you really want to know is all the dirty things I've done. The first time was in the sixth form with a boy called Aaron. Everybody else was pairing off, me included, but he was short and looked weird because his parents were really religious and made him dress like a complete prat. No girl was going to go out with him, and he knew it. He used to look so sad, watching us flirt and kiss, and every time one of the boys was boasting about what he'd been up to you'd see

Aaron lurking at the edge of the group looking like a lost puppy.

We all knew, but it didn't bother us, and girls can be real bitches about boys nobody fancies, because of course you want everybody to know that he's not good enough for you either. I don't suppose I was any better than the others, and when I saw him sneaking in behind the generator shed looking miserable I didn't follow because I was sorry for him but because I thought he was going to toss his cock and it would be really funny if I caught him and told all my friends. You see, Andy, who was cock of the walk, had managed to squeeze a bj out of my friend Gemma, and he'd told everybody, so all the girls were really pissed off and all the boys were crowing about it and teasing us, except for Aaron.

I didn't expect to find him in tears. I didn't understand at first, but I've always been soft-hearted and I asked him what the matter was, thinking he had problems at home or something. He wouldn't tell me at first, except for mumbling something about Andy, but I'm a nosy cow and I got it out of him in the end. Once he'd realised I wasn't going to laugh at him it all came out, about how none of the girls liked him and he'd never even had a kiss, and on and on. I tried to soothe him, telling him he'd find the right girl, but he wasn't having it. He said nobody would ever touch him. I said they would and he said he could prove it, because I wouldn't. I said I would and he laughed, not a funny laugh, but like he knew it was a lie.

So I kissed him. Two days later I was behind the same shed with his cock in my hand, tossing him off. He just wouldn't let up. Whatever I said he wouldn't believe it, and whatever I did it wasn't enough, until in the end it was me who told him to get it out, just to make him shut up. I did it all the way too, and ended up with a sticky hand, which was well gross. Even after that he was still saying I'd only done it because I felt sorry for him, maybe hoping I'd give him a bj like Gemma had to Andy. I wasn't going for that, and anyway, I had only done it because I felt sorry for him.

It was good though. He had a nice cock and it made me feel like I was the one in charge. Another thing, one of the things my parents always used to go on about was thinking of others before myself, and I'd done that, even if they probably hadn't been thinking of me tossing boys off when they said it.

So I was up for more, and so was he. It was always that, never anything more, just a toss, although after the second time he persuaded me to pull up my top and bra to give him something to look at while I tossed him. Unfortunately we weren't too careful about it and one day Gemma and Kristina caught us, just when I'd done it, so they saw me with my tits out and Aaron's stuff dripping down my hand. That was not good, and for the rest of my time there I was the girl who'd tossed off Aaron Goldsach.

That should have put me off, but it didn't. I liked the feeling of doing something dirty as a favour. I don't know why, and I'm sure the shrinks would have great fun with me if they knew, probably before talking me into bjs all round. That just seems to be the sort of thing that happens to me, maybe because I bring it on myself, maybe because men can guess I'm a sucker for a sob story. Not that I'm easy. If some guy comes on to me strong and I don't like him he gets turned down, and that's that. One or two have got my knee in their balls. It's just that when a guy is obviously desperate, and he's nice about it, and pushes a bit without being nasty, I usually give in.

After Aaron I tried to tell myself I wouldn't do anything like that again. It made me feel I was a bit weird, because I knew that was how other girls saw it, but underneath I still wanted to. I used to fantasise about it, inventing all sorts of situations, some of them pretty extreme, like letting a guy have me on the night before his wedding or being sent into the cell of a condemned man to spend the night with him. Not that I ever actually did anything like that, but maybe, in another world, I would have done.

What I did do was suck the guy at the next desk to me in the call centre where I got a job about a year after leaving school. It was a crap job, in a crap place, with really bad pay and lots of stupid rules. Not many people lasted long, including me, but at least I got sacked in style. The place was arranged in little cubicles, each one seating four operators, two side by side and two back to back. Next to me was Gary, who was your typical fat boy, always stuffing his face with crisps and burgers and always complaining about being fat and saying it was genetic.

Other than that he was all right, and because he'd been there a long time he showed me the ropes and taught me how to cope with the awkward bastards we'd get on the phones, even taking over from me a few times. We were the complaint centre for one of the big electrical stores, you see, and half the customers seemed to think we were personally responsible for whatever had gone wrong with their kit.

By the end of the day I'd be worn out, not physically, but mentally. I mean, just imagine having to spend eight hours solid with people going on at you for something that's not your fault and not even being able to answer them back the way you'd like to. Sometimes Gary would give me a hug, just friendly, and other times he'd go on about not having a girlfriend. I knew he was going to ask me out, and I knew I was going to turn him down. I had to.

When it happened we were doing overtime, which was the only way to earn enough. It had been a long day and he'd been really helpful, so when the big question came I found myself lying, telling him I was with somebody else. He didn't actually cry, not like Aaron, but he looked so crestfallen and he started to beg, promising to take me out to really expensive places he couldn't possibly afford and that he wouldn't try it on. I knew what he wanted, the same as Aaron and every other man, and I'd learnt a bit by then, so out came my tits and down I went, on my knees under the desk while I sucked him off.

At least we didn't get caught, but not long after we got called into the supervisor's office for a ticking off because we spent too much time talking. I pointed out that if there were no calls we might as well talk and he started to get stroppy with me, as if I was nothing. So I emptied his coffee over his head and that was the end of my job.

I still saw Gary occasionally, and a few weeks later me managed to talk me into another bj, this time at his parents' house while they were out. He was so grateful, even more than Aaron, and it became a regular thing, once a week or so. He'd call me up when it was safe and he was horny, I'd go around and we'd talk for a bit until we felt right, sometimes with his cock and balls out of his trousers for ages before I went down on him, or with me topless.

That lasted maybe six months before he started to angle for more. I said no, but he started to whine, giving me the same old routine about how he was a virgin and he'd never even seen between a girl's legs, and more. Finally he started to wear me down. First I gave him a peep, taking down my jeans and letting him look down my panties. He said he couldn't see properly, and down they came, with that odd feeling of being horny and annoyed at the same time, which I don't suppose most people would get at all.

I let him wank off while I posed like that, with my trousers and panties around my knees and my top up over my tits while he hammered away at his cock. He was nearly there when he started begging again, this time to see my bum. So I turned around, and immediately he was begging me to stick it out a bit. I knew what he wanted to see, because he was a dirty bastard, but I did it anyway, pushing my bum out to let him see between my cheeks and how I look from behind. That was too much for him.

Not the next time. Once you've gone so far it's difficult to move back, and easier to do what you've done already. So I gave him a strip, all the way, really slow and to music, until I was dancing naked in front of him. I went down on my own accord, taking him in my mouth to suck, but I'd barely started when he was begging again, to go all the way. He knew I'd done it with boyfriends, and the sneaky bastard had even brought some condoms, and he just would not shut up. So I climbed on his lap and gave him what he wanted.

– Veronica ('Ronnie'), Southampton, UK

The Way Things Are

When I discovered Becky was being unfaithful I got the biggest hard-on of my life. We were sitting in a restaurant, having a meal to celebrate her birthday. She'd just said it was a shame we were wasting her birthday in such a way and I asked what she'd rather be doing. Becky stared across the table, looked me straight in the eye and said, 'If I was working late at the office tonight, my boss could be banging me in the copier room.'

It was shocking in a lot of ways. It had been a long time since I had heard Becky say something so outrageous and there was something in the way she said it that told me she was speaking the absolute truth.

'You're banging your boss?' I gasped.

'Not tonight,' she said crossly. 'I'm here with you tonight wasting my time instead of having fun.'

I don't know if she expected me to be angry or outraged. She was studying me across the table, sipping her wine and smiling smugly. When I asked why she hadn't mentioned it before she just said, 'That's the way things are.'

'Can I watch?' I asked.

She laughed and called me a sick little pervert. Reaching for her mobile she found a picture and handed it over to me. The picture showed the familiar sight of Becky's pussy with a lean pale cock sliding into her. When she pressed the button to look at the next picture

I saw half a man's face above a picture of her pussy. His tongue was clearly sliding deep into her sex.

I almost came in my pants.

I asked the usual questions. How long has this been going on? Does this mean our marriage is over? Becky said she was just fucking the office manager until she got her promotion. It had been going on for about six months. And she admitted that he was a damned good lay. 'He's much better than you,' she said matter-of-factly.

I squirmed in my seat and told her I wanted to hear all about it. I was practically begging her to let me watch and be a part of it.

Sipping the last of her wine she stared at me and said no.

I spent the remainder of the night begging her to tell me more and let me join in. Cruelly, she kept laughing at me and saying I was a pathetic excuse for a husband. When we eventually got home and went to bed I expected her to tell me she was too tired for sex or make some excuse to frustrate me. Instead she said I could ride her if I wanted.

'It makes no difference to me,' she added. 'Your cock's so small compared to his, I doubt I'll feel it inside me.'

I came before I could get between her legs.

She went to sleep laughing and calling me pathetic.

Which was really how it all started.

Becky called me at lunchtime on the following day and told me she'd be late home from the office because she was doing some overtime. Lowering her voice on the telephone she added, 'You know that means I'm going to be getting fucked for an hour or two after work, don't you?'

My balls throbbed when she said the words. I begged her to let me come to the office and watch and, again, she called me a sick pervert. She hung up the phone and refused to take any calls from me for the rest of the day.

When she got back that evening I was desperate to know what she'd been doing and hear all the graphic details.

Becky told me to make her a drink before she went to bed. I dutifully obeyed and found her sitting in front of the TV watching soaps she had recorded whilst she was out doing overtime. I explained that the idea of her being with someone else got me really horny and she said, 'Thanks for telling me that. I wouldn't have noticed if you hadn't said something.'

I asked what she'd done with her boss and she became impatient. Standing up, taking off her panties, she tossed the white cotton at me and said, 'Sniff those and work out what I've been doing. But be quiet until I've finished watching my programme.'

The panties were warm. The crotch smelled of her pussy but the scent was stronger than anything I'd ever encountered before. Pushing them to my nose I wondered if I was also smelling the scent of another man's come on the glossy wet gusset of the panties. That thought pushed my arousal to the point of bursting.

In the commercial break she glanced at me and sneered with disapproval. I was still sniffing the panties.

'Jerk off into them,' she demanded.

I hesitated. 'I want to . . .' I began. 'I thought that tonight we could . . .'

She laughed at me. 'Your cock's not going anywhere near me tonight. You can wank in my panties if you want to come but my pussy's sore from having my boss for an hour this evening and my arsehole's too tender after having his fingers up there while he was fucking me.'

Feeling bold, and trying to match her confrontational mood, I asked, 'What about your mouth?'

She reached for her mobile and spent a moment fumbling for a specific picture. When she'd found it she passed me the phone and showed me a picture of her mouth wrapped around a large black erection.

'That was the last cock I sucked,' she explained. The date on the picture said the photograph had been taken more than a year earlier. 'I only sucked that one because I was curious to go down on a black man. I don't suck anyone's cock any more and I certainly won't be sucking yours.'

It took me less than a minute to wank myself to climax. I had her panties pushed against my nose when I came and the moment was glorious. The orgasm seemed to last for ever.

I wouldn't have believed it was possible to endure such a lifestyle for any length of time. I suppose it was made easier because Becky had her own fixed ideas about what I was allowed to do and what I wasn't.

A month after she'd first told me about her affair I got to meet her boss at her office Christmas party. I found myself shaking hands with a man who looked like a rugby player and Becky was saying, 'Arnold, this is my boss, Kevin.'

My erection sprouted instantly. The throbbing in my balls became unbearable when she said, 'Can you excuse us both, Arnold? I know it's the Christmas party but I need to show something to Kevin in the photocopier room.'

She disappeared for a full thirty minutes and I knew she was having sex with him. I thought of asking someone else at the party if they could tell me where the photocopier room might be, so I could go and discreetly watch. The thought of seeing Becky being taken by another man, watching while his rugby-player's cock pounded into her again and again, was almost too tempting to ignore.

But I knew Becky would be outraged if she discovered I had been spying on her. When I told her about that afterwards she laughed and told me I really was a pathetic specimen of manhood.

Six months later Becky got her promotion. I found out

she'd been applying for Kevin's job. When she received it, I asked her if she was still going to carry on fucking him.

'Have sex with a subordinate?' she laughed. 'God! No.' She explained that she didn't have time to have sex with Kevin any more now that she was laying the ground for another promotion as regional manager. She also added that the last time she'd had sex with a subordinate had been when she sucked and fucked the black guy from the postal room. 'Except,' she said meanly, 'for those times I've had sex with you. And that's not so much sex with a subordinate as sex with an inferior.' Her hurtful comments aroused me. I was even more excited when she explained that her plans for getting the regional manager's job involved fucking him well and often.

She showed me a picture of another stranger's cock pressing into her pussy. 'Does that excite you?' she asked.

I told her it made me very aroused.

She selected another picture, this one showing only a man's erection. I could see, from the thick thatch of dark pubes around the base, it was the same one she had shown me sliding into her pussy.

'Look at the picture and jerk off,' she demanded.

I obeyed immediately.

Becky laughed at me when I came and snatched her phone back from me. She called me pathetic because I was wanking off to pictures of another man's cock. Then she took her panties off and pushed them under my nose. 'In future,' she said, 'you're only to jerk off when you're sniffing the scent of my cunt. And then, you're only allowed to do it with my permission. Is that understood?'

I told her I understood exactly what she wanted. Even though I had just come, her authority and the scent of panties was making me hard again.

'Once a year,' she said, 'maybe on your birthday, but only when I decide, I'm going to let you slide that worthless little cock of yours into my pussy and you'll be allowed to come inside me.' She lifted her skirt to show me the crinkled folds of her shaved labia.

I could smell the raw animal scent of her arousal. I was trembling with excitement. My cock ached from the last climax and the strain of a fresh erection.

'But remember,' Becky added. 'Every other night of the year this pussy's going to be filled with whichever cock I want to have. And it won't be yours.' She pointed at the centre of her sex and then slipped her finger into the liquid folds. When the finger came out it was wet with pussy juice. She laughed and sneered at me as she daubed the wet musk under my nose.

I came again.

And that's how our relationship has been for the past three years. Becky got her job as regional manager and then got a position as deputy manger at national level. She's currently looking at a position on the board of directors and, considering the overtime she's putting in, I'm sure she'll get what she's after.

As for me, I'm not entirely happy that my wife denies me a normal sexual relationship, or that she only allows me to have sex with her once a year, or that the rest of the time she makes me wank off into her panties when they're wet at the crotch from her arousal for another man. And, as soon as the situation stops giving me the biggest hard-ons of my life, I might do something to change the situation. But, until it stops exciting me, I'm content to leave things the way they are.

– Arnold, Birmingham, UK

Sparks

I was a virgin when I started my apprenticeship and I don't mind admitting the condition was weighing me down. You know what it's like at that age: a perpetual erection, a one-track mind, and no means of release except your own right hand and whatever your over-excited imagination can conjure up.

At least work would give my friction-sore tool eight hours of welcome rest each day and something else to think about – or so I thought.

I suppose I was naïve but it never occurred to me that there were women electricians. I'd been expecting a bloke with hairy hands and a pair of dirty overalls, but what I got was Paula. She was twenty years older than me but still gorgeous. Six foot tall, legs as long as the M1 and a cleavage any porn star would have been proud of.

You might think I'd have been happy to spend my working week in the company of such a gorgeous woman, but I was so young and innocent in those days that the assignment was daily torture. I didn't know how to behave or what to say, and I walked around with a permanent erection that I was convinced at any moment would give away my pathetic condition.

But she was a patient and skilled teacher and I quickly began to learn and, after a month or so, I did start to feel a little more comfortable in her company. Every once in a while, though, she'd lean forward and I'd be treated to a view of her spectacular cleavage and my traitorous cock would rear its head again. So I took to spending my tea breaks locked in the loo, relieving my growing frustration in the hope that I might avoid disgracing myself for the rest of the day.

One day we were working in a new house, putting in the final electrics before the decorators came in. When my afternoon break came around I locked myself in the bathroom for my usual relief session and closed my eyes to conjure up my most recent memory of Paula. I'd watched her on her knees wiring up a low plug in the living room and her boobs had jiggled enticingly as she worked. I'd been so hard when I handed her a screwdriver that I swear my hand had shook, but I don't think she noticed.

I only had a few minutes so I stroked my cock as I daydreamed and quickly brought myself off. I got so involved I didn't realise at first that I'd begun to moan and gasp. It was only when I came, as my sperm shot out in long spurts across the locked bathroom door, that I realised I was making so much noise. I cleaned myself up then got out my hankie and did the same to the spunk-spattered door. I washed my hands then checked my face in the shaving mirror before venturing outside again.

I found Paula sitting at the kitchen counter drinking coffee. She pushed a mug across the work surface to me. I sat down. 'Are you all right, Mark?'

'Of course. Why?' I picked up my mug, avoiding her eyes.

'Well, you were making a bit of a noise. I wondered if you had tummy troubles.'

'Oh no . . . nothing like that,' I began, then realised that if I denied having diarrhoea I had no way of explaining away my moans. 'It was just . . . er . . . oh . . . nothing really . . .' My voice trailed away. I made the fatal mistake of allowing my mind to wander back to my wank in the loo and my cock gave a little twitch. I looked down at my crotch and noticed that in my hurry to clean up the bathroom I'd neglected to zip up my fly. I tried to fasten it, completely forgetting I was holding a mug of coffee. I upended it in my lap, staining the front of my overalls and making me leap out of my seat in pain.

'Quick!' Paula jumped to her feet. 'You'd better take those off straight away. You'll get burned otherwise.' She began unbuttoning the front of my overalls. In spite of the pain, having her bent over in front of me with her cleavage on display and her fingers fiddling with my buttons had the inevitable effect. My cock turned to granite, my legs turned to water and I began to panic. I caught her wrists and tried to stop her from undressing me, but she was bigger and stronger than me and she was determined. She slapped my hands away, finished unbuttoning my overalls and pushed them down to my ankles.

The moment she did it, it was obvious to us both that I had an erection. It tented the front of my coffee-stained boxers, making the buttons gape and practically poking her in the eye. She looked up at my face then down at my crotch and she widened her eyes in delighted surprise and began to smile.

'Better take these off too, I think.' She pushed my undies down to my ankles in a single movement, revealing my thick, upwardly-curved erection in all its purple-tipped glory. All I could do was stand there with my clothes bunched up around my ankles as she gazed at my crotch.

I hardly dared to breathe. Paula extended one finger and ran it along the seam between my balls and I trembled. She wrapped her hand around my cock and pushed back the foreskin, exposing the glistening tip. I watched in shock and delight as she stuck out her tongue and licked up a bead of pre-come from its eye. I shivered as her hot hungry tongue made contact then gasped in relief and pleasure as she opened her mouth and swallowed me to the root.

I'd never even been touched by a girl before and now I had this beautiful, sexy and experienced woman giving me a slow and delicious blowjob. I thought I'd died and gone to heaven. She snaked the tip of her tongue slowly around the underside of my helmet. She dabbled it into the eye.

Her mouth felt like warm wet velvet and her lips made obscene wet slurping noises as she sucked me. She relaxed her throat and I felt myself sliding all the way down until my balls were pressed up against her chin. Then she looked up at me and the look of naked hunger and satisfaction I saw in her eyes made me want to cream on the spot.

But I had no intention of wasting the moment. Here I was, buried up to the nuts in the mouth of the woman of my dreams and I wanted it to last. I grabbed a handful of her hair and pulled back slightly, slowing her down.

I watched her face as she sucked me slowly and sensuously. Her mouth made an obscene O and I loved watching my cock slide out of sight between her parted lips. She unbuttoned her overalls then reached behind and unhooked her bra. She pulled it away from her body and her magnificent breasts swung free. Her nipples were already erect, hard and dark, and she gasped in pleasure as she rubbed the tips with the flat of her thumbs.

She sat back, releasing my cock, and I felt bereft until she raised herself up on her knees and pressed it between her warm, soft breasts. Slowly she raised her body up and down so that my cock fucked her cleavage. She smiled with pleasure as the tip appeared then stuck out her tongue to lick it before it disappeared again.

'Is that good?' she asked.

I nodded. 'Yes . . .' My voice was a hoarse whisper. 'You've no idea how long I've wanted to do that.

'You and me both,' she answered, with a laugh.

I bent down and kissed her. Her mouth tasted of coffee. I could smell the hot musky scent of her skin. Her breath was hot on my face. I fiddled with her hair, freeing it from her ponytail until it fell around her face like a lion's mane. I broke the kiss. 'You're beautiful.'

'And so are you.' She bobbed her head and licked the head of my cock as it appeared from her cleavage then caught it in her hand before it could slip back and took it into her mouth. She began to suck me again, but this time with a hunger and urgency that I found as arousing as it was surprising.

She snaked a finger between my legs and found my arsehole. She ran the tip around the rim of my tight rosebud then gently pushed it inside, making me gasp and my legs quiver. She slowly finger-fucked me as her mouth moved up and down my erection, pushing it in a little more each time until she found my prostate and I practically hit the roof.

'Do that again,' I hissed. She pressed the tip of her finger into my G-spot as she sucked me and I moaned. After half a dozen repetitions I was ready to burst. 'That's fantastic,' I gasped. 'But if you don't stop I think I'm going to come and I'd rather like to fuck you.'

Paula straightened up and released my cock. She gently withdrew her finger and began pushing her overalls down over her hips. She struggled to her feet and lowered them as far as her ankles and tried to step out of them. But she was wearing her work boots and couldn't get them any farther. She bent down and unlaced one boot then used the toe of the other one to ease it off. She pushed me down in the chair and, hobbled by my own clothes around my ankles, I could only obey. I watched as she kicked away the leg of her overalls, freeing her socked foot. She straddled my lap and, sliding her hand between us, positioned my cock.

Her cunt was slippery and hot and I could smell the musk rising from her skin. She sat down on my cock and I felt myself sliding inside her. It was hot and tight and wet and utterly delicious. When it was all the way in, I could feel my balls mashed between our bodies and her tits pressed up against my chest. She wrapped her arms around my neck and began to move up and down, fucking me.

I'd begun to sweat. It poured down my body in rivulets. Paula's tits bounced as we fucked and I watched, mesmerised, as her fat nipples bobbed. Her cunt gripped me, squeezing and exciting me. Her hair fell in my face, smelling of honey and lavender.

Excitement throbbed in my pelvis. My balls were contracted and tight. Blood gushed in my brain. Paula had begun to moan and sigh. Mascara ran down her face. She rode me hard, pressing down on my shoulders for leverage. Her movements grew faster and more abandoned. She threw back her head and began to sob. 'I'm coming,' she cried, though I needed no announcement because she was digging her fingernails into my back and her cunt seemed to be rippling.

It felt like she was milking me, coaxing me to come inside her and I didn't need any more encouragement. I held onto her hips and moved her up and down on my erection. I was coming. I let out a long breathless groan as my cock began to jerk inside her. I was trembling all over, shaking and moaning, trying to hold onto her as she rode out her own orgasm.

Turns out that she had a thing for younger men and quite a few of the blokes on the team had been on the receiving end of her generous advances over the years. I spent the next seven years as a very happy and attentive apprentice and, when I finally got my papers, I did the decent thing and married her. Well, if you've got those kind of sparks you'd be a fool to give it up, wouldn't you?

– Mark, Dagenham, UK

Body Search

I like to holiday abroad at least a couple of times a year – mostly last-minute city breaks. After checking in my suitcase as usual this time I presented my passport and flight card at the embarkation gate. It was as I was queuing with the other passengers that I first caught her eye. I looked down the line and saw her frisking a female passenger, and she looked straight over that woman's shoulder and met my gaze with an appraising stare. I looked away self-consciously. It's never a good idea to draw the attention of airport security officers.

One by one we promised the security staff we were carrying no liquids or gels, took off our shoes and loaded the trays with our coats and keys and hand luggage, to be sent down the conveyor belt under the scanner. Then we stepped through the metal-detector. I'm used to the procedure. I did set off the metal-detector, but I often do. Too much iron in my blood, maybe. I wasn't worried.

The female security officer beckoned me to one side. 'Could you just stand with your arms out, madam?' She was wearing the regulation military-style blue shirt with jaunty cravat. Her hair was pulled back into a ponytail from her bony face and her lipstick was very dark, the colour of plums.

Funny how in this country the only people who ever call you 'madam' are the ones who scare you.

I stood obediently as she frisked me up my back, down my flanks and legs and back up my front and arms. Her hands were brisk and efficient, and they cupped my breasts only for a moment. The little squeeze, the movement of her thumbs across my nipples, might almost have been professional. My eyes widened. I could see the identity tag on her chest: SARA YATES.

This is just the sort of job for people like her, I thought. The uniform. The discipline. The control.

'That'll do, then.'

Just as I relaxed, the security man at the conveyor belt asked, 'Is this your bag, madam?'

I glanced at the black leather knapsack in his hands. 'Yes.'

'Would you mind emptying it for me?'

I took out my belongings one at a time under his instruction: sunglasses, a guidebook to Spain, a pack of toffees, some emergency toiletries and make-up. Then the little pale-pink plastic box.

'What is this?'

'Um.' I felt the blood rise to my cheeks. 'It's . . . uh . . .' The realisation of how bad this would sound hit me hard. 'It's a remote control.'

He was a big man with a blue chin and heavy brows. Those brows rose. 'A remote control?'

I wished he would keep his voice down. I nodded.

'For what?'

I glanced around, guiltily. People were starting to look over at us. I could sense the prickle of doubt and fear among those within earshot. This was far too public, and incredibly embarrassing. Hot waves were washing up and down my body. 'For something personal,' I said faintly.

'Madam,' said Security Officer Yates at my shoulder, 'we're going to have to ask you to come with us.' She put her hand on my upper arm. 'Avery, let's go to Room D. Rogers, bring her stuff.'

They led me away, the bony dark-haired woman and the tall blond man on either side of me, holding me firmly by the arms, and brawny Rogers bringing up the rear. They took me out of the hall through a door marked AUTHORISED PERSONNEL ONLY and down a corridor. This wasn't London Heathrow, just a provincial city airport, so we didn't have miles to walk. I broke before we got very far anyway.

'Look – I'm not a terrorist! It's for a vibrator. It's a remote control vibrator. I'm wearing it.'

Rogers behind me made a choking noise. Yates cast me a hard look. 'We'll see.'

'Believe me! You can look it up on the internet shop if you like. It's completely harmless!'

'I think we'd better take a look for ourselves.'

They took me into Room D, which was painted white and had a desk, an examination table, a folding screen and a toilet. There were no windows, and the neon lights hummed faintly. It was so clinical it was intimidating.

'Now let's get this straight,' said Yates, who had dropped the 'madam', 'before I put out a full security alert. You're telling me this is some sort of remote-control sex toy?'

'Yes.' I was panting and frantic.

'What sort of a transmission range does it have?'

'Uh . . . about thirty foot I think.'

Her eyebrows shot up. She looked not in the least amused. 'So you could play with yourself on the plane?'

'Yes.' I cringed. Both the men were had fixed me with disbelieving glares.

'Well, let's have a look at it then. Go over to the bench. You two, check through her things.'

I stepped to the examination table, which had a thin mattress covered in a paper sheet. She pulled the screen across behind us, separating us from the two men. 'Remove your clothes, please.'

I started to comply. I had a strong inkling that legally speaking I was in no position not to. My skirt went over the back of a plastic chair.

'Which flight were you on?'
'Uh. The seven-thirty to Barcelona.'
'And what's the purpose of your journey?'
'I'm going on holiday.'
'Alone?'
'I'm meeting a friend out there.'

Down to bra and knickers, I paused, shivering. My nipples reacted to the chill by poking through the green lace cups. She looked me over, her lips pursed. 'Bend forward over the bench.'

The tone of her voice made it clear she was relishing this. I obeyed. The paper cover felt cold against my skin; I wished they'd heated the room a little more. My skin was alive with shivers and my head was full of lurid imaginings. With my bum in the air like this I felt totally exposed. I quivered as I felt her hands on my hips, felt her pull down my lace-trimmed knickers to reveal my pussy – and the black ties about the tops of my thighs.

'Well, she's certainly wearing some sort of strap-on device,' said Yates, speaking loudly for the benefit of the other two officers. 'But it's very small.' She crouched behind me, so that she was looking straight up at the slash of my sex. 'Spread your legs.'

I eased my legs apart to the full extent that the knickers around my ankles would let me. I could feel the movement of her breath on my moist places.

'It sits over her clitoris and pubic area,' she pronounced. 'She waxes thoroughly for her holiday, by the looks of things, so she's very smooth and I've got a good clear view. The device doesn't cover her sexual opening. Doesn't inhibit access. It rather looks like she's been telling us the truth. Rogers – do you have the remote to hand?'

'Uh. Yeah.' His voice had thickened. I could imagine the two men staring at the screen between us.

'Let's test it out. Switch it on. Low setting.'

There was a moment's hesitation. Then: 'Right you are.'

The clit vibe purred into life. I spasmed with shock and shot upright; she was on me in a heartbeat, slamming me face down onto the mattress again. 'Don't you dare move!' she snarled into my ear. 'Lie still!' Hand between my shoulder-blades, she could pin me easily. I whimpered.

'That's better. Now you arc going to stay there while I have a look at you. Aren't you?'

'Yes.'

She swung round, one hand lingering warningly on the small of my back, so that she could see the vibe in action. It hummed between my legs like a bee doing its honey-dance on the comb. I could feel the tickle spread in waves through my body.

'Well, it certainly seems to be having an effect,' mused Yates. 'She's looking flushed. I think I might as well check that she hasn't got any hidden surprises for us, while we're here.'

I shut my eyes in dread. I heard a drawer open, the sound of her fumbling with objects within.

'You don't have any allergy to latex, do you, madam?'

'No,' I whispered.

'That's good. We like to keep you comfortable. Now, my fingers may be a little cold.' Silky latex-clad digits tucked up behind the humming vibrator, stroking the length of my slot to find moisture. Then she pushed a finger deep inside me, withdrew it for a moment then plunged in two. I gasped, accommodating the demands on my interior geography as her fingers scissored apart, twisted, and explored me thoroughly.

'Vaginal examination reveals no foreign bodies,' she mused. 'Just that she's got a tight wet snatch. Very wet. This little toy of hers seems to be working.'

The pumping intrusion of her hand made me groan. As soon as she heard that she withdrew.

'And a rectal.'

More fumbling, which I did not look for the source of. My eyes were closed, my face burning, my hands leaving damp imprints on the paper sheet. I was helpless to stop the throbbing at my clit, and Rogers seemed to be amusing himself playing with the speed-settings, keeping my body on the edge of sensation at every moment.

Yates squirted cold wet lube into my bum-crack, stroking it around my tight anal freckle with gloved fingers. It had almost warmed through by the time she slid her longest finger through the pursed entry of my bottom.

Sweat sprang out on my skin. I heaved against her, willing myself to open, not to fight the invasion, not to be hurt.

'Ah; she's hot in here. And it's way tighter than her pussy.'

Like little electrical snakes the impulses of sensation wriggled and flickered through the depths of my body, radiating from my violated anus. I was slackening already, my bum-hole welcoming her, my arousal building to a wave too top-heavy to stop. The copious lube was running down into my sex. The vibe felt like a nail upon which my whole body was hanging, being driven deeper and deeper into me.

And that bitch Yates knew it. 'Turn the vibe off!' she snapped, pulling out of me with a slurp.

Suddenly everything was still. There was no nail. I hung in mid-air, desperate, and sobbed.

'Now,' she said conversationally, peeling off her gloves. She came round to my head and lifted my face from the mattress. 'You're a very stupid girl, aren't you? You got onto an international flight at a time when everyone's terrified of terrorist bombs, wearing a remote device. Do you know what trouble you could've got into?'

I swallowed.

'You could have put this whole airport into lockdown and evacuation. You could have blocked every flight path over the whole of Britain. You think the rules don't apply to you, girl, because it's so obvious you don't look like a terrorist is supposed to. You think they don't apply to you because you wanted to play a naughty little game with yourself on the plane. You're a dirty little tramp, aren't you?'

'Yes.'

'You're a dirty, *silly* little tramp, aren't you?'

'Yes.'

'Right. And now I don't suppose you want me to call the police, do you?'

I tried to shake my head.

'So, dirty girl, we're going to teach you a lesson right here. So you won't forget and do anything so silly again. That's what you want, isn't it?'

'Yes,' I croaked.

'Rogers,' she said, smiling, 'there are condoms in the top drawer of that desk. Bring them through.'

I shut my eyes and pressed my face to the mattress. I could hear the snap of a drawer being closed, the movement of the screen across the tiled floor as they pulled it aside and readjusted it to make room for all four of us in here. I heard their loud breathing. Two men, looking down at my bare body, my spread thighs, my splayed pussy. In that cold room the heat of their eyes burned my skin, flushing me pink all over. I could smell their musk, their sudden sweat, their maleness.

'Jesus,' said one of them appreciatively. I recognised Rogers's voice.

'Nice one, Yates,' said Avery.

Suddenly there were hands on my bum; more than one pair, exploring me. They were surprisingly gentle about it, as if unsure of themselves. I bucked and quivered as they squeezed. A fingertip found my lubricated arsehole and quivered there vigorously. I wailed in response and one of them slapped my cheek.

'Not so loud.'

'Better give me that remote, Rogers,' said my female tormentor. 'You'll need to be putting a rubber on. Avery, go round to her head.'

A foil packet was torn open. Avery came round the table to stand near my head. I was at just the right height to look his cock in the eye as he opened his flies and released it from the tight blue fabric of his trousers. He had blond pubes and a long slim prick that he stroked lovingly. His glans was flushed and rosy, its slit already oozing.

'Pass us one,' he urged.

'You won't need a condom,' Yates told him. 'Come on her face or down her throat; it's your choice. She'll take it willingly either way. Rogers: snatch or ass, up to you.'

'What!' I moaned.

'Shut her up,' instructed Yates. Avery obeyed, stuffing his cock between my lips to make a most effective gag. I could smell shower-gel in his pubes as he pushed all the way forward into me, lifting one knee onto the table to get closer.

Then Yates turned the vibe back on. Just on the low setting, to start with, but it was enough to remind my body of what it had so nearly had moments before, the vibe humming a tune that my pussy couldn't help but dance to. My moan of protest changed note. My throat yielded to Avery, my mouth moulding about his hot length.

'Don't forget to let her breathe,' Yates admonished dryly. She put her hand on the small of my back, firmly, to feel me quiver. I found her touch unbearably provoking, yet soothing too. My spine flexed as she pushed down, sending my bum up another notch and putting my sex on display.

I felt the broad head of Rogers's cock slipping up and down my sex lips, bumping against the plastic vibrator. I could picture the glossy latex stretched tight over a prick as thickset as its owner. My tongue slid around Avery's knob-end and he gasped and sank his hand in my hair.

'Take her,' ordered Yates. 'Now.' She turned the vibe up to full speed.

Rogers thrust forward into me in one motion – not into my arse but, as she put it, my 'snatch'. There was no resistance; I was just too juicy, too ready, though that didn't stop me groaning around Avery's cock as I yielded deliciously to his girth. My expectations weren't disappointed; he was thick enough to make lights flash behind my eyes.

Then I had no breath left to waste on noise, because I had to cope with both of them pumping into me at once, shaking the air out my lungs until they found a mutual rhythm. My bum bounced under Rogers's heavy hands and his balls slapped against me. Avery's solid meat slid over my tongue. Yates held me down and tuned the vibrations to my clit up and down in long pulses that shook me not from the outside, as the two men were doing, but from within my own core.

I came. I couldn't help myself. I came around the cocks of two strangers, my drawn-out cry entirely muffled by the cock working my mouth. Yates felt my crisis through her hand. She was merciless, and expert. She let me plunge down from the peak of one orgasmic wave, and then caught me up on the vibe and thrust me to the next crest so that I could fall again. She was relentless. There was no let-up, nowhere for me to escape to, no chance to rest. I just kept coming. My vision started to turn red.

'Fuck her,' she chanted. 'She's coming; fuck her *now.*'

Mashing my face into his belly, Avery unloaded down my throat, pulled out and let the last gouts splash on my cheek. Rogers saw and hit his mark too, thundering into my body so hard the table squealed on the tiled floor, gasping, 'Fuck – yes – oh fuck – oh *fuck.*'

The vibe went still. I collapsed. Rogers more or less fell over me. I don't think he was used to such vigorous activity at work. It took me nearly as long to stop gasping.

'Clean Mr Avery's cock,' said Yates.

So, with his spunk still on my face like pearly tears, I licked his cock clean.

'Say thank you,' she said.

'Thank you,' I whispered. He grinned, bemused.

'To both of them.'

Rogers slid from me, leaving a considerable void, skinned off his condom, knotted it and flicked it into the toilet basin. I slithered to my knees, kissed the tip of his blunt instrument and thanked him too.

'Now take the vibe off. There can't be any more fizz left in you for the flight and I have to confiscate it. For safety reasons.'

I nodded, and peeled the straps down my legs before handing it over. 'Thank you.'

She smiled at last.

They got me onto my flight just before the gate closed. I was last in, and everyone watched as I hurried down the aisle, flushed and dishevelled, to collapse into my seat. The engines began to whine and I stared blindly as the flight attendants ran through the lifejacket drill.

I'd have to get myself cleaned up, of course, once we were in the air and the seatbelt signs went off. I'd have to be pristine for Barcelona. Maybe I could find somewhere in Arrivals to take a shower and buy fresh clothes. There would be time, of course. Sara's own flight was due to land three hours after mine and she'd expect me to be neat and clean and ready to serve her. She'd be so hot for me, after what she'd seen.

I shifted in my seat, my swollen sex wanting comfort. I smiled to myself. My girlfriend is a strict mistress who derives immense satisfaction from loaning me out to people, though this was the first time she'd involved her work colleagues. As always, the major part of my own pleasure had come from submitting to her will.

Not all of it, though.

– Vivienne, Manchester, UK

The leading publisher of fetish and adult fiction

TELL US WHAT YOU THINK!

Readers' ideas and opinions matter to us so please take a few minutes to fill in the questionnaire below.

1. **Sex:** Are you male ☐ female ☐ a couple ☐?

2. **Age:** Under 21 ☐ 21–30 ☐ 31–40 ☐ 41–50 ☐ 51–60 ☐ over 60 ☐

3. **Where do you buy your Nexus books from?**

☐ A chain book shop. If so, which one(s)?

____

☐ An independent book shop. If so, which one(s)?

____

☐ A used book shop/charity shop

☐ Online book store. If so, which one(s)?

____

4. **How did you find out about Nexus books?**

☐ Browsing in a book shop

☐ A review in a magazine

☐ Online

☐ Recommendation

☐ Other __________________________________

5. **In terms of settings, which do you prefer? (Tick as many as you like.)**

☐ Down to earth and as realistic as possible

☐ Historical settings. If so, which period do you prefer?

____

☐ Fantasy settings – barbarian worlds

☐ Completely escapist/surreal fantasy

- ☐ Institutional or secret academy
- ☐ Futuristic/sci fi
- ☐ Escapist but still believable
- ☐ Any settings you dislike?

____

- ☐ Where would you like to see an adult novel set?

____

6. In terms of storylines, would you prefer:

- ☐ Simple stories that concentrate on adult interests?
- ☐ More plot and character-driven stories with less explicit adult activity?
- ☐ We value your ideas, so give us your opinion of this book:

____

____

____

7. In terms of your adult interests, what do you like to read about? (Tick as many as you like.)

- ☐ Traditional corporal punishment (CP)
- ☐ Modern corporal punishment
- ☐ Spanking
- ☐ Restraint/bondage
- ☐ Rope bondage
- ☐ Latex/rubber
- ☐ Leather
- ☐ Female domination and male submission
- ☐ Female domination and female submission
- ☐ Male domination and female submission
- ☐ Willing captivity
- ☐ Uniforms
- ☐ Lingerie/underwear/hosiery/footwear (boots and high heels)
- ☐ Sex rituals
- ☐ Vanilla sex
- ☐ Swinging

☐ Cross-dressing/TV
☐ Enforced feminisation
☐ Others – tell us what you don't see enough of in adult fiction:

____

____

____

8. **Would you prefer books with a more specialised approach to your interests, i.e. a novel specifically about uniforms? If so, which subject(s) would you like to read a Nexus novel about?**

____

____

____

9. **Would you like to read true stories in Nexus books? For instance, the true story of a submissive woman, or a male slave? Tell us which true revelations you would most like to read about:**

____

____

____

10. **What do you like best about Nexus books?**

____

____

11. **What do you like least about Nexus books?**

____

____

12. **Which are your favourite titles?**

____

____

13. **Who are your favourite authors?**

____

____

14. Which covers do you prefer? Those featuring: (Tick as many as you like.)

- ☐ Fetish outfits
- ☐ More nudity
- ☐ Two models
- ☐ Unusual models or settings
- ☐ Classic erotic photography
- ☐ More contemporary images and poses
- ☐ A blank/non-erotic cover
- ☐ What would your ideal cover look like?

____

15. Describe your ideal Nexus novel in the space provided:

____

____

____

____

16. Which celebrity would feature in one of your Nexus-style fantasies? We'll post the best suggestions on our website – anonymously!

____

THANKS FOR YOUR TIME

Now simply write the title of this book in the space below and cut out the questionnaire pages. Post to: Nexus, Marketing Dept., Thames Wharf Studios, Rainville Rd, London W6 9HA

Book title: ____

NEXUS NEW BOOKS

THE PERSIAN GIRL

Felix Baron

Sir Richard Francis Burton was a soldier, spy, explorer, linguist, diplomat, master of disguise and the greatest swordsman of his time. He was also a notorious rake and, during the period of his life recounted in *The Persian Girl*, he carouses and womanises his way around the world. From the depraved 'governess' Abigail and her debauched young wards, to the Ethiopian Amazon who takes him prisoner, Burton's journey leads him to his greatest challenge of all – schooling a dozen lusty young wenches in the more arcane arts of the bedchamber.

£7.99 ISBN 978 0 352 34501 1

To be published in November 2008

BARE, WHITE AND ROSY

Penny Birch

Natasha Linnet has a weakness for older men, preferably those with sufficient confidence to take her across their knees. The directors of old-fashioned wine merchants Hambling and Borse seem ideal for the task, and they want her to work for them. It's an offer too good to refuse, but Natasha quickly finds that she is expected to give a great deal more than she had bargained for, to a great many more people and in a number of unexpected ways. Only the temptations being dangled in front of her make it possible for her to put up with what is being inflicted from behind.

£7.99 ISBN 978 0 352 34505 9

To be published in December 2008

GIRLFLESH CASTLE

Adriana Arden

Vanessa Buckingham has discovered strange contentment in the bizarre and secretive underworld of commercially organised slavery. Having accepted her own submissive nature, Vanessa is now happily working for the powerful Shiller Company as a 'slave reporter' for *Girlflesh News*. She has also found a lover in the form of the beautiful slavegirl Kashika. But there are forces at work that wish to destroy Shiller's carefully run 'ethical' slave business. Shiller's rival and arch-enemy – the media mogul Sir Harvey Rochester – has not given up trying to take over the operation. Having failed to use Vanessa as his unwitting pawn to expose Shiller, Sir Harvey now turns to more extreme methods.

£7.99 ISBN 978 0 352 34504 2

NEXUS BOOKLIST

Information is correct at time of printing. To avoid disappointment, check availability before ordering. Go to www.nexus-books.co.uk.

All books are priced at £6.99 unless another price is given.

NEXUS

☐ ABANDONED ALICE	Adriana Arden	ISBN 978 0 352 33969 0
☐ ALICE IN CHAINS	Adriana Arden	ISBN 978 0 352 33908 9
☐ AMERICAN BLUE	Penny Birch	ISBN 978 0 352 34169 3
☐ AQUA DOMINATION	William Doughty	ISBN 978 0 352 34020 7
☐ THE ART OF CORRECTION	Tara Black	ISBN 978 0 352 33895 2
☐ THE ART OF SURRENDER	Madeline Bastinado	ISBN 978 0 352 34013 9
☐ BEASTLY BEHAVIOUR	Aishling Morgan	ISBN 978 0 352 34095 5
☐ BEING A GIRL	Chloë Thurlow	ISBN 978 0 352 34139 6
☐ BELINDA BARES UP	Yolanda Celbridge	ISBN 978 0 352 33926 3
☐ BIDDING TO SIN	Rosita Varón	ISBN 978 0 352 34063 4
☐ BLUSHING AT BOTH ENDS	Philip Kemp	ISBN 978 0 352 34107 5
☐ THE BOOK OF PUNISHMENT	Cat Scarlett	ISBN 978 0 352 33975 1
☐ BRUSH STROKES	Penny Birch	ISBN 978 0 352 34072 6
☐ CALLED TO THE WILD	Angel Blake	ISBN 978 0 352 34067 2
☐ CAPTIVES OF CHEYNER CLOSE	Adriana Arden	ISBN 978 0 352 34028 3
☐ CARNAL POSSESSION	Yvonne Strickland	ISBN 978 0 352 34062 7
☐ CITY MAID	Amelia Evangeline	ISBN 978 0 352 34096 2
☐ COLLEGE GIRLS	Cat Scarlett	ISBN 978 0 352 33942 3
☐ COMPANY OF SLAVES	Christina Shelly	ISBN 978 0 352 33887 7
☐ CONCEIT AND CONSEQUENCE	Aishling Morgan	ISBN 978 0 352 33965 2
☐ CORRECTIVE THERAPY	Jacqueline Masterson	ISBN 978 0 352 33917 1
☐ CORRUPTION	Virginia Crowley	ISBN 978 0 352 34073 3

☐ CRUEL SHADOW	Aishling Morgan	ISBN 978 0 352 33886 0
☐ DARK MISCHIEF	Lady Alice McCloud	ISBN 978 0 352 33998 0
☐ DEPTHS OF DEPRAVATION	Ray Gordon	ISBN 978 0 352 33995 9
☐ DICE WITH DOMINATION	P.S. Brett	ISBN 978 0 352 34023 8
☐ DOMINANT	Felix Baron	ISBN 978 0 352 34044 3
☐ DOMINATION DOLLS	Lindsay Gordon	ISBN 978 0 352 33891 4
☐ EXPOSÉ	Laura Bowen	ISBN 978 0 352 34035 1
☐ FORBIDDEN READING	Lisette Ashton	ISBN 978 0 352 34022 1
☐ FRESH FLESH	Wendy Swanscombe	ISBN 978 0 352 34041 2
☐ THE GIRLFLESH INSTITUTE	Adriana Arden	ISBN 978 0 352 34101 3
☐ THE INDECENCIES OF ISABELLE	Penny Birch (writing as Cruella)	ISBN 978 0 352 33989 8
☐ THE INDISCRETIONS OF ISABELLE	Penny Birch (writing as Cruella)	ISBN 978 0 352 33882 2
☐ IN DISGRACE	Penny Birch	ISBN 978 0 352 33922 5
☐ IN HER SERVICE	Lindsay Gordon	ISBN 978 0 352 33968 3
☐ INSTRUMENTS OF PLEASURE	Nicole Dere	ISBN 978 0 352 34098 6
☐ JULIA C	Laura Bowen	ISBN 978 0 352 33852 5
☐ LACING LISBETH	Yolanda Celbridge	ISBN 978 0 352 33912 6
☐ LEAH'S PUNISHMENT	Aran Ashe	ISBN 978 0 352 34171 6
☐ LICKED CLEAN	Yolanda Celbridge	ISBN 978 0 352 33999 7
☐ LONGING FOR TOYS	Virginia Crowley	ISBN 978 0 352 34138 9
☐ LOVE JUICE	Donna Exeter	ISBN 978 0 352 33913 3
☐ MANSLAVE	J.D. Jensen	ISBN 978 0 352 34040 5
☐ NEIGHBOURHOOD WATCH	Lisette Ashton	ISBN 978 0 352 34190 7
☐ NIGHTS IN WHITE COTTON	Penny Birch	ISBN 978 0 352 34008 5
☐ NO PAIN, NO GAIN	James Baron	ISBN 978 0 352 33966 9
☐ THE OLD PERVERSITY SHOP	Aishling Morgan	ISBN 978 0 352 34007 8
☐ THE PALACE OF PLEASURES	Christobel Coleridge	ISBN 978 0 352 33801 3
☐ PETTING GIRLS	Penny Birch	ISBN 978 0 352 33957 7

☐ PORTRAIT OF A DISCIPLINARIAN	Aishling Morgan	ISBN 978 0 352 34179 2
☐ THE PRIESTESS	Jacqueline Bellevois	ISBN 978 0 352 33905 8
☐ PRIZE OF PAIN	Wendy Swanscombe	ISBN 978 0 352 33890 7
☐ PUNISHED IN PINK	Yolanda Celbridge	ISBN 978 0 352 34003 0
☐ THE PUNISHMENT CAMP	Jacqueline Masterson	ISBN 978 0 352 33940 9
☐ THE PUNISHMENT CLUB	Jacqueline Masterson	ISBN 978 0 352 33862 4
☐ THE ROAD TO DEPRAVITY	Ray Gordon	ISBN 978 0 352 34092 4
☐ SCARLET VICE	Aishling Morgan	ISBN 978 0 352 33988 1
☐ SCHOOLED FOR SERVICE	Lady Alice McCloud	ISBN 978 0 352 33918 8
☐ SCHOOL FOR STINGERS	Yolanda Celbridge	ISBN 978 0 352 33994 2
☐ SEXUAL HEELING	Wendy Swanscombe	ISBN 978 0 352 33921 8
☐ SILKEN EMBRACE	Christina Shelly	ISBN 978 0 352 34081 8
☐ SILKEN SERVITUDE	Christina Shelly	ISBN 978 0 352 34004 7
☐ SINDI IN SILK	Yolanda Celbridge	ISBN 978 0 352 34102 0
☐ SIN'S APPRENTICE	Aishling Morgan	ISBN 978 0 352 33909 6
☐ SLAVE OF THE SPARTANS	Yolanda Celbridge	ISBN 978 0 352 34078 8
☐ SLIPPERY WHEN WET	Penny Birch	ISBN 978 0 352 34091 7
☐ THE SMARTING OF SELINA	Yolanda Celbridge	ISBN 978 0 352 33872 3
☐ STRIP GIRL	Aishling Morgan	ISBN 978 0 352 34077 1
☐ STRIPING KAYLA	Yolanda Marshall	ISBN 978 0 352 33881 5
☐ STRIPPED BARE	Angel Blake	ISBN 978 0 352 33971 3
☐ TEMPTING THE GODDESS	Aishling Morgan	ISBN 978 0 352 33972 0
☐ THAI HONEY	Kit McCann	ISBN 978 0 352 34068 9
☐ TICKLE TORTURE	Penny Birch	ISBN 978 0 352 33904 1
☐ TOKYO BOUND	Sachi	ISBN 978 0 352 34019 1
☐ TORMENT, INCORPORATED	Murilee Martin	ISBN 978 0 352 33943 0
☐ TRAIL OF SIN	Ray Gordon	ISBN 978 0 352 34182 2
☐ UNEARTHLY DESIRES	Ray Gordon	ISBN 978 0 352 34036 8
☐ UNIFORM DOLL	Penny Birch	ISBN 978 0 352 33698 9
☐ WEB OF DESIRE	Ray Gordon	ISBN 978 0 352 34167 9
☐ WHALEBONE STRICT	Lady Alice McCloud	ISBN 978 0 352 34082 5

☐ WHAT HAPPENS TO BAD GIRLS	Penny Birch	ISBN 978 0 352 34031 3
☐ WHAT SUKI WANTS	Cat Scarlett	ISBN 978 0 352 34027 6
☐ WHEN SHE WAS BAD	Penny Birch	ISBN 978 0 352 33859 4
☐ WHIP HAND	G.C. Scott	ISBN 978 0 352 33694 1
☐ WHIPPING GIRL	Aishling Morgan	ISBN 978 0 352 33789 4
☐ WHIPPING TRIANGLE	G.C. Scott	ISBN 978 0 352 34086 3
☐ THE WICKED SEX	Lance Porter	ISBN 978 0 352 34161 7
☐ ZELLIE'S WEAKNESS	Jean Aveline	ISBN 978 0 352 34160 0

NEXUS CLASSIC

☐ AMAZON SLAVE	Lisette Ashton	ISBN 978 0 352 33916 4
☐ ANGEL	Lindsay Gordon	ISBN 978 0 352 34009 2
☐ THE BLACK GARTER	Lisette Ashton	ISBN 978 0 352 33919 5
☐ THE BLACK MASQUE	Lisette Ashton	ISBN 978 0 352 33977 5
☐ THE BLACK ROOM	Lisette Ashton	ISBN 978 0 352 33914 0
☐ THE BLACK WIDOW	Lisette Ashton	ISBN 978 0 352 33973 7
☐ THE BOND	Lindsay Gordon	ISBN 978 0 352 33996 6
☐ THE DOMINO ENIGMA	Cyrian Amberlake	ISBN 978 0 352 34064 1
☐ THE DOMINO QUEEN	Cyrian Amberlake	ISBN 978 0 352 34074 0
☐ THE DOMINO TATTOO	Cyrian Amberlake	ISBN 978 0 352 34037 5
☐ EMMA ENSLAVED	Hilary James	ISBN 978 0 352 33883 9
☐ EMMA'S HUMILIATION	Hilary James	ISBN 978 0 352 33910 2
☐ EMMA'S SUBMISSION	Hilary James	ISBN 978 0 352 33906 5
☐ FAIRGROUND ATTRACTION	Lisette Ashton	ISBN 978 0 352 33927 0
☐ THE INSTITUTE	Maria Del Rey	ISBN 978 0 352 33352 0
☐ PLAYTHING	Penny Birch	ISBN 978 0 352 33967 6
☐ PLEASING THEM	William Doughty	ISBN 978 0 352 34015 3
☐ RITES OF OBEDIENCE	Lindsay Gordon	ISBN 978 0 352 34005 4
☐ SERVING TIME	Sarah Veitch	ISBN 978 0 352 33509 8
☐ THE SUBMISSION GALLERY	Lindsay Gordon	ISBN 978 0 352 34026 9
☐ TIE AND TEASE	Penny Birch	ISBN 978 0 352 33987 4
☐ TIGHT WHITE COTTON	Penny Birch	ISBN 978 0 352 33970 6

NEXUS CONFESSIONS

Title	Author	ISBN
☐ NEXUS CONFESSIONS: VOLUME ONE	Various	ISBN 978 0 352 34093 1
☐ NEXUS CONFESSIONS: VOLUME TWO	Various	ISBN 978 0 352 34103 7
☐ NEXUS CONFESSIONS: VOLUME THREE	Various	ISBN 978 0 352 34113 6

NEXUS ENTHUSIAST

Title	Author	ISBN
☐ BUSTY	Tom King	ISBN 978 0 352 34032 0
☐ CUCKOLD	Amber Leigh	ISBN 978 0 352 34140 2
☐ DERRIÈRE	Julius Culdrose	ISBN 978 0 352 34024 5
☐ ENTHRALLED	Lance Porter	ISBN 978 0 352 34108 2
☐ LEG LOVER	L.G. Denier	ISBN 978 0 352 34016 0
☐ OVER THE KNEE	Fiona Locke	ISBN 978 0 352 34079 5
☐ RUBBER GIRL	William Doughty	ISBN 978 0 352 34087 0
☐ THE SECRET SELF	Christina Shelly	ISBN 978 0 352 34069 6
☐ UNDER MY MASTER'S WINGS	Lauren Wissot	ISBN 978 0 352 34042 9
☐ UNIFORM DOLLS	Aishling Morgan	ISBN 978 0 352 34159 4
☐ THE UPSKIRT EXHIBITIONIST	Ray Gordon	ISBN 978 0 352 34122 8
☐ WIFE SWAP	Amber Leigh	ISBN 978 0 352 34097 9

NEXUS NON FICTION

Title	Author	ISBN
☐ LESBIAN SEX SECRETS FOR MEN	Jamie Goddard and Kurt Brungard	ISBN 978 0 352 33724 5

- - - - - - ✂ -

Please send me the books I have ticked above.

Name ....

Address ....

....

....

.... Post code ....

Send to: **Virgin Books Cash Sales, Thames Wharf Studios, Rainville Road, London W6 9HA**

US customers: for prices and details of how to order books for delivery by mail, call 888-330-8477.

Please enclose a cheque or postal order, made payable to **Nexus Books Ltd**, to the value of the books you have ordered plus postage and packing costs as follows:

UK and BFPO – £1.00 for the first book, 50p for each subsequent book.

Overseas (including Republic of Ireland) – £2.00 for the first book, £1.00 for each subsequent book.

If you would prefer to pay by VISA, ACCESS/MASTERCARD, AMEX, DINERS CLUB or SWITCH, please write your card number and expiry date here:

....

Please allow up to 28 days for delivery.

Signature ....

Our privacy policy

We will not disclose information you supply us to any other parties. We will not disclose any information which identifies you personally to any person without your express consent.

From time to time we may send out information about Nexus books and special offers. Please tick here if you do *not* wish to receive Nexus information. ☐

- - - - - - ✂ -